KT-462-442

DAUGHTER OF SILENCE

A twenty-four-year-old girl shoots a man down in broad daylight in cold blood – a vendetta killing that has its roots in wartime Italy sixteen years before.

Carlo Rienzi, the lawyer who takes up her case, is also conducting a vendetta – an emotional vendetta against his beautiful, faithless wife, and against her father, a brilliant lawyer who has crippled her emotionally by his demanding, selfish love.

But in the end, it is not his wife he destroys but the woman he has come to defend. For her crime the girl risks a sentence of twenty years, but there is a greater danger even than this lying in wait for her . . .

MORRIS WEST

Daughter of Silence

FONTANA BOOKS
by agreement with Heinemann

First published in 1961 by William Heinemann Ltd.
First issued in Fontana Books 1976
Second Impression November 1976

© Morris L. West, 1961

Made and printed in Great Britain by
William Collins Sons & Co Ltd Glasgow

For Hilda

Alta vendetta d'alto silenzio è figlia.
Noble vengeance is the daughter of deep silence.
(Alfieri: *La Congiura de' Pazzi*, Act I. Sc. I.)

CONDITIONS OF SALE
This book is sold subject to the condition that
it shall not, by way of trade or otherwise, be lent,
re-sold, hired out or otherwise circulated without
the publisher's prior consent in any form of
binding or cover other than that in which it is
published and without a similar condition
including this condition being imposed on the
subsequent purchaser

Chapter One

IT WAS bright noon, high summer, in the upland valleys of Tuscany: a torpid time, a season of dust and languor, of stripped flax and larks in the wheat-stubble, and new wines coming to vintage in the country of the elder gods. It was an hour of bells, undulant in a dry air, tranquil over the tombs of dead saints and the feuds of forgotten mercenaries. It was a persuasion to darkness and drawn shutters; since who but dogs and Americans would expose their foolish foreheads to an August sun at midday?

In the village of San Stefano the first strokes of the angelus were sounding over the square. The bell-ringer was old and the music of his chimes was muted. The village was drowsy and replete with a good harvest, so the last passages of its morning life were muted too.

An old man stopped, crossed himself and stood with bowed head as the triple tones rang out from the white campanile. A tubby fellow in a white apron with a checker-board napkin over his arm stood at the door of the restaurant and picked his teeth with a match. A mule-faced policeman made a tentative step outside his door, squinted languidly round the square, spat, scratched himself and then wandered back to his wine and cheese.

Water welled sluggishly from the mouths of tired dolphins and spilled into the shallow basin of the fountain, while a skinny boy sailed a paper boat in the eddies. A charcoal-burner trundled his handcart over the cobbles. The cart was piled high with little bundles of twigs and brown bags filled with charcoal. A small girl was perched on top of them, tousle-haired, serious of mien, like a woodland elf. A barefoot woman, with a baby on her hip, came out of the wine-shop and headed for the alley at the far end of the piazza. Five miles away, the towers and tumbled roofs of Siena reared themselves, hazy and magical against a copper sky.

It was a placid tableau, curiously antique, sparsely peopled, its animation geared to the low pulse-beat of country living. Here, time flowed sluggishly as the fountain, and the only change was the cyclic mutation of age and the seasons. This, one understood, was a tribal enclave, where tradition was more important than progress, where custom was nine points of the law, and old loves were cherished as sedulously as old hates and the tangled loyalties of blood and bondage.

There was a road in and a road out, the one leading to Arezzo, the other to Siena, but their traffic was small and seasonal. The trunk routes of tourism and commerce had always by-passed San Stefano. The valley farms were small and jealously reserved to their peasant owners, so there was no welcome for migrants. Those who went away were the restless or the footloose or the ambitious, and the village was happily quit of them.

Before the last echo of the bell had died away, the square was empty. Shutters were closed, curtains were drawn. The dust settled back into the cracks of the cobbles, the paper boat swam rudderless round the fountain and the cry of the cicadas rose, strepitant and monotonous, from the circling fields. The first watch of the day was over. Peace – or what passed for peace – came down on the village.

It was, perhaps, ten minutes later when the bell-ringer came out of the church: an elderly friar in the dusty habit of St Francis, with a white tonsured head and a ruddy face lined and seamed like a winter apple. He stood a moment in the shadow of the portico, mopping his brow with a red handkerchief; then he twitched his cowl over his head and padded across the square, his sandals flapping tic-tac on the parched stones.

Before he had gone a dozen yards, an unfamiliar sight stopped him in his tracks. A taxi with a Siena number-plate pulled into the piazza and rolled to a halt outside the restaurant. A woman got out, paid off the driver, and watched him drive out of sight.

She was young, no more than twenty-five. Her dress marked her as a city-dweller: tailored costume, white blouse, fashionable shoes, a handbag slung by a leather strap over one shoulder. She wore no hat and her dark hair hung in waves to her shoulders. Her face was pale, calm and singularly beautiful, like that of a wax madonna. In the empty, sunlit square she looked uncertain and vaguely lonely.

6

For a while she stood, looking round the square, as if orienting herself in a once-familiar territory; then with a firm, confident step, she walked across to a house between the wine-shop and bakery and rang the bell. The door was opened by a stout matron dressed in black bombazine with a white apron tied round her middle. They talked for a few moments, and the stout one made a gesture inviting her to enter. She declined and the matron went away, leaving the door open. The girl waited, fumbling for something in her handbag, while the friar watched, curious as any countryman about any stranger.

It was perhaps thirty seconds later when the man appeared in the doorway – a tall, thickset fellow in shirt-sleeves, with a grizzled head, a sallow, lined face, and a table-napkin stuck in his shirt-front. He was still chewing on a mouthful of food, and in the clear light the friar could see a small dribble of sauce at the corner of his mouth. He looked at the girl without any sign of recognition, and asked her a question.

Then she shot him in the chest.

The impact spun him around and flung him against the door-jamb, and in a horrible suspended moment the friar saw her pump four more shots into him and then turn away, walking unhurriedly towards the police station. The echoes were still shouting around the piazza when the friar began to run, tottering and stumbling, to offer a final absolution to a man who was already beyond it.

Five miles away, in Siena, Doctor Alberto Ascolini was sitting for his portrait – an exercise in futility, an illusion of immortality to which he submitted himself with irony.

He was a tall man, sixty-five years of age, with a pink lively face and a mane of snow-white hair that flowed down in careful disarray over his collar. He wore a silk suit and a silk cravat fastened with a diamond pin. Both the suit and the cravat were immaculately tailored but deliberately old-fashioned as if age and incongruous animation were his stock-in-trade. He looked like an actor – a very successful actor – but he was in fact a lawyer, one of the most successful advocates in Rome.

The artist was a slim, dark girl in her late twenties with

7

hazel eyes, a frank smile and expressive, elegant hands. Her name was Ninette Lachaise. Her apartment was a high attic chamber that looked over the roof-tops of the old city towards the campanile of the Vergine Assunta. One end of it was a studio, meticulous in its order and cleanliness. The other was her living quarters, furnished with the gleanings of provincial craft, waxed and gleaming with Gallic housewifery. Her pictures were an index to her character – full of light, spare in detail, stylized, yet ample in movement, a lineal development of the primitive Tuscan tradition to a twentieth-century idiom.

She was working in charcoal now, making a series of swift bravura sketches of her subject as he sat, half in sunlight, half in shadow, telling scandalous stories of the Roman courts. It was a virtuoso performance on both sides. The old man's stories were full of extravagant wit, clever malice and sly bawdry. The girl's sketches were avid and percipient, so that it seemed as if a dozen men lived inside the sleek pink skin of this very intelligent mountebank.

Ascolini watched her with shrewd, affectionate eyes, and when he had come to the end of his stories he grinned and said with mock pathos: 'When I am with you, Ninette, I mourn my youth.'

'If you have nothing else to mourn, *dottore*,' she told him with gentle irony, 'then you're a fortunate man.'

'What else is there to regret, my dear, but the follies one is incapable of committing?'

'Perhaps the consequences of those one has already committed.'

'Eh! Eh! Ninette!' Ascolini fluttered his eloquent hands and laughed dryly. 'No lectures this morning, please! This is the beginning of my holiday; I come to you to be diverted.'

'No, *dottore*.' She smiled at him in her grave fashion and went on sketching with swift, firm strokes. 'I've known you too long and too well. When you come to drink coffee or buy me lunch at the Sordello, then you are content with the world. When you offer me a commission like this or pay me too much for my landscapes, then you have problems on your mind. You offer me a fee to solve them. It's a bad habit, you know – it does you small credit.'

His smooth, youthful face clouded a moment, then he grinned crookedly. 'But you still accept the fee, Ninette. Why?'

'I sell you my pictures, *dottore*, not my sympathy. That you get for nothing.'

'You humble me, Ninette,' said the old man tartly.

'Nothing humbles you, *dottore*,' she told him bluntly. 'And this is where all your troubles begin – with Valeria, with Carlo and with yourself. There now!' She made a last brisk stroke on the canvas and turned to him, holding out her hand. 'The words are said, the sitting is over. Come and look at yourself.'

She led him to the easel and stood, holding his hand while he surveyed the sketches. He was silent for a long time, then with no hint of raillery he asked her: 'Are these all my faces, Ninette?'

'Only the ones you show me.'

'You think there are others?'

'I know there must be. You are too various a man, *dottore*, too dazzling in each variety.'

'And which of them is the real Ascolini?'

'All of them – and none of them.'

'Read them to me, child.'

'This one? The great advocate, the noble pleader who dominates every court in Rome. He changes a little, as you see. Here he is the darling of the *salons*, the wit who makes the men blush and the women squirm when he whispers in their willing ears. That one? A moment from the Sordello: Ascolini drinking wine with the law students and wishing he had a son of his own. There he becomes the chess-player, moving people like pawns, despising himself more than he despises them. In the next one there is a memory – of youth perhaps, and an old love. And last of all, the great advocate as he might have been, had not a country priest pulled him out of a ditch and opened the world to him: a peasant with a load of sticks on his back and the monotony of a lifetime in his eyes. . . .'

'It is too much,' said the old man flatly. 'From one so young it is too much and too frightening. How do you know all this, Ninette? How do you see so many secrets?'

For a moment she looked at him with sombre, pitying eyes. Then she shook her head. 'They are not secrets, *dottore*. We are what we do. It is written in our faces for the world to read. For myself? I am a foreigner here. I came from France like the old soldiers of fortune, to plunder the riches of the South. I live alone. I sell my pictures – and wait for someone to whom I can give myself with confidence. I know what it is to be solitary and afraid. I know what it is to reach out for love and grasp an illusion. You have been kind to me and you have shown me more of yourself than you know. I've often wondered why.'

'Simple enough!' There was a harsh note in his rich actor's voice. 'If I were twenty years younger, Ninette, I should ask you to marry me.'

'If I were twenty years older, *dottore*,' she told him softly, 'I should probably accept – and you would hate me for it ever afterwards.'

'I could never hate you, my dear.'

'You hate everything you possess, *dottore*. You love only what you cannot attain.'

'You're brutal today, Ninette.'

'There are brutal things to be faced, are there not?'

'I suppose there are.'

He released her hand and walked over to the window, where he stood watching the sun pour down over the towers and roof-tops of the old city. His tall frame seemed bowed and diminished, his noble face became pinched and shrunken, as if age had come upon him unaware. The girl watched him, caught in a rush of pity for his dilemmas. After a while she prompted him quietly: 'It's Valeria, isn't it?'

'And Carlo.'

'Tell me about Valeria.'

'We're not two days arrived from Rome and she's started an affair with Basilio Lazzaro.'

'There have been other affairs, *dottore*. You encouraged them. Why should this one bother you?'

'Because it's late in the day for me, Ninette! Because I want grandchildren in my house and a promise of continuity, and because this Lazzaro is scum who will end by destroying her!'

'I know,' said Ninette Lachaise softly. 'I know it only too well.'

'It is news already in Siena?'

'I doubt it. But I was once in love with Lazzaro myself; he was my grand illusion.'

'I'm sorry, child.'

'You must not be sorry for me – only for yourself and Valeria. Carlo too, for that matter. Does he know yet?'

'I doubt it.'

'But he knew about the others?'

'I think so.'

'You laughed about that, I remember, *dottore*. You made a joke about your daughter putting horns on a foolish husband. You said she was following in her father's footsteps. You were proud of her conquests, and her cleverness.'

'He is a fool,' said Ascolini bitterly. 'A sentimental young fool who didn't know what time of day it was. He deserved a lesson.'

'And now?'

'Now he's talking of leaving me and setting up his own legal practice.'

'And you don't approve of that?'

'Of course not! He's too young, too inexperienced; he'll wreck his career before it's half begun.'

'You wrecked his marriage, *dottore*; why should you care about his career?'

'I don't, except that it involves my daughter's future, and the future of their children if they have any.'

'You're lying, *dottore*,' said Ninette Lachaise, sadly. 'You're lying to me. You're lying to yourself.'

Surprisingly, the old advocate laughed and flung out his hands in an almost comic despair. 'Of course I'm lying! I know the truth better than you do, child. I made a world in my own image and I don't like the look of it any more, so I need someone to break it over my head and make me eat the pieces.'

'Perhaps this is what Carlo is trying to do now?'

'Carlo?' Ascolini exploded into contempt. 'He's too much of a boy to control his own wife. How can he compete with a perverse old bull like me? I would like nothing better than he should ram my nonsense down my neck, but he's too much a gentleman to do it! ... Eh!' He shrugged off the discussion and walked back to take her hands in his own. 'Forget all this and go paint your pictures, my dear. We're not worth helping – any of us! But there's one thing —'

'What is it, *dottore*?'

'You're dining with us tonight at the villa.'

'No – please!' Her refusal was sharp and emphatic. 'You're welcome here any time, you know that, but keep me out of your family. They're not my people; I'm not theirs.'

'It's not for us, it's for yourself. There's someone I'd like you to meet.'

'Who?'

'He's my house-guest. His name's Peter Landon. He's a doctor and he comes from Australia by way of London.'

'A barbarous country they tell me, *dottore*, full of strange animals and giants in shirt-sleeves.'

Ascolini laughed. 'When you meet this Landon for the first time you may be inclined to believe it. He fills a room when he walks into it. When he talks it seems brusque and too certain for politeness. Then you realize that he is talking pure Tuscan, and that what he says makes a deal of sense, and that he has lived more variously than you or I. There is a strength in him too and, I think, a touch of discontent.' He laid an affectionate hand on her cheek. 'He could be good for you, my dear.'

She flushed and turned away. 'Are you turning match-maker, *dottore*?'

'I am more fond of you than you know, Ninette,' he told her soberly. 'I should like to see you happy. Please come.'

'Very well, *dottore*, I'll come, but you must promise me something first.'

'Anything, child.'

'You will play no comedies with me, no plots like you make with your own family. I could never forgive you that.'

'I could never forgive myself either. Believe me, Ninette.' He took her face in his old hands and kissed her lightly on the forehead. Then he was gone, and she stood a long time looking out over the roof-tops of the town to the tumbled hillsides of Tuscany, where the wine is sweetened by the blood of ancient sacrifices and the cypresses grow out of the eyes of dead princes.

At the Villa Ascolini, perched high on a terraced hill above the village of San Stefano, Valeria Rienzi was drowsing behind closed shutters. She had heard no bells, no shots, no echo of the tumult that followed them. The only sounds that penetrated her room were the bourdon of the cicadas, the clip-clip of a gardener's shears and the pale, plangent music that Carlo was playing in the *salone*.

She had no thought of death this summer noon. The beat of her blood was too strong for such dreary irrelevance. She had only to flex her long body on the bed, twitch the silk robe against her skin, to feel the sweetness and the itch of living. She was in fact thinking of love, which she understood as a pleasant if transient diversion, and of marriage, which she recognized as a permanent, if occasionally irksome, condition.

Marriage meant Carlo Rienzi, the handsome, boyish husband playing his sad piano below stairs. It meant discretion, public propriety, a matronly care for her husband's career. It meant a surrender of liberty, an expense of tenderness which she rarely felt, demands on a body which Carlo had never understood how to waken, exacerbation of a spirit too wilful and too lively to match his melancholy and uncertain temperament. Marriage meant Rome and Roman rectitude – legal dinners and cocktail parties for those who handed fat briefs to her father and his fledgeling son-in-law.

Love, in the context of a summer holiday in Tuscany, meant Basilio Lazzaro, the swarthy, passionate bachelor who made no secret of his fondness for young wives. Love was an antidote to boredom, an affirmation of independence. It was a rich joke to share with an understanding father, a goad to prick a too youthful husband into man's estate.

At thirty, Valeria Rienzi was prepared to count her blessings: good health, good looks, no children, a manageable husband, an urgent lover, a father who saw all, understood all and forgave everything with a cynic's indulgence.

It was a pleasant contemplation in the warm, private twilight of her bedroom where painted fauns and dryads disported themselves on the ceiling. There was music whose sadness touched her not at all. There was a promise of a whole summer's diversion, and if Basilio proved too demanding there was the visitor, Peter Landon. She had not measured him yet, but there would be time enough to test this fellow from the New World in the devious, sardonic games of the Old.

And yet . . . and yet . . . there were uneasy ripples on the Narcissus pool, dark currents stirring under the lily-pads. There were changes in herself which she did not fully understand – a sense of emptiness, a demand for direction, a compulsion to new and more passionate encounters, vague fear and occasional poignant regret. Time was when conspiracy with her father assured her of absolution for even her wildest follies. Now it was no longer an absolution but a kind of wry-mouthed tolerance as though he were less disappointed in her than in himself.

He made no secret now that he wanted her settled and breeding a family. The problem was that he still had no respect for Carlo, and could show her no way to restore her own. What he demanded was a new conspiracy: seduction of a husband made indifferent by the indifference of his wife, a loveless mating to bring love to an old epicure who had affected to despise it all his life. It was too much for too little. Too little for her, too much for him – and for Carlo one deception too many.

Time was when he had pleaded with her for love and for the fulfilment of children. Time was when he would barter the last shreds of pride for a kiss and a moment of union. But not now. He had grown older these last months, colder, less dependent, more absorbed in a private planning of his own.

Part of it he had told her. He was determined to leave Ascolini's office and set up his own practice in advocacy. This done, he would offer her a home of her own, a household separate from her father. Afterwards? It was the afterwards that troubled her, when she must stand alone, without buttress, without absolution, subject to the verdict of a wronged husband and the determination of her own turbulent desires.

This was the nub of the problem. What did one want so much that the wanting was a torment in the flesh? What did one need so much that one was prepared to reject all else to attain it? Twenty-four hours ago she had heard the same question from the unlikely lips of Basilio Lazzaro.

She had been standing at the door of his bedroom, fully dressed, with gloves and bag in hand, watching him button a shirt over his brown barrel-chest. She had noted the slack satisfied ease of his movements, his swift indifference to her presence, and she had asked, plaintively: 'Why, Basilio – why must it always be like this?'

'Like what?' asked Lazzaro irritably as he reached for his tie.

'When we meet it is like the overture to an opera. When we make love it is all drama and music. When we part it's . . . it's like paying off a taxi.'

Lazzaro's dark handsome face puckered in a frown of puzzlement. 'What do you expect, *cara*? This is the way it is. When you drink the wine, the bottle's empty. When the opera's over, you don't wait around for the cleaners. You've had your fun. You go home and wait for another performance.'

'And that's all?'

'What else can there be, *cara*? I ask you – what else?'

Which was a neat riddle, but she had found, then or now, no adequate answer. She was still puzzling over it when the ormolu clock sounded a quarter after midday, and it was time to bathe and dress for lunch.

The square of San Stefano was seething and populous as an ant-heap. The whole village was out, babe and beldame, crowding about the house of the dead man, chaffering round the fountain, arguing with the doltish policeman who stood guard at the door of the station. There was nothing riotous in their behaviour, nothing hostile in their attitude. They were spectators only, involved by curiosity in a melodrama of puppets.

15

From the window of his office Sergeant Fiorello watched them with a canny professional eye. So far, so good. They were excited but orderly, milling about the square like sheep in a pen. There was no danger of immediate violence. The detectives from Siena would arrive to take over the case in an hour. The family of the murdered man was absorbed in a privacy of grief. He could afford to relax and attend to his prisoner.

She was sitting, slumped in a chair, head bowed, her body shaken with rigors. Fiorello's lean, leather face softened when he looked at her, then he poured brandy into an earthenware cup and held it to her lips. She gagged on the first mouthful, then sipped it slowly. In a few moments the rigors subsided and Fiorello offered her a cigarette. She refused it and said in a dead, flat voice: 'No, thank you. I'm better now.'

'I have to ask you questions. You know that?' His voice for so burly a man, was oddly gentle. The girl nodded indifferently.

'I know that.'

'What's your name?'

'You know it already. Anna Albertini. I used to be Anna Moschetti.'

'Whose gun is that?'

He picked up the weapon and held it out to her flat in the palm of his hand. She did not flinch or turn away, but answered simply: 'My husband's.'

'We'll have to get in touch with him. Where is he?'

'In Florence. Vicolo degli Angelotti, number sixteen.'

'Is there a telephone?'

'No.'

'Does he know where you are?'

'No.'

Her eyes were glazed; she sat bolt upright in the chair, pale and rigid as a cataleptic. Her voice had a formal, metallic quality like that of a subject in narcosis. Fiorello hesitated a moment, and then asked another question: 'Why did you do it, Anna?'

For the first time a hint of life crept into her voice and eyes. 'You know why. It doesn't matter how I say it, or how you will write it down. You know why.'

16

'Then tell me something else, Anna. Why did you choose this time? Why not a month ago or five years? Why didn't you wait longer?'

'Does it matter?'

Fiorello toyed absently with the pistol that had killed Gianbattista Belloni. His own voice took on a brooding, reflective quality, as if he too were reliving events remote from this place and this moment.

'No, it doesn't matter. Very soon you will be taken away from here. You will be tried, convicted and sent to prison for twenty years because you killed a man in cold blood. It's just a question to fill in time.'

'Time . . .' She took hold of the word as if it were a talisman, key to a lifetime's mysteries. 'It wasn't like looking at a clock or tearing pages off a calendar. It was like – like walking along a road . . . always the same road . . . always in the same direction. Then the road ended . . . here in San Stefano, outside Belloni's house. You understand that, don't you?'

'I understand it.'

But the understanding had come too late – and he knew it. Sixteen years too late. The road had swung full circle and now, like his prisoner, he was stumbling over milestones that he had thought past and forgotten. He laid the gun down on the desk and reached for a cigarette. When he came to light it he found that his hands were trembling. Ashamed, he stood up and busied himself laying out bread and cheese and olives on a plate, pouring a glass of wine and setting the rough meal in front of Anna Albertini. He said gruffly: 'When they take you to Siena you'll be questioned again, for many hours probably. You should try to eat now.'

'I'm not hungry, thank you.'

He knew that she was in shock, but her passivity angered him unreasonably. He blazed at her: 'Mother of God! Don't you understand? There's a man dead a couple of doors down the street. You killed him! He's the Mayor of this town and there's a crowd outside that would tear you in pieces if someone spoke the right word. When the black-suit boys come from Siena they're going to fry you like a fish in a pan. I'm trying to help you, but I can't force you to eat.'

'Why are you trying to help me?'

There was no malice in the question, only the vague and placid curiosity of the ailing. Fiorello knew the answer only too well, but for the life of him he could not give it. He turned away and walked again to the window while the girl sat picking at the food, aimless and pathetic as a bird which has been caged for the first time.

There was a flurry in the street now. The little friar had left the house of the dead man and was hurrying towards the police station. The people pressed about him, tugging at his habit, besieging him with questions, but he waved them away and stumbled breathlessly into Fiorello's office.

When he saw the girl he stopped dead in his tracks and his eyes filled up with an old man's impotent tears. Fiorello said boldly: 'You know who she is, don't you?'

Fra Bonifacio nodded wearily. 'I think I guessed it the first moment I saw her in the square. I should have expected all this. But it's been such a long time.'

'Sixteen years. And now the bomb explodes!'

'She needs help.'

Fiorello shrugged and spread his hands in a motion of despair. 'What help is there? It's an open-and-shut case. Vendetta. Premeditated murder. The penalty's twenty years.'

'She needs legal counsel.'

'The State supplies that to needy prisoners.'

'It's not enough. She needs the best we can find.'

'Who pays, even if you can find someone to handle a hopeless brief?'

'The Ascolini family is staying at the villa for the summer. The old man's one of the great criminal advocates. At least I can ask him to interest himself in the case. If not he, perhaps his son-in-law.'

'Why should they care?'

'Ascolini was born in these parts. He must have some legal loyalties.'

'Loyalties!' Fiorello vented the word in a harsh chuckle. 'We have so few of our own, why should we expect them from the *signori*?'

For a moment it seemed as if the little priest would accept

the familiar proposition. His face sagged, his shoulders drooped. Then a new thought engaged him and when he turned back to Fiorello his eyes were hard. He said quietly: 'There is a question for you, my friend. When Anna is brought to trial, how will you testify?'

'On the evidence,' said Fiorello flatly. 'How else?'

'And on the past? On the beginning of this monstrous business?'

'I stand on the record.' Fiorello's face was blank, his eyes cold as agate-stones.

'And if the record lies?'

'Then I am not aware of it, *padre*. I'm paid to keep the peace, not to rewrite old history.'

'Is that your last word?'

'It has to be,' said Fiorello with odd humour. 'I can't hide myself in a cloister like you, *padre*. I can't afford to go beating my breast and making novenas to Santa Caterina when things don't turn out the way I'd like. This is my world. Those folks out there are my people. I have to live with them the best way I can. This one' – he made a curt gesture towards the girl – 'whatever we do, she's a lost cause. I suppose, anyway, that makes her the Church's business.'

Seconds ticked away as the two men faced each other, priest and policeman, each committed to his separate road, each caught in the consequence of a common history, while Anna Albertini sat a pace away, pecking at her food, remote and contained as a moon-dweller. Then, without another word, the old friar turned away, lifted the telephone and asked to be connected to the Villa Ascolini.

In the noonday quiet of the *salone*, Carlo Rienzi was playing Chopin for the visitor, Peter Landon. They made a curious pair: the burly Australian with his freckled, quirky face and his ham-fist clamped round the bowl of his pipe; the Italian, slim, pale, incongruously beautiful, with sensitive lips and a dreamer's eyes touched with mystery and discontent.

The piece was one of the early nocturnes, tender, limpid, plangent, and Rienzi was interpreting it with simplicity and fidelity. The notes fell pure as water-drops; the phrases were shaped with love and understanding – and with no slur of bravura or false sentiment. This was the true discipline of art: the submission of the executant to the composer's talent, the subordination of personal emotion to that recorded by the long-dead master.

Landon watched him with shrewd, diagnostic eyes and thought how young he was, how vulnerable, how oddly matched with his cool, civilized wife and the flamboyant old advocate who was his master in the law.

Yet he was not all youth, nor wholly unscarred. His hands were strong yet restrained on the keys. There were lines on his forehead and incipient crow's feet at the corners of his eyes. He was on the wrong side of thirty. He was married. He must have suffered his share of the exactions of life. He played Chopin like one who understood the frustrations of love.

For Landon himself, the music woke echoes of a private discontent. A man from the New World, he had assumed without effort the urbanities of the Old. Ambitious, he had abandoned a promising practice in his own country to climb the risky slopes of reputation in London. A rebel by nature, he had disciplined his tongue and his temper and accommodated himself to the stratagems of the most jealous profession in the most jealous city in the world. He had hitched himself to the coat-tails of eminence and now, by industry, talent and diplomacy, had established himself as a senior consultant in psychiatry and a specialist in criminal psycho-pathology.

It was much for a man a year short of forty, but it was still two paces away from the closed perimeter of greatness. Two paces – and yet this was the longest leap of all. One needed a springboard to make it: the opportune case, the fortunate meeting with counsel in need of advice, the moment of illumination in research.

So far opportunity had eluded him and he had lapsed by slow degrees into frustration and the tart dissatisfaction of those who are challenged always within the stretch of their talent.

It was a kind of crisis, and he was wise enough to recognize it. There was a climacteric in every career: a season of resentment, indecision and danger. Many a hapless politician had lost a seat in Cabinet because he lacked patience or discretion. Many a brilliant scholar had missed preferment because he was a mite too brusque with his seniors. In the closed brotherhood of the British Medical Association a man had to swallow his pride and cultivate his friends. And when one ventured into the new science of the spirit, one made sedulous deferment to one's colleagues of the scalpel and the stethoscope. If one were an outlander one was doubly careful, doubly dependent upon the quality of one's performance and the validity of one's research.

So he had chosen a strategy for himself – withdrawal: this sabbatical year among the experts of Europe; three months with Dahlin in Stockholm on institutional practice with the criminally insane, a term with Gutmann in Vienna exploring the nature of responsibility, and now a brief vacation with Ascolini, famous for his use of medico-legal testimony.

And afterwards? He too had his questions about afterwards because now he was faced with a new aspect of the crisis: the ennui of the middle years. How much should a man pay for the fulfilment of ambition? And when he had paid, how much could he enjoy – and with whom? The old, sad music mocked him with its tale of lost hopes and dead loves and the clamour of forgotten triumphs.

There was a long, synoptic moment while the last overtones died away, then Rienzi swung round on the stool to face him. His lips puckered into a boyish, uncertain smile. 'There now, Peter! You've had your music! Money on the table! It's time to pay the piper.'

Landon took the pipe out of his mouth and grinned at him. 'What's the price?'

'Some advice. Some professional advice.'

'About what?'

'About myself. You've been here a week now. I like to think we've become friends. You know some of my problems. You're shrewd enough to guess the rest.' He flung out his hands in an abrupt gesture of appeal. 'I'm caught, Peter! I'm married, in a country where there is no divorce. I'm in love with a wife who has no passion for me. I work for a man whom I admire greatly – and who has as little respect for

21

me as if I were the junior clerk. What do I do about it? What's the matter with me? You're the psychiatrist! You're the fellow who probes the hearts of his patients. Read my wife's and Ascolini's.'

Landon frowned and stuck his pipe back in his mouth. Professional instinct warned him against such untimely intimacies. He had a dozen evasions to discourage them. But the man's distress was patent and his solitude in his own household was strangely poignant. Besides, he had spent more than courtesy on his father-in-law's house-guest, and Landon had been touched to an unfamiliar gratitude. He hesitated a moment and then said carefully: 'You can't have it two ways at once, Carlo. If you want a psychiatrist – and I don't think you do – then you should consult one of your own countrymen. At least you'll have a common language and a set of common symbols. If you want to bellyache to a friend, that's something different.' He chuckled dryly. 'Generally it's a better prescription, too. But if you tell my patients, I'll be out of business in a week!'

'Call it a bellyache, if you want,' said Rienzi in his brooding, melancholy fashion, 'but don't you see, I'm trapped like a squirrel in a cage?'

'By marriage?'

'No. By Ascolini.'

'You don't like him?'

Rienzi hesitated a moment and when he answered there was a world of weariness in his voice. 'I admire him greatly. He has a singular variety of talents and he is a very great advocate.'

'But?'

'But I see too much of him, I suppose. I work in his office. My wife and I live in his house. And I am oppressed by his eternal youth.'

It was an odd phrase, but Landon understood it. He had a momentary vision of the first cocktail party in Ascolini's Roman apartment when father and daughter played to their small but distinguished audience while Carlo Rienzi walked solitary on the moonlit terrace. He found himself more gently disposed to this young-old man with the too-sensitive

22

mouth and the restrained artist's hands. He asked quietly: 'Do you have to live with him?'

'I am told,' said Rienzi with soft bitterness, 'I am told that I am in his debt. I am indebted to him for my career. In Italy today the law is an overcrowded profession and the patronage of a great man is rare to find. I am indebted to him also for my wife. And she is in debt to him, being an only daughter whose father has given her love, security and the promise of a rich estate.'

'And Ascolini exacts payment?'

'From both of us.' He made a small, shrugging gesture of defeat. 'From me a loyalty and a conformity with his plans for my career. From my wife a – a kind of conspiracy in which her youth is spent on him instead of on me.'

'How does your wife feel about this?'

'Valeria is a singular woman,' said Rienzi flatly. 'She understands duty, filial piety and the payment of debts. Also she is very fond of her father and finds much pleasure in his company.'

'More than in yours?'

He smiled at that: the boyish, uncertain smile that lent him so much charm. He said gently: 'He has much more to offer than I, Peter. I cannot read the world with my fingertips. I am neither assured nor successful though I should like to be both. I love my wife, but I am afraid I have more need of her than she of me.'

'Time may change that.'

'I doubt it,' said Rienzi sharply. 'In this conspiracy there are others involved.'

'Other men?'

'Several. But I am less worried by them than by my own deficiency as a husband.' He stood up and walked to the french doors that gave on to the balcony and the garden terraces. 'Let's walk a little, shall we? It's more private outside.'

For a while they were silent, pacing an alley of cypresses, through whose green pillars they saw the sky within hand's reach and the countryside spread in a multichrome of dark olives, green vineyards, brown fallow and ripe corn shaken by the wind. Cynically, Landon thought that time wrought its changes all too slowly, and that for Carlo Rienzi there was need of swifter remedies. He prescribed them, curtly: 'If your wife makes horns for you, you don't have to wear them. Hand her back to her father and get yourself a judicial separation. If you don't like your job or your patron, change them. Dig ditches, if you must, but cut yourself free – now!'

'I wonder,' asked Rienzi with bleak humour, 'why it is always the sentimentalists who have the pat answers. I expected better of you, Peter. You're a professional. You should understand more than others the obliquities of love and possession: why sometimes a half loaf is better than a basketful of pastry; why hope deferred is often a stronger bond than conquest shared.'

Landon flushed and gave him the tart reminder: 'If a man likes to scratch, he won't thank you for curing his itch.'

'But do you have to tear out his heart to cure him? Cut off his head to teach him reason?'

'Not at all. You try to help him to enough maturity to choose his own remedy. Or, if there is no remedy, to wear his affliction with dignity.'

The words were hardly out before he regretted them, being vain of a tolerance which he did not possess, ashamed of a brusqueness with which clinical practice had endowed him. This was the penalty of ambition: that a man could not sympathize without demeaning himself. This was the irony of self-love: that he could not pity what he had not endured in his own flesh – the kiss given but not returned, the passion spent but unrequited. Rienzi's mild answer was the bitterest reproach of all: 'If I lack dignity, Peter, you must not blame me too much. The meanest actor can play a king. It takes a great one to wear the horns and have his audience weep. If I have not rebelled before this, it is because opportunity was lacking, not courage. It is not as easy as you think to receive the dilemmas of loyalty and love. But I'm plotting revolution, believe me! I know, better than you, that my only hope with Valeria is to beat Ascolini on his own ground – to destroy the legend which he has built up for her and which is the source of his power over her. Strange, isn't it? To prove myself a lover, I must prove myself a lawyer first. I need a brief, Peter, just one good brief. But where the hell do I get it?'

Before Landon had time to frame a reply or an apology, a servant came to call Rienzi to the telephone and the physician of souls was left pondering the problems of love in an old land where passions run in crooked channels and youth carries on its back five thousand years of violent history.

Landon was glad to be alone. A man devoted to the mechanics of success, he found too much company exacting, too many new impressions a burden on the imagination. He felt the need of some restoration before committing himself to an afternoon with his very intelligent but very demanding hosts.

Carlo Rienzi was an attractive fellow, and one could not grudge a gentleness for his dilemmas and indecisions; but it was the problem of all friendships in Italy that one was expected to be involved, to take sides in the most trivial or grandiose issue, to have a care for every sorrow and a blush for every indiscretion. If one were not careful, one was spent like a plenty-purse, sucked dry and left gasping while one's friends waxed riotous on love or pity.

It was a relief therefore to be quit of people and enjoy the simple tourist pleasure of looking at the view from the garden.

The first impact was breathtaking: a bright and palpitating air that challenged the leap of heart and spirit; hills at eye-level, stark against the sky, tufted with pine and chestnut, craggy with ancient rocks and the crumbling castles of Guelph and Ghibelline; a hawk, high-wheeling against the blue; dark pines like spearmen marching the upland slopes.

For all his crust of egotism and ambition Landon was not a gross man. One could not walk the secret ways of the human spirit without a talent for wonder, a minimal grace of compassion, and a small well of tears for man caught in the terror of discontinuity. There were tears rising in him now at the sudden wonder of this old land, peopled with noonday ghosts.

This was the true climate of mysticism, savage yet tender, soft with tillage yet stark with relics of ancient and bloody conflicts.

Here the little Brother Francis was wedded in a wonderful union with the Lady Poverty. Here came the mercenaries of

Barbarossa: pikemen from England, bowmen from Florence, bandits from Albania, motley yet terrible in the massacre of Montalcino. The poet-king of Luxembourg, Henry of the love-songs, died here under the cypresses. On the hill of Malmarenda, crowned with four trees, was held that monstrous feast of feasts which ended in the butchery of the Tolomei and the Salimbeni. And under the ancient roofs of Siena the Lady Catherine revealed the sweet substance of her spirit – 'Charity does not seek itself for itself . . . but for God. Souls should be united and transformed by charity. We must find among thorns the perfume of roses about to open.'

It was a place of paradox, a field of fusion for historic contrarieties: beauty and terror, spiritual ecstasy and gross cruelty, medieval ignorance and the cold illumination of the age of unreason. Its people, too, were a complex of many strains: ancient Etruscan, Lombard German and soldier of fortune from God knows where. Medieval saints, Florentine humanists, Arab astrologers had all contributed to their inheritance. Their merchants traded from Provence to the Baltic and students came from the four corners of Europe to hear Aldo Brandini lecture on the regimen of the human body.

For Landon it was a strange processional vision – part landscape and part the dredging of old memory – but when it passed he felt a mite more understanding, a shade more tolerant of the passionate, involute people with whom he had broken bread. He did not have to share the damnation they imposed upon themselves. He could forgive them – provided he did not have to live with them.

He caught a drift of perfume and the sound of a footfall and a moment later Valeria Rienzi was standing beside him on the path. She was dressed in a modish summer frock. Her feet were bare in sandals of gold leather and her hair was tied back from her face with a silk ribbon. She looked pale, he thought. There were shadows about her eyes and a hint of weariness in her lips; but her skin was clear as amber and she greeted him with a smile.

'You know, Peter, that's the first time I've seen you looking like that.'

'Like what?'

'Unguarded, unwary. Almost like a boy watching Pulcin-
ella in the square.'

Landon felt himself blushing, but he grinned and tried to
shrug off the comment. 'I'm sorry. I didn't know I looked –
wary. I don't mean to be, I assure you. You must find me a
very stuffy fellow.'

'Anything but stuffy, Peter.' As if it were the most natural
gesture in the world she linked hands with him and began
strolling down the garden walk at his side. 'On the contrary,
you're a very exciting man. Exciting and perhaps a little
frightening, too.'

He played games with too many women not to recognize
this simple gambit; but his vanity was tickled and he decided
to play it a little longer. He asked innocently. 'Frightening?
I don't understand.'

'You're so complete . . . so contained. You live from yourself to yourself. You're like my father in many ways. You
understand so much that there seems to be nothing other
people can give you. You both take life like a dinner party.
You eat it, get up satisfied and then pass on. I wish I could do
that.'

'I should have said you did it very successfully.'

He delivered the stroke lightly like a fencer opening a
friendly match. To his surprise she frowned and said seriously :
'I know. I do it very well. But it isn't real, you see. It's like a
pupil going through a lesson that he knows by heart. My
father's a good teacher. So is Basilio.'

'Basilio?'

'He's a man I've been seeing lately. He makes an art of
irresponsibility.'

The gambit was not so familiar after all. Landon decided
that it might be wise to quit the game before it began in
earnest. He said, lamely : 'There's a lot of talk about the art of
living. In my experience it's mostly artifice : powder and
patches and carnival masks.'

'And what's underneath?'

'Men and women.'

'What kind?'

'All kinds – most of them lonely.'

27

As soon as he had said it, he knew that he had made a mistake. This was the beginning of every affair – the first intimacy, the chink in the mailcoat that left the heart bare to the blade. And the blade came probing more swiftly than he had dreamed.

'That's what I read in your face, wasn't it, Peter? You were lonely. You're like that bird up there – high, free, with all the world spread under your wings – and yet you were lonely.' Her fingers tightened on his palm; he felt the warmth of her body and caught the heady drift of her perfume. 'I'm lonely too.'

He was a physician and he understood the uses of pain. He asked coolly: 'With so much, Valeria? With your father and Carlo – and Basilio thrown in for good measure?'

He was prepared for anger and even for a slap in the mouth; but she simply disengaged herself and said with icy scorn: 'I expected better of you, Peter. Because I hold your hand and tell you a little of the truth about myself, does that make me a whore? I make no secret of what I do or of whom I like. But you – you must despise yourself very much. I'm sorry for any woman who tries to love you.'

Then, as if the one shame were not enough, Carlo was standing in the middle of the path and saying with wintry politeness: 'You'll have to excuse me from lunch, I'm afraid. There's been some trouble in the village. I've been asked to help. I'm not sure when I'll be back.'

He did not wait for their comments but left them quickly, hostile actors on an empty stage, without script, prompter or any predictable resolution to their conflict. Awkward as a schoolboy, Landon stammered through an apology. 'I don't know what I can say to beg your pardon. I – I can only try to explain. In my work a man gets bad habits. He sits like a father confessor listening to people's miseries. Sometimes he comes to feel a little bit like God sitting in the judgement seat. That's one problem. The other one is that patients always try to turn their psychiatrist into something else: a father, a mother, a lover. It's a symptom of sickness. We call it transference. We develop defences against it – a kind of clinical brutality. The trouble is we sometimes use the same weapon against people who are not our patients at all. It's a kind of cowardice. And you're right when you say I despise myself for it. I'm very sorry, Valeria.'

For a while she did not answer him but stood leaning against a stone urn, stripping the petals from a wis⁺aria blossom and scattering them at her feet. Her face was averted so that he could not read her eyes and when finally she did speak her voice was studiously grey.

'We're all cowards, aren't we, Peter? We're all brutal when someone probes at the little fester of fear inside us. I'm brutal to Carlo, I know that. He in his own fashion is cruel to me. Even my father, who is as brave as an old lion, makes a purgatory for those he loves. And yet we are necessary to each other. With no one to hurt, we can only hurt ourselves and that is the last terror of all. But how long can we live like this without destroying one another?'

'I don't know,' said Peter Landon sombrely, and asked himself at the same moment how long a man could endure the goads of ambition, how high he could climb alone before he toppled into disillusionment and despair.

Chapter Two

THE POLICE STATION in San Stefano was fusty with cigarette smoke and the smell of stale wine and country cheese. Sergeant Fiorello sat ostentatiously detached, copying out a deposition. Fra Bonifacio stood fumbling at his cincture while Carlo Rienzi explained himself to Anna Albertini: 'Fra Bonifacio has told me a little of your history, Anna. I'm anxious to help. But there are things you must understand first.' His voice took on the patient expository tone of a dominie instructing a dullard pupil. 'You must realize, for instance, that a lawyer is not a magician. He can't prove black is white. He can't wave a wand and wipe out things that have happened. He can't bring dead people back to life. All he can do is lend you his knowledge of the law and his voice to plead your case in court. Then a lawyer must be acceptable to his client. You must agree to engage his services. Do I make myself clear?'

It might have been an illusion but it seemed for a moment as if a ghost of a smile twitched at the pale lips of the girl. She said gravely: 'I haven't had much education, but I do understand about lawyers. You mustn't treat me like a child.'

Rienzi blushed and bit his lip. He felt very young and very gauche. But he recovered himself and went on, more firmly: 'Then you must understand what you've done – and what the consequences are.'

Anna Albertini nodded in her placid, detached fashion. 'Oh yes. I've always known what would happen. It doesn't worry me.'

'Not now, perhaps, but later, when you stand in court and hear the sentence. When they take you away and dress you in prison clothes and lock you behind bars.'

'No matter where they put me, it doesn't matter. I'm free now, you see – and happy.'

For the first time the old friar entered the discussion. He said gently: 'Anna, child, today is a strange and terrible day. You cannot say at all how you may feel tomorrow. In any case, whether you want it or not, the court will see that you have a lawyer. I think it's better that you have someone who may care a little, like Mr Rienzi here.'

'I haven't any money to pay him.'

'The money will be provided.'

'Then I suppose it's all right.'

Rienzi was shocked by her indifference and he said testily: 'We'll need something more formal than that. Will you tell Sergeant Fiorello that you accept me as your legal representative?'

'If that's what you want.'

'I heard.' Fiorello looked up with a grin. 'I'll put it in the record, for what it's worth. But I think you're wasting your time.'

'That's what I don't understand,' said Anna Albertini with odd simplicity. 'I know there's nothing you can do for me. So why do you and Fra Bonifacio take the trouble?'

'I'm trying to pay a debt, Anna,' said the friar softly.

30

Carlo Rienzi gathered up his notes, stuffed them into his pocket and stood up. He said briskly: 'You'll be taken into Siena and charged there, Anna. After that they'll either put you in the remand cells in the city prison, or more probably send you out to the women's house of correction at San Gimignano. Wherever you are, I'll come to see you tomorrow. Try not to be too frightened.'

'I'm not frightened,' said Anna Albertini. 'Tonight I think I shall sleep without nightmares.'

'God keep you, child.' Fra Bonifacio made the sign of blessing over the girl's dark head and turned away.

Rienzi was already at the door talking with Fiorello.

'When we start preparing the defence, I'd like to come and talk to you, Sergeant.'

'Out of order, I'm afraid.' Fiorello's face was a blank, official mask. 'I'll be called for the prosecution.'

'Then we'll talk in court,' said Rienzi curtly and walked out into the buzzing, sunlit square, with the little Franciscan at his heels.

The crowd parted before them. Everyone stared, pointing and whispering as if they were side-show monsters, until they disappeared into the cool confessional shadows of the church of San Stefano.

Lunch at the Villa Ascolini was a three-cornered match, dominated by the flamboyant wit of the old advocate. Carlo's absence was accepted with a shrug and, Landon guessed, a measure of relief. The trouble in the village was dismissed with a gesture of deprecation. Neither Ascolini nor Valeria asked what it was, but when Landon pressed them Ascolini read him an ironic homily on the vestigial practice of the feudal system.

'. . . We live most of the year in Rome, but our ownership of the villa makes us by definition the padronal family. When we return here, we pay a kind of tribute to our dependency. Sometimes it is a demand for new endowments to the church or the convent. Sometimes we become patrons to a more or less brilliant student. Occasionally we are asked to arbitrate in a local dispute – which is probably what has happened

31

today. But whatever the circumstance, the principle is the same: the lords pay a tax to the lowly for the privilege of survival; the lowly use the lords to protect them from a democracy they distrust and bureaucracy they despise. It's a reasonable bargain.' He sipped delicately at his wine and added the afterthought, 'I am happy that Carlo begins to assume his share of the tribute.'

Valeria smiled tolerantly and patted the man's sleeve. 'Take no notice of him, Peter. He's a malicious old man.'

Landon grinned and began dissecting a peach. Ascolini's pink face wore an expression of patent innocence. He said, blandly: 'It's the privilege of age to test the mettle of youth. Besides, I have great hopes for my son-in-law. He's a young man of singular talent and cultivation.' His shrewd, youthful eyes quizzed Landon over the rim of his glass. 'I hope he has been entertaining you properly.'

'Better than I deserve.' Landon was grateful for the change of subject. 'He drove me out to Arezzo yesterday.'

Ascolini nodded approval. 'A noble city, my friend. Too much neglected by the tourists. Petrarch's town and Aretino's.' He gave a small, amused chuckle. 'You're a student of the soul, Landon. There's a parable for you: the great lover and the great lecher spring from the same soil; the scholarly poet and the satirist scribbling dirty words on public buildings; the Sonnets to Laura and the *Sonetti Lussuriosi*. You've read them, of course?'

'I've read Petrarch,' Landon told him with a grin. 'But they don't reprint Aretino these days.'

'I will lend you a copy.' Ascolini waved an eloquent hand. 'It's a scatological classic which cannot fail to interest a psychiatrist. While you are here, please make yourself free of the library. It's not a large collection, but you may find it interesting and curious.'

'That's kind of you. I didn't know you were a collector.'

'Father is a dozen men rolled up in one,' said Valeria dryly.

Again Ascolini gave his spry, old man's chuckle. 'I collect experience, Mr Landon, as I once collected women, who are the key to experience. But I'm too old for that now. So I have books, an occasional picture and the vicarious drama of the law.'

'You're a fortunate man, *dottore*.'

Ascolini fixed him with a bright, ironic eye. 'Youth is the fortunate time, my dear Landon. The best fortune of age is a wisdom to value what is left: the last of the wine, the richness of memory, the ripeness of the season. It is a thing I have tried to explain to Carlo – and to my daughter here – that it is better to be a tree growing quietly in the sun than the monkey scrambling wildly after the fruit.'

'I wonder,' asked Landon with affected innocence, 'whether you were always content to be the tree, *dottore*.'

'I knew I was right about you, my friend. You've dealt with the law too long to be taken in by an old advocate's tricks. Of course I wasn't content; the higher the fruit, the faster I wanted to climb. But the fact is still the same. It is better to be the tree than the monkey. But how do you put an old truth into a young head?'

'You don't try,' said Landon with some tartness. 'Young heads are made to be beaten on walls. Most of them survive it.'

Surprisingly, Ascolini nodded agreement and said, with an air of regret: 'You're right, of course. I'm afraid I've intruded too much into the lives of these young people. They don't always understand the affection I have for them.'

'What we don't understand, Father . . .' Valeria's voice was high and tight as a fiddle-string, 'what you don't understand either, is the price you exact for it.'

As she stood up, her trailing sleeve caught the rim of her glass so that the crystal shattered on the pavement and the wine splashed red on the grey stones. Landon addressed himself with studious care to the last remnants of his peach until the old man challenged him with sardonic humour: 'Don't let yourself be embarrassed, my friend. Don't try to play the urbane Anglo-Saxon with people like us. This is what we are. This is how we have lived for a thousand years. We make great pictures from our lecheries and grand opera of our most murderous tragedies. You're a student of the human drama. You have a box seat. If we're happy to parade our follies, you have a perfect right to applaud the comedy. Come, my dear fellow, let me pour you a brandy. And if you find it hard to forgive me, remember I'm a peasant who used the law to make himself a gentleman.'

There was no resisting so much urbanity and in spite of himself Landon was charmed back into laughter. But later, as he stretched out on the big Florentine bed to take the ritual siesta, he found himself trying to write his own version of the Rienzi chronicle.

The old advocate was too complex a character to be defined by the somewhat naïve snobberies of a still feudal society. A peasant he might be, with a peasant's shrewdness and harsh ambition, but he was no beggar on horseback. He might have been hewn from rough material, but he was granite-hard and polished by the disciplines of a crowded world. His career was founded on the follies of other men, and passions too ignoble would have destroyed him long since. Landon felt that he owned more stature than either Carlo or Valeria would admit in him. He could see the old man strong in love, hate or a perversion of either, but he could not judge him petty.

Valeria? Here too there was a different reading from the one Carlo had given. He saw her as a kind of intransigent princess, half-awakened to love, yet still enchained by the tyrant magic of childhood. For Carlo there was still an innocence, even in her affairs. But Landon was reminded of the girls Lippo Lippi used for his virgins and angels, with smooth cheeks and limpid eyes and the memory of a thousand nights on their lips. It was a distasteful thought, but he could not rid himself of it. When one sat by the confessional couch one looked at women with calculation and one learnt, sometimes painfully, that innocence was rare and had many counterfeits. Valeria might not be loose, but she was certainly inclined to other satisfactions than those offered by a young and uncertain husband. Landon saw her maternal yet childless, cool but not passionless; not dominated by her father but sustained, like him, by some inner reserves, so that she needed less than other women but could give much more if the mood and the moment were right.

He lapsed into languid contemplation of what such a mood

34

and such a moment might be – and found himself looking into the well of his own emptiness.

All that he saw in these people he had avoided in his own life: cuckoldry, cruelty, the itch in the flesh, the fear of losing what one could only pretend to possess, the vampire tyranny of age, the perverted surrender of youth. He had set himself a limited goal and stood now within measurable reach of it. He had enjoyed women but had never submitted to them. He had preserved the ethics of a healing art while using the art for his own advancement. He had money, position, leisure. He was amenable neither to wife nor mistress. He was free, disciplined – and empty of the wine of life which these others spent with such passionate indiscretion.

Suddenly, it was they who were rich and he the mendicant at their gates; and he wondered, as beggars must, whether he had not lost the stomach for feasting, even were the feasting offered to him.

When the afternoon heat poured like lava over the land, when peasant and burgher burrowed like moles in flight from the sun, Ninette Lachaise packed paints and canvases into her battered car and headed for the open country.

It was an artist's pilgrimage, hardly less painful than that made long ago by the brotherhood of shell and staff. The land was as hot as a chafing-dish; the roads were a dusty misery; the hills, burnt umber, gathered the heat and diffused it in parching waves over the lowland, where the vines drooped and the runnels dried and the olive branches hung listless in the slack air. The cattle gave up their grazing and huddled under the sparse shade, eyes glazed, thirsty tongues lolling. The rare human, caught unaware on cart-track or tillage, seemed shrunken and desiccated as a gnome trudging some lunar landscape.

Yet over it all lay the pervasive miracle of light: the high dazzle of the southward sky, the white flare of stucco and tufa outcrop, bronze shadows in the clefts of the mountains, sheen of pond-water, ochre of roof-top, jewel-fire from bird-wing or locust flight. And this was the justification for the pilgrimage – the harsh newness of aspect, the sudden extension of

35

space, the separation of mass and contour, so that one saw through to the bones of creation and glimpsed the massive articulation of its parts.

For Ninette Lachaise there were other justifications, too. Every pilgrimage was, by definition, a discipline for the spirit, a tempting of the unknown and a stretch towards the unattainable.

Four years before, she had come, in flight, to this city whose devotees called it 'The Home of Souls'. She had fled a Parisian household dominated by an ailing mother and an elderly father whose recreation was a regret for the vanished glories of the military life. She had fled the sterilities of the post-war ateliers and a youth which was a foretaste of old age. Two things had happened swiftly: her painting had exploded into a startling maturity, and a week after her first exhibition she had tumbled headlong into a love affair with Basilio Lazzaro.

He was a professional amorist, indifferent as a bull, and the affair had lasted six stormy months. They had parted without regret; and she was left, bruised but awakened, aware of her capacity for passion but dubious of another total surrender. She had learnt another wisdom too. This was a man's country and there was no salvation for a woman in promiscuous or ill-considered loving. So she had made the disciplines of art a discipline for the flesh as well, while she waited, too cautiously for the most part, on the moment of fortunate meeting.

But it was not enough to wait, unknowing, on the fairy-tale promise of love, Prince Charming and happiness-ever-after. There were elements in her nature and her situation which, as yet, she did not fully understand. How far might her talent drive her? How soon might she challenge the legend of woman's incapacity for greatness in creation? How much equality did she need to survive after the first flush of courtship and bedding? Why was she drawn to men like Ascolini – the cynical and the wise – and why did she so mistrust the young ones, all ardour and so little endowed with understanding? What was the profit in recording visions for others to enjoy while the green years waned into the loneliness of autumn?

Since Ascolini's visit, all these questions and a dozen others had moved into sharp focus like the crags and crenellations of the Tuscan hills. It was a measure of her uneasiness that she had accepted his invitation to dine at the villa – with Valeria, who was now playing lover to Basilio Lazzaro, and with an unknown outlander who was being presented like bloodstock for her inspection.

Then, abruptly, the humour of the situation took hold of her and she began to laugh – a clear, free sound that rang across the valley, startled the cropping goats and flushed a ground lark into the shimmering summer air.

In the library of the villa, Alberto Ascolini, advocate and actor, staged a reconciliation with his daughter. It was a scene he had played many times and his role had the patina of long practice. He stood, leaning against the mantel, trim, dapper and impressive, with a glass of brandy in his hand, a small conspiratorial smile twitching the corners of his mouth. Valeria sat, curled in his armchair, chin on hand, her feet tucked under her like a small girl. He shrugged eloquently and said: 'Child, you mustn't resent me too much. I'm a perverse old goat who laughs at his own jokes. But I love you tenderly. It's not easy for a man to be father and mother to a girl-child. I know my failures better than you. But that I should seem to sell my love – this is new to me. Painful, too. I think you should explain yourself a little.'

Valeria Rienzi shook her head. 'You're not in court now, Father. I'm not going into the witness-box.'

'Perhaps not, child.' His tone was unruffled, touched only with a hint of sadness. 'But you put me in the dock. Surely I have the right to hear the indictment? How do I make you pay for love?'

'You take a share of everything I do.'

'Take? Take?' The noble brow wrinkled in puzzlement and he ran a hand through his white mane. 'You make me sound like a tax-gatherer. I have a care for you – true! I have an interest in your happiness – is this an exaction? Have I denied you anything, even the right to be young and foolish?'

For the first time she tilted up her head to face him, half hostile, half appealing. 'But don't you see, half of it has always been for yourself. Carlo? He was your creation first. You groomed him and handed him to me like a pet pony, but you always had one hand on the bridle. The others? They were yours, too – diversions for the unhappy bride, *cavalieri serventi* provided by the indulgent father. They were romances to recall your own youth.'

'And you accepted them, my dear. You were grateful, as I remember.'

'You taught me that, too.' The words came out in a rush of bitterness. 'Say thank you for the sweetmeats like a good girl. . . . But when I wanted and took something for myself – like Basilio – ah, that was different!'

For the first time a flush of anger showed in his pink, shining cheek. 'Lazzaro is scum! No fit company for a woman of breeding!'

'Breeding, Father? What is our breeding? You were a peasant's son. You married poor and regretted it when you came to reputation. You despised my mother and you were glad when she died. Me? You know what I was to be? The model of the woman you wanted but never had. You know why you never married again? So that no one could ever match you. So that you could always despise what you needed and own what you loved!'

'Love?' Ascolini laid down the word with bleak contempt. 'Tell me about love, Valeria. You have loved Carlo perhaps? Or Sebastian? Or the South American, or the son of the Greek who had money running out of his ears? Or have you found it rutting in a third-floor apartment with this Lazzaro fellow?'

She was weeping now, head buried in her hands, and he thought that he had won. He said gently: 'You and I should not hurt each other, child. We should be honest and say that what we have between us is the best we have known of love. For me it is all I have known worth having. For you there will be more, much more, because the world is still young for you. Even with Carlo there can be something, but you must make at least half the step towards it. He's a boy, you're a woman, rich with experience. But you must begin to prepare like a woman for a home and children. In a year or two I shall want to retire; Carlo will naturally step into my practice. You will have a secure estate. And there must be children with whom you can enjoy it. The locust years will come to you too, my dear, as they have already come to me. It is then you will need the little ones.'

Slowly she heaved herself out of the chair and then stood, facing him with the brutal question: 'And whose children will they be, Father? Carlo's? Mine? Or yours?'

Abruptly she turned away and left him alone in the vaulted library with two thousand years of wisdom on the shelves and no remedy at all against winter and disillusion.

There was a legend in San Stefano that Little Brother Francis had built the first chapel there with his own hands. The frescoes in the church commemorated the event, and in the cloisters of the brown friars there was a garden with a shrine where the *Poverello* stood with outstretched arms welcoming the birds who came to bathe in the fishpond at his feet. The air was cool, the light subdued, and the only sounds were the splash of water in the pond and the flapping of sandalled feet along arches of the colonnade. Here, seated on a stone bench, Carlo Rienzi found himself listening to the confession of Fra Bonifacio.

It was a chastening experience, like watching a man read his own indictment in open court or hearing a physician diagnose his own malignancy. The old man's face was scored and shrunken, his back bent as if by a heavy load. As he stumbled through his exposition, his knotted fingers laced and unlaced the cord of his cincture.

'I told you earlier, my son, that what happened today was the last chapter of a very long story. There are many people involved in it. I am one of them. Each of us bears a measure of guilt for what happened today.'

Rienzi held up a warning hand. 'Let's wait here a moment, Father. Let me show you first a little of the law. Murder was done here today. On the first evidence the crime was a premeditated act of revenge for a wrong done some years ago to Anna Albertini. There is no dispute about the act, its circumstances or its motive. The prosecution has an iron-clad case. The defence has only two pleas: insanity or mitigation. If we plead insanity we have to prove it by psychiatric testimony, and the girl's case is hardly better than if she suffers the normal penalty for murder. If we plead mitigation we have a choice of two grounds: provocation or partial mental infirmity. A court is not a confessional. The law takes only a limited cognizance of the moral guilt of an act. It concerns itself with responsibility, but in the social order and not in the moral one.' He smiled and spread his hands in deprecation. 'I read your lectures, Father. Forgive me. But this time our roles are reversed. For my client's sake, you must not lead me into irrelevance.'

The old man digested the thought slowly and then nodded approval. 'Every act of violence is a kind of madness, my son, but I would doubt whether you will find Anna Albertini legally insane. As to mitigation, here I think I can help you, though I cannot say how you may use what I tell.' He paused a moment and then went on slowly. 'There are two versions of this history. The first is the one which will be presented in court, because it is a matter of official record. The second —' He broke off and waited a long moment, staring down at the backs of his knotted, freckled hands. 'I know the second version, but I cannot tell it to you, because it came to me first under the seal of confession. I can only say that it exists and that you will have to ferret it out for yourself. Whether you can prove it is another problem again. And even then I am doubtful whether it will have validity in court.' His voice trembled and his eyes filled up with the rheumy tears of age. 'Justice, my son! How often is it abrogated by the very processes and the very people who are meant to preserve it! You saw Anna today. She is twenty-four years old. The last time I saw her was sixteen years ago – a child of eight putting flowers on her mother's grave and scratching an inscription on the cemetery wall with a piece of tin. It's still there. I'll show it to you afterwards.'

For all his professional detachment and his private preoccupations, Rienzi was moved by the pathos of the old man's situation. He himself was a man familiar with guilt, familiar too with the impotence to purge it. This was the tragedy of the human condition: that every single act was contingent upon another in the past and spawned a litter of consequences for the future. Sin might be expiated, forgiveness might be granted, but the consequences spread out, ripples in a limitless pool, currents eternally moving in a dark sea.

Rienzi prompted the friar gently: 'The official story, Father – where does it begin? Where is it written? Who tells it?'

'Everyone in San Stefano. The record is in Sergeant Fiorello's files, attested by half a dozen men. It begins in the last year of the war, when the Germans were in control of this area, and Gianbattista Belloni was the leader of a Partisan band operating in the hills. It was, as you know, a time of confusion, suspicion and blood-feud. Anna was living in the village with her mother, Agnese Moschetti, who was the widow of a man killed in the Libyan campaign. For a while there was a small detachment of Germans quartered in the village and some of them were billeted in Agnese Moschetti's house. When they moved out, she was accused of consorting with them and of betraying Partisan movements and personnel. She was arraigned before a drumhead court martial of Partisans, found guilty and executed by a firing-squad. Gianbattista Belloni presided at the court and signed the order for the execution. After the armistice, the proceedings of the court martial were attested and recorded in the police records of the village. A few years later, Belloni was made Mayor of the village and decorated with a gold medal by the President for gallantry in the service of his country . . .'

He broke off and wiped his lips as if to erase an unpleasant taste. Rienzi asked him: 'And what does the record say about Anna Albertini?'

'Her existence was noted,' said the old man dryly. 'And the fact that she was handed in to the care of Fra Bonifacio of the Order of Friars Minor, who had her sent away to Florence in the care of relatives.'

'Where was she while her mother was tried and executed?'

'The record makes no mention of that.'

'But you know?'

'Under the seal.'

'Anna herself never told you?'

'From the time of her mother's death until this day I

never heard a single word from her lips. Neither did anyone else in the village. At her mother's grave she did not even cry.'

'She's married now. Do you know anything about her husband?'

'Nothing. The police have sent for him, of course.'

'Other relatives?'

'The aunt who took her to Florence. I'm not even sure she's alive.' His old shoulders drooped despairingly. 'It's been sixteen years, my son. Sixteen years. . . .'

'You told me she wrote something on the cemetery wall. Could I see it, please?'

'Of course.'

He led Rienzi round the circuit of the cloisters, through a creaking postern and into the walled confine of the Campo Santo, where marble cherubs and wreathed columns and shabby immortelles gave their mute testimony to mortality. The grave of Agnese Moschetti was marked by a rough headstone which recorded only the date of her birth, the date of her death, and the last pathos: *'Requiescat in pace.'* There was hardly a pace between the headstone and the crumbling wall of the cemetery, and they squatted and wedged themselves close to the ground to read the painful childish etching: 'Belloni, one day I will kill you.'

Rienzi stared at the words for a long time, then asked sharply: 'Has anyone else seen this?'

'Who knows?' The old man shrugged helplessly. 'They've been there so many years.'

'Produce them in court,' said Rienzi softly, 'and we are dead before we begin. Find me a mallet and a chisel, man – and hurry!'

At three-thirty in the afternoon Landon woke from an uneasy doze to find Carlo Rienzi sitting in his armchair smoking a cigarette and flipping through a magazine with moody disinterest. His shoes were dusty, his shirt crumpled. His face looked drawn and tired. He gave Landon a telegraphic account of the events in San Stefano and ended with the wry summation: 'So that's it, Peter. The dice are cast. I've accepted the brief. I've found a pair of associates to act with me and give me entry to the Sienese courts. I have my first case.'

'Have you told your wife or Ascolini?'

'Not yet.' He gave a little lopsided grin. 'I've had enough excitement for a while. I'll leave the announcement until after dinner. Besides, I wanted to talk with you first. Would you do me a favour?'

'What kind of favour?'

'Professional. I'd like to retain you informally as psychiatric adviser. I'd like you to see the girl, make your own diagnosis and then indicate a possible use of medical evidence.'

'That's a tall order.' Landon frowned dubiously. 'It raises questions of ethics and medical politeness and my own status under the law.'

'If you were assured that informal consultation would give no offence?'

'Then I'd consider it. But I would still owe your father-in-law the courtesy of an explanation. After all, I'm his guest.'

'Would you wait until after I've spoken with him?'

'Naturally. But there's something I'd like to ask you, Carlo . . .' He hesitated a moment and then put the bald question: 'Why this case? On the face of it, the odds are all against you. It's your first brief and I don't see that you have a hope in hell of winning it.'

Rienzi's drawn face relaxed into a rare, boyish smile, and then grew serious again. He said quietly: 'It's a fair question, Peter, and I'll try to answer it, as I've already answered it for myself. It's a *naïveté* to believe that legal eminence is founded only on victories. The lost cause is often more profitable than the safe brief. New light on classic antimonies, contentious applications of accepted principles, a strategy that takes advantage of the perennial paradox of legality and justice – these are the foundations of reputations in advocacy. It's like medicine, you see. Who makes the greatest name – the fellow who cures an apple-colic or the man who massages ten seconds of life into a failing heart? There's no cure for death, my dear Peter, but there is a high art in its deferment. In law there is a correlative art of illumination, and on this great careers are built. Ascolini's for instance. And, I hope, mine.'

Landon was shocked by the cool cynicism of the exposition. He could not believe that this was the nostalgic poet who had played Chopin, the pained lover whose world had blown up in his face. His lips seemed too young to have framed the argument, his heart too young to have surrendered to so bleak an ambition. Yet, in all justice, Landon had to agree with him. He had undertaken to beat Ascolini on his own ground, that narrow field of contention where the law defines itself by contradiction as an instrument of rule or an instrument of justice. Carlo Rienzi could only contend on the traditional terms, divesting himself of feeling as he divested himself of the common dress, clothing himself in the black inhuman habit of the inquisitor.

Still, Landon had committed himself to friendship and he had to know how far Rienzi understood his own commitment. So he faced him harshly with a new question: 'Do you understand what you're saying, Carlo? You've engaged yourself to a client – and on the basis of hope. Not a great hope, maybe, but at least a small one. It's a personal relationship that reaches far beyond legality.'

'No, Peter!' His denial was swift and emphatic. 'It is based simply and solely on legality. I cannot make moral judgements on the state of my client's soul. I cannot commit myself to sympathy or sentiment in her regard. It is my function to induce such sympathies in others, to advocate favourable judgement by others, to bend every provision of the law to her advantage. These are her claims on me. I can admit no others. I am neither priest nor physician, nor custodian of sick minds.'

If he were as precise and as eloquent as this on the floor of the court there could be great hopes for him. But Landon wondered how many were the pupil's words and how many were the master's. He wondered, too, how far Rienzi understood that the detachment of the great lawyer or the great surgeon was the fruit of bitter experience, the mature conviction of ultimate futility. He asked himself whether it were not as great a mistake for Rienzi to commit himself too early to the detachment of age as to surrender too readily to the compassions of youth. But he was the spectator and Rienzi was the actor, so he shrugged and said lightly: 'I should stick

44

to my own cobbling. Anyway, if your client is as beautiful as you tell me you'll make an impressive pair in court.'

Rienzi's face clouded and he said thoughtfully: 'She's like a child, Peter. She's twenty-four but she talks and thinks like a child – simple and unaccountable. I doubt she's going to be much help to me or to herself.'

'An insanity plea?'

Rienzi frowned. 'I'm no expert, but I doubt it. This is why I need your expert advice. I confess I'm relying more heavily on mitigatory evidence which I hope to dig up in San Stefano.'

'Investigations like that can be expensive.'

'Fra Bonifacio has undertaken to raise the expenses for the defendant. But I shouldn't be surprised if I have to meet some of them from my own pocket.'

'You're gambling a great deal, aren't you?'

'The biggest gamble of all is Valeria,' said Rienzi gravely. 'But I am resigned to that, so the rest is bagatelle.' He held out his hand. 'Wish me luck, Peter.'

'All the luck in the world, Carlo. Go with God.'

Rienzi gave him a swift, searching look. 'I think you mean that.'

'I do. I'm no great example of devotion, but I know that no matter how far you fall you'll never quite fall out of the hand of God. You may need to remember it some time.'

'I know,' said Rienzi moodily. 'Tonight I think I shall need it most of all.'

Then he was gone and Landon felt an oddly poignant grief for him. There were swords at his back and a battle looming ahead, but Landon could not shake off the uneasy conviction that he was fighting with the wrong weapons and for the wrong cause – and that victory for Carlo Rienzi might well prove the subtlest defeat of all.

Ascolini's dinner party began, genially enough, with cocktails in the library. The old man was urbane and eloquent, Valeria was affectionate to him and attentive to her guests, if a shade more reserved than the occasion seemed to demand. For Landon, his fellow guest was a pleasant surprise. He found her decorative, diverting and agreeably feminine. She had none of the studied languor of her Italian cousins, none of their giddy coquetry which promised much but was apt to be niggardly in fulfilment. She talked well and listened with flattering interest – and she was more than a match for the ironic malice of the advocate.

Ascolini was making a patent comedy out of his role of matchmaker. He said heartily: 'We must provide some diversion for you, Landon. A pity you're not in the marriage market. You'd be the rage of the town.'

'Don't you provide for bachelors in Siena?'

Ascolini laughed and tossed the question to Ninette Lachaise. 'How would you answer that, Ninette?'

'I would say that bachelors generally manage to provide for themselves.'

'It's a legend,' said Landon with a grin. 'Most bachelors get what they ask for and end by finding it isn't what they want.'

'We have our legends, too,' said Ascolini with tart humour. 'Our virgins are virtuous, our wives content, our widows discreet. But love is always a lottery. You buy the ticket and wait on your luck.'

'Don't be vulgar, Father,' said Valeria calmly.

'Love is a very vulgar business,' said Doctor Ascolini.

Ninette Lachaise raised her glass in a toast. 'To your conquest of Siena, Mr Landon.'

He drank to it cautiously. There was no coquetry in her frank brown eyes, but a faint smile clung to the corners of her mouth. Good-humoured women were rare enough in his life, and the intelligent ones were either boresome or unbeautiful. He toyed with the thought that with this one he could risk more than he had ever dared before of confidence, intimacy and perhaps even love. He saw Ascolini watching with a smile of thin amusement, and wondered if the thought were patent to the old man. Then Carlo came in, immaculate and apparently in the best of humour, to pour himself a drink and join in the conversation.

The change in the climate was immediate and startling and yet curiously hard to define. It was as if half the lights in the room had been switched off, so that they stood in a rosy glow of amiability. Ascolini became suddenly benign and Valeria took on an aura of prosy tenderness. The talk lost its edge and lapsed into comfortable digression. It was the kind of conspiracy which is practised on the ailing; the vague euphoria which is imposed on those for whom the impact of the world has proven too harsh.

Carlo himself seemed unaware of it, and Landon was quite prepared to admit that his own perception might have been heightened by fatigue and that cautious suspicion which one brings to a new situation. The fact remained that from the last cocktail till the first cup of coffee he could not remember one single significant phrase or gesture. But when the brandy was poured and the servant had retired, Carlo Rienzi took the stage and light came up again to full glare.

'With the permission of our guests I should like to make a family announcement.' Valeria and her father exchanged a swift, questioning glance and Valeria shrugged her ignorance. Carlo went on, calmly: 'I haven't discussed this with either of you, because I felt it was my private decision. Now it is made and I hope you will accept it. I was called to the village today, as you know. The Mayor was murdered by a former village girl, Anna Albertini. It's a long story that I won't bother you with now. The end of it is that Fra Bonifacio asked me to undertake the girl's defence. I agreed to do it.'

Ascolini and Valeria watched him blank-faced. He waited a moment and then turned to Ascolini with the not ungraceful compliment: 'I have served a long apprenticeship under a great master. Now it is time I made my own road. I'm resigning, *maestro*, to wait for my own briefs and plead my own causes.' He fished in his pocket and brought up a small package which he handed to the old man. 'From the student to the master, a gift which says my thanks. Wish me luck, *dottore*.'

Landon felt a singular respect for him at that moment and prayed that they would be kind to his shortcomings. Whatever the basis of their tacit union against him, he had acquitted himself like a man.

Rienzi waited, standing in a pool of silence while his wife and her father sat with heads bowed and eyes downcast to the table. Then he too sat down and Ascolini began to open the package with sedulous deliberation.

Finally the gift was revealed: a small, gold fob watch of exquisite Florentine workmanship, hung on a close-linked chain. Ascolini showed no sign of pleasure or regret, but held the watch in his hands and spelt into Italian the classic Latin of the inscription: 'To my illustrious master, from his grateful pupil, this gift and my first case are dedicated.'

Ascolini let the watch drop from his hands so that it swung like a pendulum from its intricate chain. His eyes were hooded, his voice a dusty contempt: 'Keep it, boy – or send it to the pawnbroker. You may need it sooner than you think.'

He laid the watch carefully on the table, pushed back his chair and walked from the room. Carlo watched him go, then he turned to Valeria and said, quite calmly: 'And you, *cara*? What do you have to say?'

Slowly she raised her head and looked at him with eyes full of condemnation. She said softly: 'I am your wife, Carlo. Wherever you go, I must walk too. But you've done a terrible thing tonight. I'm not sure that I can ever forgive you.'

Then she too walked out, and Landon, Ninette and Rienzi sat facing each other over the wreckage of the dinner party. Carlo cupped his hands round the warm bubble of the brandy goblet and raised it to the level of his lips. He gave them a small, crooked smile and said: 'I'm sorry you both had to see that, but it was the only way I could guarantee my own courage.' Then he added the saddest words they had ever heard: 'Strange, you know . . . all my life I was afraid of being alone, and all my life I was alone and never knew it. Strange!'

'All my life,' said Peter Landon moodily, 'I have dealt with sick minds. I don't think I've ever been so shocked.'

Ninette Lachaise laid a cool hand on his wrist and said calmly: 'That's your mistake, I think, Peter. These people are not sick, only selfish. Their whole life is a battle, one against the other. Each wants too much for too little. They're entrenched like enemies in their own egotism.'

'You're a wise woman, Ninette.'

'Too wise for my own good, perhaps.'

They were sitting in her car, half a mile from the gates of the villa where three separate lights burned yellow in the blank walls and the moonlight shone cold on the spear-points of the cypresses. When Carlo had left the dining-room, Landon had felt suddenly stifled by the atmosphere of hostility, and with unaccustomed humility he had begged Ninette to lend him her company for a while before bed-time. She had agreed calmly and driven him out along the winding road to a spot where the land fell away into a pool of darkness and the hills climbed steeply towards the late, faint stars.

He felt no need of caution with this woman, and she made no drama of this first intimate nocturne. He was thankful to her and he sensed in her quiet talk a return of this gratitude of the lonely. It gave him pleasure to open to her a thought that had puzzled him for a long time. 'You know the rarest thing in the world, Ninette? A man or woman wise enough to look the world in the eye and accept it, good or bad, for what it is at that moment. When people come to me or when I am summoned to them in prison or hospital, it's because I am the last milestone in their long flight from reality. Their flight is a symptom of sickness – and the sickness is the subtlest one of all: fear! They're afraid of loss, of pain, of loneliness, of their own natures, of the obligations which any normal life lays on them.'

'And what's your cure, Peter?'

'Sometimes there is no cure. Sometimes the mechanisms of the mind seize up or refuse to work except in a psychotic groove. For the rest, I try to take them by the hand and lead them back, step by step, to the moment of primal terror. While I am doing it I try to rebuild their courage to face it. If I succeed, they begin to be well again. If I fail . . .' He hesitated a moment and sat staring out over the dark valley where a sparse huddle of lights marked the village of San Stefano '. . . If I fail, then the flight begins once more.'

'And where does it end?'

'In nothingness. In the ultimate negation of being, when the world contracts to the dimensions of a man's own navel,

49

when there is no splendour, no profusion, and even a capacity for love is destroyed. There are times,' he added softly, 'when I wonder if I am not destroying in myself what I'm trying to build in others.'

'No, Peter!' The warmth in her voice surprised him. 'I watched you tonight with Carlo. You were careful of him. You had the grace to be gentle. So long as you keep that, you needn't be afraid.'

'But how do you renew in yourself what you spend on others?'

'If I could be sure of the answer to that,' said Ninette softly, 'I would feel safer than I do now. But I think – no, I believe – that the spending is the growing too, that the flowers fall to make the fruit grow, and that this is the way it was intended to be from the beginning.' She laughed lightly and withdrew her hand. 'It's late and I'm getting sentimental. Go to bed, Peter. You're a disturbing man.'

'May I see you again?'

'Any time. You'll find me in the phone book.'

'I think I may leave the villa tomorrow.'

'Where will you go?'

'If it weren't for Carlo I'd go back to Rome. But I've promised to help him with his case and I can't retract now. I'll probably get myself a room in Siena.'

'I'm glad of that,' said Ninette Lachaise simply. 'It gives me a little hope, too.'

She turned and kissed him lightly on the lips and when he held her to him she pushed him away gently. 'Go home, Peter. Golden dreams.'

He stood watching a long time as her rickety car clattered down the hillside; then he turned away and trudged back to the iron gates of the villa, where a sleepy gate-keeper bade him a truculent good night.

He slept badly that night and woke, stale and sour, to raw summer in Tuscany. A shave and a bath refreshed him, but he could not shake off the burden of being a guest in a hostile house. He wished fervently that he had not obliged himself either to Ascolini or Rienzi; but the damage was done and he had at least the comfort of a partial retreat. He packed his bags for a swift departure after breakfast and then walked out to take the early morning air on the terrace.

To his surprise he found Valeria Rienzi there before him. There was more than a hint of embarrassment in her greeting. 'You're up early, Peter.'

'I had a restless night. And it is a beautiful morning.'

She made a rueful mouth and said quietly: 'I'm glad to find you here. I want to apologize for last night. We behaved very badly.'

He was in no mood for a fencing match, so he shrugged and said boldly: 'I don't need an apology. This is your house. You're free to behave in it any way you want. But I think Carlo deserved better.'

'I know that.' She accepted the reproof without protest. 'I hurt him very badly. I've told him I'm sorry.'

'Then there's nothing more to be said. The rest is private to you both.'

'You're very angry, aren't you?' Her hand imprisoned his against the stone balustrade and she turned on him the charm of a very penitent smile. 'I don't blame you. But Carlo took me by surprise. I'm sorry that you had to be involved.'

'I'm not involved and I'm not angry. Not now. But I think it's better that I leave after breakfast.'

She made no attempt to dissuade him but nodded assent. 'Carlo told me. I can understand how you feel. He told me, too, that you had promised to stay a few days in Siena. I'm grateful for that. He needs a friend just now.'

'I think he needs his wife more.'

She flushed at the reproach and turned away, covering her face with her hands. Landon waited, half guilty, half glad, staring over the cypresses to the distant crags of Amiata. In a little while she was composed again, but there was a winter in her voice and her look was sombre when she turned to him. 'Perhaps I deserved that. Perhaps, for Carlo's sake, you have the right to say it. But now will you do me a favour?'

'What sort of favour?'

'Walk with me in the garden. Talk with me a while.'

'Of course.'

'Thank you.'

She took his hand and led him down the broad stone steps that gave on to the garden walks. By the classic contrivance of the old gardeners they followed the contour of the land, winding imperceptibly downwards through ranks of pines, rose arbours, banks of flowering shrubs and pergolas trailing the purple blossom of wistaria. Sometimes the house was hidden, sometimes the walk was screened, as if for the privacy of old lovers, but always the valley was in view. There was no sound but the buzzing of insects, the occasional chitter of a bird and the brisk rustle of a lizard from the leaves to a warm rock.

'Sometimes at night,' said Valeria, 'we hear nightingales in the garden. Father and I come out very softly and listen. First one starts, then another, until the whole valley seems full of singing. It is so very beautiful.'

'Lonely too, sometimes.'

'Lonely?' She looked up at him in mild surprise.

'For the one who sits inside playing Chopin in the dark.'

'Carlo?'

'Who else?'

'You don't understand, do you?'

'I'd like to, but I don't have to. After all, it's not my affair.'

'Carlo has made it so. And I'd like to explain myself.'

'Listen to me, Valeria!' He stopped pacing and faced her under the branch of a grey fig tree where a robin surveyed them with a beady, critical eye. 'Understand who I am and what I am. I'm a healer of sick minds. I spend the best part of my life listening to other people's troubles and getting paid for it. If I extend myself outside the consulting-room I give myself no chance at all of a normal life. I'm often touched by people's misfortunes, but I can't be obliged because I have so little to give. By the same token, you owe me no explanation, even if you choose to do hand-springs on the roof of the Duomo. Now, if that's understood, I'll listen. If I can help, I will. After that – *basta*! Enough for me, enough for you, too.'

'I wish I had half your detachment.' Landon was startled by the bitterness of her tone. 'But you're right. There are no claims on you. I talk; you listen; you go away. *Basta!* But you're not half so cold as you want others to believe.' She took his hand again and made him fall into step beside her while the robin flirted cheekily along the fringe of their progress. He found himself admiring the assurance with which she entered on subjects and issues that earned her no credit at all. She did not minimize or attempt to make a drama. There was an essential simplicity in her which was damnably disconcerting. She said first of all: 'I know, Peter, that you find something unnatural in my relation with my father. It colours what you think about my marriage with Carlo.'

'Let's settle on another word – "unusual" – and start from there.'

'Very well – "unusual". You're more courteous than some of my friends.'

'It's the way of the world. People gossip. They love the smell of scandal.' It was a banality, but she thought on it gravely for a few moments, then asked him: 'Do you find it scandalous, Peter?'

He smiled and shook his head. 'I'm a doctor, not a censor of morals. I take the clinical view. Find out all the facts before you make a diagnosis.'

'Then here is the first fact, Peter. For a long time I lived only in one world and I found it very satisfying. I had no mother, but a father who loved me tenderly and who opened the world to me door by door. Each new revelation was a kind of wonder. He denied me nothing, yet somehow managed to teach me the disciplines of enjoyment. He did what most fathers cannot do – taught me to understand what it means to be a woman. He answered every question I ever asked and I never found him out in a lie. Was it unnatural that I should love him and be glad to have him near me?'

'No, not unnatural, but perhaps unfortunate.'

'Why do you say that?' For the first time he caught an edge of anxiety in her voice.

'Because, generally, it is the shortcoming of parents which forces a child to find wholeness elsewhere – in a wider world, with other people, with other kinds of love. It is not your relationship which is unnatural, only that you should find it complete and sufficient. Your father's a very remarkable man, but he's not all men nor all the world.'

'That's what I found out,' said Valeria Rienzi quietly. 'Does that surprise you?'

'A little.'

'I told you I had never found him out in a lie. Until recently that was true. It dawned on me quite slowly. Always he had told me that all his care and counsel was directed to my well-being. Instead I found that my well-being was a fund set for himself. I was a capital he had created to replenish the youth he had lost.' Her face clouded and she stumbled, shamefaced, to the conclusion. 'He wants me to be all the things I can't be – wife, mistress, son . . . and a mirror image of Alberto Ascolini!'

'And what do you want to be, Valeria?'

'A woman! My own woman.'

'Not Carlo's?'

'Anybody's who can give me the identity my father has taken from me!'

'Can't Carlo do that?'

For the first time he heard her laugh; but there was no humour in it, only an unhappy irony. 'You feel so much for Carlo, don't you, Peter? He's a boy! A passionate boy! And when you've lived with a man all your life, it isn't half enough!'

'He looked very much like a man last night,' said Peter Landon flatly.

'You didn't go to bed with him,' said Valeria Rienzi. He was still digesting that sour little morsel when she offered him another one. 'What's your prescription, Doctor, when a girl wants to be kissed and tumbled in the hay, and all she's offered are chocolates for breakfast!'

Then, because he was challenged in his own manhood, because he was sick of playing the wise owl while others played '*baciami*' in the bushes, he took her in his arms and kissed her and tasted the sweetness of her mouth mixed with the salt tang of blood.

'Charming!' said Doctor Ascolini with dry good humour. 'Quite, quite charming – if a trifle indiscreet.' Landon broke away roughly and saw the old man standing in the middle of the path, his pink face bright with merriment. 'I must disapprove on principle, but in the circumstances I find it a commendable diversion for both of you.'

'Oh – go to hell!'

Sick with anger and humiliation, Landon pushed past Ascolini and hurried away. The rich actor's laugh followed him like the laughter of a child delighted with the antics of a painted clown.

Chapter Three

WHEN LANDON reached the terrace, breakfast was already laid and Carlo Rienzi was working through coffee and a stack of morning newspapers. He greeted Landon with grave courtesy, passed him a cup of coffee and a dish of warm country bread, then told him calmly: 'I saw what happened, Peter. It was almost as if it were contrived that I should.' He pointed down into the garden where Ascolini and his daughter were clearly visible through a gap in the shrubbery. 'You understand now, perhaps, what it is that I have to fight.'

Landon felt himself blushing under a new humiliation. He said awkwardly: 'It was my fault. I'm sorry it happened.'

Rienzi waved aside the apology. 'Why blame yourself? It's happened before. It will happen again.'

Unreasonably, Landon was angry with him. 'Then why are you so damned complacent about it? Why don't you punch me on the nose? And if my wife were unfaithful I'd break her neck, or walk out!'

'But she is not your wife, Peter,' said Rienzi in a flat voice. 'She is mine – and I am half responsible for what she is. You've known her for a few days. I've lived with her for years. You judge her as you would judge any other wife who wants to play hot cockles in the summertime. But in her this is a kind of childish wilfulness in which her father has indulged her for his own purposes. She is never wilful with him, you see, although she often resents it. The pattern of order and authority has been set, as it would have been set with us in a normal marriage. Outside the pattern Valeria recognizes no claim, no obligation. The world and all the creatures thereof were made for the sole use and benefit of the Ascolini family.'

'And do you think you can break the pattern and reset it?'

'I know I must try.'

'I wish you luck!'

Rienzi smiled and shook his head. 'Peter, my friend, don't play the cynic with me. I know what you are and how you feel. This is a marriage – not a very satisfactory one, but it's a contract binding until death and I must make it work as best I can. In the beginning I made a bad mistake. I had too much love, too little wisdom. Now I am wiser and there is, I think, still enough love. You must not despise me because I try to do a good thing. You must not despise Valeria because she has never been taught what is good.'

The dignity of the man, the pathos of his situation, shamed Landon more than he cared to admit, but there was still a warning to be given: 'It takes two to keep a contract, Carlo. You may do all that you hope, and more – and you can still fail with Valeria. You should at least be prepared.'

He shrugged and said with a kind of sad self-contempt: 'What have I to lose, Peter?'

'Hope.'

For a long moment Rienzi stared at him, then nodded a bleak assent. 'This is the last terror, Peter. You must not ask me to face it yet. Start your breakfast and let's see what the Press has to say about our client.'

The affair at San Stefano had made headlines in every morning paper. Their accounts were lurid, full of gory rhetoric and sadistic detail. The photographs ran the gamut of vulgarity, from a grisly shot of the dead man lying in state in the parlour to a close-up of Anna Albertini being bundled into a police car with her skirt rucked up to her thigh. But, out of the welter of ill-chosen words, the lines of the story emerged clearly enough.

The dead man was Gianbattista Belloni, formerly a peasant farmer, then a Partisan leader and later Mayor of San Stefano and a landowner of ample means. After the war he had been decorated with a gold medal and a citation from the President for distinguished military service. He was married, with two grown sons. His wife's name was Maria. All local testimony confirmed him as a man of good character, generous habits and modest eminence. His murder had raised the village to passionate resentment.

Anna Albertini – named variously in the Press as 'the young assassin', 'the beautiful but ensanguined murderer', 'the killer of Satanic charm' – was born Anna Moschetti, daughter of a conscripted soldier killed in the Libyan campaign and a mother executed by the Partisans for collaboration with the Germans. She was twenty-four years of age and had lived away from San Stefano for sixteen years. At twenty she had married a young Florentine named Luigi Albertini who worked as night-watchman in a textile factory.

On the day of the murder, she had made breakfast for her husband, then, when he was asleep, had taken his gun and left the house. She had caught an early train which arrived in Siena just before midday. She had hailed a taxi at the station and driven to San Stefano to murder Belloni. The motive for her crime was manifest: vendetta – reprisal for her mother's death on the man who had presided at the drumhead court.

The newspapers made much of this motive. Most of them discussed it with singular sobriety and one leading journal spread itself in an editorial condemning in the strongest terms 'any revival of this ancient and malevolent practice' and demanding 'the utmost vigilance on the part of the police and the judiciary lest any false benignity should seem to justify the barbarity of the blood-feud which has disfigured so many pages of our history'.

Which, it seemed to Landon, was fair enough. The *lex talionis* marked rock-bottom in human relations. It was a bloody, mutinous, wasteful cult which had no counterpart even in the jungle. Wherever it was practised, communities lived in daily terror, one step from breakdown and chaos. In this affair he had to admit that his sympathies were all on the side of the angels. And no matter how Carlo Rienzi framed his plea, the angels would give him a rough passage through the court.

In the last journal of all he came on a startling photograph of Anna Albertini: a two-column plate, marred somewhat by

57

hasty etching, but still a portrait of tragic beauty and terrible innocence. There was no malice in the softly curving lips, no hate in the eyes, but almost a touch of wonder at some magnificence invisible to others. If the old moralists spoke truth when they said that the eyes were windows of the soul, then Anna Albertini's soul was a mirror of primitive purity. Carlo Rienzi leaned across the table and tapped the photograph with a coffee spoon.

'That's exactly how she looks, Peter, and you have to tell me what goes on behind that face.'

'I'll need time,' said Landon, in dry, professional fashion, 'time and a certain freedom in consultation. That part's up to you.'

'I'll have to consult with Galuzzi. He's the consultant to the Department of Justice on Mental Health. If he agrees, we won't have too much trouble with the prison authorities. It may take a little time to arrange a meeting with him, but I'll do it as soon as I can. I've arranged a lodging for you in Siena. I'll get in touch with you there.'

'It's an awkward situation for everybody,' said Landon with sour discomfort. 'It's best I leave the villa.'

'You told me you wanted to talk with Ascolini before you did any work with me.'

'I'll dispense myself from the courtesy. I don't think it matters now.'

'Good,' said Carlo briskly. 'Let's get your bags and hit the road.'

The drive into Siena was a short and barren one for both. Carlo was preoccupied and Landon was moody and exacerbated. The splendid countryside slipped by unnoticed and Rienzi soon gave over his half-hearted attempts at diversion. When they arrived, he installed Landon in an astonishing *pensione* with the arms of the Salimbeni over the portal, immense rooms with coffered ceilings and a thirteenth-century fountain playing in the courtyard. As a final gesture he announced that the rent was paid for a week. When Landon blushed at so much generosity, Rienzi laughed. 'Call it a bribe, Peter. I need you here. You've seen the worst of us. Now I'd like to show you the better side. Today you need time to yourself and so do I. I'll pick you up here at nine-thirty tomorrow morning. Stay out of mischief!'

Landon had no heart for mischief just then, but he was glad when Rienzi was gone. He needed time and privacy to shake off the depression which had been laid upon him. The day was still young and he decided to wander round the city. Its lovers had named it long ago 'The Home of Souls'. He hoped it might do something for his own, which presently was in a very sorry state.

In fact, it did nothing at all but make him feel more miserable. There is a disease which afflicts many travellers, an endemic malaise whose symptoms are an acute melancholy, a sense of oppression by what is old and distaste for what is new. The faces one sees take on a sinister character, like the cartoons of da Vinci. The gaudy cavalcade of history becomes a procession of spavined caricatures shambling forward to the tolling of the *miserere* bell. One is conscious of solitude and strangeness. The effort of communication in an alien tongue becomes an intolerable burden. The food presents itself as a garbled mess. One longs for the thinnest wine of one's own country.

There is no remedy for the disease. One tolerates it like a recurrent bout of malaria, and then it goes away, with no perceptible harm to mind or body. The best treatment is to ignore it and keep moving; to go through the motions of interest and activity. A pretty girl is a great help. A half-bottle of brandy is an unreliable substitute.

But Landon had drunk too much brandy the night before and was too jaded to go looking for the fillies in a new town! So, after two hours of footloose wandering, he settled for an indifferent lunch, a siesta and a phone call to Ninette Lachaise. Her reaction was immediate and warm. She would be delighted to see him. They should meet for dinner at the Sordello, a cavernous, lively resort near the Campo, frequented by artists and students from the faculties of the University.

When they met she greeted him affectionately. When they made their entrance into the smoky cellars heads were turned and there was a whistling chorus of approval which made Landon feel a foot taller and singularly grateful to Ninette Lachaise.

For the practised traveller or the practising bachelor there was no time for long overtures in friendship. One either achieved a quick rapport or abandoned the effort. One became jealous of time because so much was dispersed on the mechanics of getting from one place to another. Even a railway ticket was a warrant for the minor death of parting. When one boarded an aircraft one was launched into a suspension which was a troubling image of eternity. So one resented those who demanded proof of identity, elaborate tokens of aptitude for their company. One was impatient of women who doled out their smiles and made a grand opera out of an invitation to dinner. And one sometimes despised oneself for so much need of company on the pilgrim road.

When Landon explained it to Ninette Lachaise she accepted it as a compliment and gave him her own good-humoured version of the theme. 'It's the penalty of freedom, Peter, the tax we pay for being bachelors or artists. When the strolling players come to town, husbands keep a close eye on their wives. When the pedlars come with their trays of novelties, honest merchants tighten their purse-strings and keep their daughters at home. You are still Scaramouche, *chéri*; I am still Pierrette, light in love and ready to seduce their sons to the altar. It is only when we are old and famous that they want to have us to dinner.'

'And yet they need us, Ninette It's only people like you and I who can show them how to hold up the world by the heels and spit in its eye.'

She laughed happily and bit into an olive. 'Of course they need us, Peter, but not quite as we want to be needed. The walls are bare without a picture or two. It's as fashionable to have an analyst today as it used to be to have a personal confessor. For the rest' – her fine hands embraced the chattering concourse in the cellar – 'they would rather we stayed in Bohemia and came out only at carnival time. I'm sure we're happier there, anyway.'

'What happens when we get old?'

She shrugged and pouted like a true Parisienne. 'If we are old and foolish we hit the pavement and the bottle. If we are old and wise we still come back sometimes, ancient masters to receive the homage of youth . . . like that one, for instance.'

She pointed across the room to a shadowy corner where a white-haired man sat with half a dozen students who listened to him with rapt attention. On the hat-stand beside the table were hung three or four of those curious medieval caps whose colour denoted the Faculty of Law. At the same moment the old man turned his head and Landon saw with a shock of surprise that it was Doctor Ascolini. He was too far away, too absorbed in his séance, to notice Landon, but Landon felt a faint flush of embarrassment mount to his cheeks. Ninette quizzed him, smiling: 'You haven't told me what happened this morning, Peter. Do you want to talk about it?'

He did. He talked through the soup and the *pasta*. He talked through one bottle of wine and ordered another, while Ascolini sat, eloquent and honoured, among his student entourage, while Ninette probed with an occasional question towards the core of the provincial drama. When he had finished, she laid one slim hand over his and asked gently: 'Do you want to know what I think, Peter?'

'I do.'

'Then I think Valeria is more than half in love with you. Carlo leans on you too much for his own good, and Ascolini respects you more than you know.' Before he had time to challenge her, she went on: 'I think, too, that you are more deeply touched by all this than you admit. You like to play the misanthrope, but the mask slips off because it doesn't fit you very well. Underneath, you are a soft man, too easily hurt by malice and mistrust. You judge these people too curtly. You make all your pictures black and white, with no room for half-tones.'

'You mean Ascolini?'

'All of them, but Ascolini first, if you want.'

A burst of laughter went up from the old man's table and Landon saw him tapping the shoulder of the youth who had caused it. He saw him signal the waiter for another bottle of wine and then bend attentively to the question of another student. Ninette Lachaise asked another question: 'How do you read that, Peter? What brings him here?'

61

'You said it yourself. The old master receives the homage of youth!'

'Is that all, *chéri*? No kindness? No fear? No loneliness?'

Landon surrendered ruefully. 'All right, Ninette. You win. So the devil has a gentle heart – but not for his own.'

'Has he shown you his heart, Peter? Or have you read it only through someone else's eyes?'

The reproof was so gentle that he had perforce to accept it. He grinned at her and said: 'You're the artist. Your eyes are sharper than mine. Maybe you should read him for me.'

'I know him, Peter,' she said calmly. 'I have known him for a long time. He buys my pictures and he comes often to look at what I'm doing, to drink coffee and talk.'

For no good reason, Landon felt a pang of jealousy that this malign old mountebank should enjoy the privacy of Ninette's house. But Siena was a small town and he had fewer rights in the girl than Ascolini. He shrugged and said: 'I know he has a lot of charm.'

Ninette Lachaise refilled his glass and handed it to him with a laugh. 'Drink your wine, *chéri*. It is you who will be seeing me home, not the venerable doctor. But seriously, there is a tragedy in his life. He has a daughter who disappoints him and a son-in-law who resents him.'

Now it was Landon's turn to laugh. 'Valeria disappoints him? What's he got to grumble about? He made her in his own image.'

'Self-portraits are not always the best art, Peter.' Her lovely hands reached out and turned his face towards her. Her eyes challenged him, half in jest, half in earnest. 'We all love ourselves, Peter, but we are not always happy with what we see in the mirror. Are you?'

He capitulated as gracefully as he could. He took her hands and kissed them, and said lightly: 'You win, Ninette. You're a better advocate than Ascolini. I'll reserve judgement.'

'Would you do me a favour?'

'Name it.'

'Let me ask Ascolini to our table for a drink.'

To refuse would have been a grossness. Besides, he wanted to see more of this woman and a few minutes of embarrassment were a modest price for the privilege. She gave him a swift, grateful smile and walked across the room to another chorus of whistles and applause. Ascolini greeted her with lavish courtesy and, after a few moments of talk, walked back with her to Landon's table. He held out his hand and said, with the old wilful irony: 'You're keeping better company, my friend. I'm glad to see it.'

'We have much in common,' said Ninette Lachaise.

'You're a fortunate fellow, Landon. If I were twenty years younger, I should take her away from you.' He sighed theatrically and settled into his chair. 'Ah youth! Youth! A fugal time! We prize it only when we have lost it. Every one of these boys wants to be as wise as I am. How can I tell them that all I want is to be as lusty as they?'

Landon poured wine for him and drank the toast he made to Ninette. They talked desultorily for a few moments and then abruptly Ascolini said: 'I seldom make apologies, Landon, but I owe you this one. I'm sorry for what happened in my house.'

'It's forgotten. I'd like you to forget it, too.'

Ascolini frowned and shook his white mane. 'You must not promise too much, my friend, even in courtesy. It is not possible to forget, only to forgive – and that is difficult enough, God knows.' As curtly as he had raised the subject, he dropped it and turned to another. 'You've been with Carlo today, Landon?'

'I have.'

'You're embroiled in the affair then?'

'Hardly embroiled.' Landon's tone was testy. 'I've offered Carlo my professional advice on the side of the defence.'

'Carlo is fortunate in his friends,' said Ascolini dryly.

'More fortunate than in his family, perhaps!'

Before the old man had time to answer, Ninette Lachaise moved into the argument. 'You are both my friends. I will not have you quarrel in my company. You, Peter, have too quick a tongue. And you, *dottore*' – she laid a restraining hand on his sleeve – 'why do you make yourself a monster with horns and tail and fire coming out of your ears? You have the same loyalties as Peter, though you will not admit them.'

For Landon it was a reminder to better manners from

someone whose respect he wanted. He tried awkwardly to repair the breach. 'Please, Doctor! I'm a stranger caught up in a family affair against his will. I'm irritable and confused. Carlo gave me his confidence in the first instance, so, naturally, I'm prejudiced in his favour. But really none of it is my concern. Only a fool wants to arbitrate a domestic dispute.'

The old man surveyed him with a bright, ironic eye. 'Unfortunately, Landon, it is not arbitration we need, but forgiveness of our sins and a grace of amendment. I am too old and too proud to ask for it, Carlo is too young to admit the need. And Valeria . . .' He broke off to sip his wine and consider how he should express the thought. 'I have opened the world to her – and robbed her of the innocence to understand it. You're the wise woman, Ninette; how do you prescribe for a sickness like ours?'

'You may not buy any more pictures if I tell you.'

'On the contrary, I may surprise you and buy them all.'

'Then, *dottore mio*, here is my prescription. Unless you want to end by killing each other, someone has to say the first gentle word. And you are the one who has the least time left.'

For a long moment Ascolini was silent. The fire went out of his eyes, his pink cheeks sagged, and Landon understood for the first time how old he was. Finally, he stood up, took the girl's hand and pressed it to his lips. 'Good night, child. Sleep in peace.' To Landon he said formally: 'If you will lunch with me at Luca's tomorrow I should like to talk with you.'

'I'll be there.'

'One o'clock, then. Enjoy yourselves with my blessing.'

They watched him across the room, picking his old man's way between the crowded tables, until the students stood to welcome him back like sons careful of an honoured parent.

Landon felt Ninette's eyes on him, but he had nothing to say and he sat staring down at the checked tablecloth, abashed and faintly ashamed. Finally, she said, with a touch of tenderness: 'There are other places, other people, Peter. Let's go and find them.'

There were no whistles as they walked out. Even the Sordello had its private chivalries, but Landon could not say whether it was the aegis of Ascolini that protected them or whether even then he had the look of a man fallen in love – a noble occasion in Tuscany, only a trifle less solemn than a funeral or the coronation of a Pope.

It was three in the morning when he walked Ninette home from the last place and the last people. In the shadow of her doorway, they kissed and clung together, drowsy and passionate, until she pushed him away and whispered: 'Don't rush me, Peter. Promise me you won't rush me. We're not children and we know where this road goes.'

'I want it to go a long way.'

'I, too. But I need time to think.'

'May I come tomorrow?'

'Tomorrow – any day!'

'You may get sick of me and turn me out.'

'And then I'll curse myself and call you back. Now go home, *chéri*, please!'

The old city lay magical under a summer moon, her columns silver, her towers serene, her fountains full of faint stars. Her bells were silent, but her squares were murmurous with ancient friendly ghosts. One of them asked him a question which he thought to have heard before: 'What happens, my friend, when the world blows up in your face?'

In a third-floor room near the Porta Tufi, Valeria Rienzi lay awake and watched the moon-shadows lengthen over the roof-tops. Beside her in the tumbled bed, Basilio Lazzaro slept and snored, his heavy, handsome face slack with satisfaction. Even in repose, there was a gross, animal vitality about him: in the broad barrel-chest, tufted with swart hairs, in the flat belly and the thick, muscly shoulders. He was like a stud beast, bred for coupling, proud of his potency, graceless but dominant in the act of union.

Yet even while she despised him she could not regret him. His violence bruised her, his egotism angered her, yet he never failed to bring her to a kind of fulfilment. He did not ask her to be other than she was, an attractive woman, apt for mating, happy to play lovers' games and not ask too many questions about love. There was a panic urgency in his wooing that brought her swiftly to excitement. He was content with submission but delighted with co-operation.

He did not demand, like Carlo, that she play the seducer or, like her father, that she should relive an episode in prurient fiction. He was simple as the animal he resembled; and his simplicity was a guarantee of her freedom. She could go or stay. If she stayed, there was a price. If she went, there were twenty other women to be called with a snap of his stubby fingers. He treated her like a whore and made her feel like one, but at least she was not involved beyond the night's contract.

He was purge for her confusions, a partner and a symbol of her rebellion. Yet he would never be permanent or sufficient to her. Which brought her by a round turn face to face with the answered question: what else was left when the opera was over?

Her father had one answer: convenient marriage and a clutch of children with whom she could decline gracefully into the middle years. But his answer was coloured by an old man's demand for possession and continuity. When the children came, he would bind them to him with affection and hold them over her like a reproach.

Carlo? His answer was different again. Marriage was a contract, love a mutual bargain. He held up his love like a posy of flowers and demanded to be kissed for the offering. If he brought off a victory in this case or another he would become more arrogant, but no less demanding to lay it at her feet as the price of love. In a sense his exaction was more brutal than Lazzaro's, who gave and took and went away. Carlo loved himself in her, as a child loves itself in a mother, and, self-centred as a child, demanded a gratuitous gift of affection.

He was full of uncertainty, but he could not tolerate uncertainty in her. He had submitted, in his own fashion, to Ascolini's tyranny, but he refused to understand how much more subject she herself had become. He demanded allegiance to his own rebellion, but could never understand that hers must be made elsewhere and in subtler fashion. He too wanted children – but as a proof and not as a fruit of loving.

But these were not the only answers, and she knew it. She

was wilful and demanded to be tamed, passionate and in need of satisfaction. There were fears buried deep inside her that he wanted shared, by someone cool and wise but unpaternal. There were shames to be talked out and memories to be accepted without reproach; so that when the time came to give, she could give gratefully and freely – whether as wife or mistress made no matter.

As the moon waned and the pale shadows climbed from floor to ceiling, she thought of Peter Landon and the brief, passionate interlude with him in the garden. Given time and the occasion, she could draw him to her again, unless – and the thought gave her a sharp pang of jealousy – unless Ninette Lachaise were to take him first.

Peter Landon was not the only subject of contention between herself and this interloper from over the border. She had watched for a long time the growth of Ascolini's affection for her, sensed his unspoken regrets that his daughter could not match the footloose Bohemian, painting in her garret. Even Lazzaro talked of her with a kind of regret. And tonight, with a perverse enjoyment, she had made him talk again.

She had flattered him and tickled his sensuality, until in the end he had revealed with a base man's vanity the intimate details of his affair with Ninette Lachaise. It was a shameful victory at best, but a wise Valeria might well turn it into a nobler one. Love was a war in which the spoils were to the subtle and the knowing – and a man once kissed was already half disarmed.

Spilt milk could not be poured back into the pitcher, lost innocence could never be restored. But Landon was no innocent either and perhaps . . . perhaps . . . The cold grey of the false dawn was creeping into the eastern sky as she dressed hurriedly and crept down the stair to where her car was parked in the alley. Basilio Lazzaro would wake and find her gone – and would smile with relief at having found a woman who knew the rules of the game.

Punctually at nine-thirty the next morning, Carlo Rienzi arrived at the *pensione* to read Landon the report of the first day's activity. The opening summary of it was unpromising.

Anna Albertini had been charged with premeditated murder and lodged in the women's house of correction at San Gimignano. Carlo had interviewed her and found her quite unco-operative. The thing was done. She was content. She did not want to talk about it any more. Her husband was to be produced as a witness for the prosecution and no one in San Stefano was prepared to open his mouth except in support of police evidence. Fra Bonifacio's expectations had exceeded his purse and Rienzi would have to pay his colleagues' expenses from his own pocket.

There was one entry on the credit side. Professor Galuzzi would be happy to welcome his distinguished colleague from London and to open informal discussions on the psychiatric aspects of the case. Carlo and Landon were bidden to coffee with him at his rooms in the University.

Landon warmed to him from the first moment of meeting. He was a lean, tall fellow in his late forties with grey hair, a grey goatee, gold pince-nez and a faintly pedantic address. But the pince-nez concealed a shrewd, twinkling eye, and the pedantry masked a quick wit and a ready sympathy. Landon had the feeling that he might be a formidable and expert fellow in court. His private summation was brisk but genial: 'A formula exists under which Mr Landon might be called in an Italian court as an expert witness for the defence. For my part – and please don't mistake my intentions – I would advise against it. Local sympathies, even among the judiciary, might run against a foreign expert. On the other hand, I should be happy to have my distinguished colleague work with me as a clinical observer on the case.' He bent sedulously over his coffee. 'Of course if my distinguished colleague chose to advise defence privately, that would be his own affair.'

'You go further than I had hoped, Professor,' said Rienzi cautiously.

'But you don't understand why?' Galuzzi surveyed him with a bright, birdlike eye. 'Is that it? I think perhaps Mr Landon will understand me better than you do. We are both medical men. Our prime concern is to care for the health of the human mind and, when we meet with the law, to mitigate the consequences of any mental infirmity that may exist. Don't misunderstand me!' He held up a warning hand. 'When I am called to the witness-stand, I must answer fully and truthfully any questions which are asked on the subject of my clinical knowledge. I'm not a judge. I cannot determine what use the court may make of my testimony. If you felt it necessary to call other experts to challenge my diagnosis, they would of course be given full facilities to examine the accused.'

'It's a fair offer, Carlo,' said Landon warmly. 'I'm flattered by it. I think you should be grateful. Tell me, Professor, have you seen Anna Albertini yet?'

'Not yet. I make my first visit to her this afternoon. For that I should like to be alone. Afterwards it will be easier to introduce you as a visiting observer. However, I do have one item of interest. As you know, every new prisoner is submitted to a medical examination by the prison doctor. The purpose of the examination is to detect the presence of communicable disease which may infect other inmates. Anna Albertini has been given a clean bill of health. It is also noted in the record that she is *virgo intacta*.'

Rienzi gaped at him. 'But she's been married four years.'

'Interesting, isn't it?' Galuzzi's goatee bobbed up and down as he laughed. 'Something for you, also, to sleep on, Mr Landon! And there is another thing. No sign of depression or mania. No violence, no hysteria. My colleague at the prison describes the accused as calm, good humoured and apparently content. But we shall see. . . .' He hesitated a moment and then asked: 'Would you do me a favour, Mr Landon?'

'Of course.'

'Your work is not unknown here, and you speak excellent Italian. I should like to improve our acquaintance – and perhaps, if it is not too much of an imposition, have you lecture to some of my senior students.'

'I'd be delighted. You can contact me at any time at the Pensione della Fontana.'

'I'll be in touch with you.' He scribbled the address on a desk pad, then stood up. 'And now, if you'll excuse me, gentlemen, I have a lecture in five minutes.'

As they made their tortuous way back to the centre of the

city, Carlo was voluble in his satisfaction with the meeting, but Landon added a rider or two of caution. 'Don't lean too much on this kind of thing, Carlo. I like Galuzzi. He's a pleasant fellow, freer than most with the courtesy of the trade. But the courtesy doesn't cost him anything – and in the witness-box he'll stand up like a rock, because his professional reputation is at stake.'

'I keep forgetting,' said Rienzi wryly, 'that you must have been through this kind of thing many times. Tell me one thing: is it likely that your diagnosis of a case would vary much from Galuzzi's?'

'I doubt it. There might be some divergence of opinion on a complex disorder. There might be a greater divergence on the question of treatment. But it seems to me you're begging the question. You're assuming that all abnormal conduct is a symptom of mental illness. There are some extreme practitioners who hold that view. I don't. I'm sure Galuzzi doesn't, either. If your client is insane, we'll both agree on the point – and your case will be over in twenty minutes. If she's not, then you're back to mitigatory circumstances.'

'That's what I'm working on now. But so far I've met only closed doors.'

'There's one that might open.'

'What's that?'

'Anna Albertini's husband.'

'He's refused to talk to anyone but the police, and he's already gone back to Florence.'

'Take a drive up there and ask him why his wife's still virgin after four years of marriage.'

'My God!' said Rienzi softly. 'My God, it might just work!'

'It's always a reasonable bet. Challenge a man in his virility and he's only too ready to talk. Whether he gives you the truth is, of course, another matter.'

'If we knew what inhibited the marriage we would have some leading questions to ask Anna herself. And from there ...'

'From there,' said Landon with a grin, 'you cook your own dinner, Carlo. I can help you stir the soup, but in the end you're the fellow who has to eat it and talking of eating, Ascolini's asked me to lunch with him today. I met him last night with Ninette Lachaise.'

'The old, old charm!' said Rienzi resentfully. 'Honey for the flies. If you were a woman, he'd have you in bed before sunset. Don't sell me out, Peter!'

He said it with a smile, but Landon was instantly and bitterly angry. 'To hell with you, Carlo! If that's the way you read a simple politeness, to hell with you!'

Ignoring Rienzi's protest, he turned and hurried away, plunging into a tangle of alleys, stumbling over refuse and runnels of filthy water until he emerged, breathless and furious, into the blinding sunlight of the Campo. When he looked at his watch it was only midday, so he turned into a bar, drank two brandies and smoked half a dozen tasteless cigarettes until it was time for lunch with Alberto Ascolini.

He found the old man in the favoured corner of Luca's, enthroned in a red-plush chair at the feet of a Renaissance nude. A brace of waiters hovered at his elbow, attentive and obsequious, while Ascolini sipped yellow vermouth and made notes in a pocket-book covered with purple morocco. Landon could not repress a smile at the care with which he stage-managed every occasion. Peasant he might be, but he had the knack of imposing distinction even on the baroque splendour of Luca's, which is part restaurant, part club and part monument to the vanished pomps of the nineteenth century.

He greeted Landon absently, had an aperitif in his hand in ninety seconds, and then asked him bluntly: 'Have you been reading the papers, Landon?'

'I have.'

'What do you make of the affair?'

'Barring insanity, I can't imagine a simpler case for the prosecution.'

'And the defence?'

'Has a hopeless task. I've said as much to Carlo.'

'Does he agree?'

'Not altogether.'

'He must have other information, then.'

'It would seem so.'

He let it rest there and smiled – a canny old swordsman disengaging after the first perfunctory passes. 'Let's call a truce, Landon. I have, believe me, no wish to embarrass you. And I would like you to trust me a little. It may be hard for you to understand, but I do have a very real interest in Carlo's welfare.'

Landon digested that for a moment and then said, carefully: 'It might help us both if you would explain that interest.'

Ascolini leaned back in his chair, spreading his soft hands and joining them, fingertip to fingertip, in an episcopal gesture. His eyes filmed over like those of a dozing bird and his voice took on a dusty, didactic quality.

'As one of your English writers has said, Landon, youth is wasted on the young. When one is old, one resents the waste. One also has the means to indulge the resentment, as I have done in Carlo's case. This is the problem of age, my friend – and you will face it sooner than you imagine: the catalogue of available pleasures contracts so that one clings even to one's baseness for want of more robust diversion. I am not proud of this. Neither can I say that I am sorry for it. I explain it to you as an experience. I am a jealous man, my friend: jealous of what I have, jealous of what I have lost, jealous of the extravagance with which the young indulge their conscience or their illusions. Take Carlo, for instance. In his marriage he plays the patient gentleman. That is a folly with all women – most foolish with a woman like Valeria. With me he plays the respectful pupil, the dutiful son-in-law. He refuses to see that I am an old hard-head, who needs his nose rubbed in the dust. The old bulls, Landon! They stand, diminished but defiant, waiting for the one last fight which will ennoble them even while it destroys them and despising the uncertain youngsters who refuse the combat. Does this make any sense to you? You of all people should understand.'

'I do understand,' Landon told him quietly. 'I'm grateful that you've explained it. But there's something you should understand, too. Carlo has begun his fight. What he has done so far is his challenge to you. You must not despise him because he fights in another fashion than yours.'

'Despise him?' The old man was suddenly vehement. 'For the first time I begin to respect him!'

'Then why humiliate him as you did when he offered you a gift and his thanks?'

Ascolini gave him a wintry smile and shook his head. 'You too are still young, my dear Landon. When the old bulls fight they use all the dirty tricks.' He shrugged off the argument as if he had no further interest in it. 'Now let me order you dinner and a wine to put blood in your veins. You'll need it with a woman like Ninette Lachaise.'

The waiters came scurrying at his signal and they were served like princes of a nobler age. As they ate, the old man talked, quietly and persuasively, of his peasant boyhood in the Val d'Orcia, of his education at the hands of the parish priest, his student days at the University of Siena, his struggle to find a foothold in Rome, his first successes, his eclipse under the Fascist régime, his rise to new eminence after the war.

The narrative was bold and vivid, touched sometimes with sardonic humour, sometimes with poignant regret for the simplicities of a lost time. He talked, without rancour of the failure of his marriage, of his desire for a son, and of his hopes for the daughter who had arrived instead.

By the time they reached the fruit and the cheese, Landon had the picture of a man who had attained greatly but who had lost, somewhere along the road, the key to happiness. Of himself, Ascolini said whimsically: 'I have eaten the apples of Sodom, my friend, but I cannot regret them too much because I can still remember the taste of good fruit and of some noble wines.' Of Valeria he said bleakly: 'I tried to arm her with knowledge against the day when love might fail her. I have understood too late that it was my love which failed her first. I wanted to possess in her what her mother had failed to give me. What I found, finally, was a replica of myself. But . . .' He shrugged and swept away regret with the crumbs on the tablecloth. 'This is life. One must wear it with good grace or walk out of it with dignity. I have elected to wear it.'

To which Landon had nothing to say. He could neither comfort the man nor judge him. So he asked a question: 'Do you think Carlo can ever re-establish himself with Valeria? Will she ever content herself with him?'

'I don't know. As it lies now, Carlo would seem to be the lover, she the one who accepts love but sets no value on it. It may be that, if the love were withdrawn, she might be afraid and reach out to hold it. If not – *chi sa*? There are women who play games with their hearts and seem to live satisfied.'

'Do you care which way it goes?'

He fixed Landon with a cold, lawyer's eye and said, emphatically: 'I care greatly, though not, perhaps, for the reason you think. I want this marriage to last – and last as happily as possible, not for Carlo's sake, not for Valeria's, but because I want a grandchild – some promise, at least, of continuity.' Before Landon had time to comment, he hurried on. 'That is why I have asked you here today. I want Carlo to know that he has my support in this case and in his relations with Valeria.'

Landon stared at him in blank disbelief. Everything that had happened in the last forty-eight hours gave the lie to what the old man was saying. As if aware of Landon's thought, Ascolini brought out from his pocket a buff-coloured envelope and pushed it across the table. 'I'd like you to see that Carlo gets this. It contains a cheque for a million lire and some notes which I have made on the case. I'd like you to explain to Carlo my attitude and urge him to accept the money and the advice to further this client's cause. Will you do it?'

'No!'

'You don't believe me? Is that it?'

'I think you're making a mistake.'

'Why?'

'First, I don't believe Carlo will accept. Second, even if he did accept, you would put him in your debt again. His triumph – if any – would still belong partially to you.'

'You think that's what I want?'

'No. But on your own confession you would use it. The old bulls – remember?'

For a long while Ascolini sat silent, staring down at the

74

table, drawing meaningless patterns with a fork on the white cloth. Then he picked up the envelope, put it back in his pocket and said quietly: 'Perhaps you're right, Landon. You have no good reason to trust me, and I have no right to salve my vanity by making you a messenger. Will you do me at least one favour?'

'If I can, certainly.'

'Tell Carlo what I have said, what I have offered.'

'You see him every day. Why not tell him yourself?'

'I hope that you may explain me better than I can explain myself.'

'I'll try, but I can't guarantee how he will judge.'

'Of course not. Who can guarantee that even the judgement he makes on himself is not a lie to make life bearable?' He gave Landon a cool, ironic smile. 'You, for example, Landon, you can take a man's mind to pieces and put it together again like a watch. Have you explained to yourself why you are so deeply committed to our affairs?'

It was so neatly done that Landon had to laugh at the sheer virtuosity of the man. Besides, it was a fair question and it was time he gave it a fair answer. He thought about it for a moment and then said, soberly: 'Sympathy is part of it. I like Carlo and I think he deserves better. Ambition is part of it, too. You know that I've been looking for a theme of original research to herald my return to London. This case might provide me one. More than that' – he spread his hands palms downward on the tablecloth and studied them intently for a few moments – 'in a sense, I too am in crisis – a crisis which I think you will understand. I have been too long solitary and self-sufficient. My involvement is, I believe, part of a subconscious drive to community and competition.'

Ascolini nodded approval. 'I appreciate your frankness, Landon. Let me ask you a little more. How do you regard me?'

'With singular respect,' said Landon.

'Thank you. I believe you mean it.' He waited for a fraction of a second and then probed more shrewdly. 'How do you regard Valeria?'

Again Landon felt the swift rise of anger but he fought it

75

down and said in a flat voice: 'She's an attractive woman and she has her own problems.'

'Do you think you can solve them?'

'No.'

'Do you think she may create problems for you?'

'Any woman can create problems for any man.'

Landon grinned crookedly into his wine-glass. Ascolini frowned and resumed his tracing on the tablecloth. After a few moments he looked up. 'Strangely enough, Landon, at another time I should not have disapproved of an association between you and Valeria. I think you are the kind of man she needs. But now, for all the reasons that I have explained to you, I would set my face against it.'

'I, too,' said Landon lightly. 'I have hopes elsewhere.'

The old man brightened immediately. 'Ninette Lachaise?'

'Yes.'

'I'm glad to hear it,' said Ascolini with grave satisfaction. 'I have a great affection for Ninette. I should give much to see her happy. For this reason only I say to you, be very sure of yourself – and don't try to have it all on your own terms. Thank you for your patience, Mr Landon, and your company.'

For all Ascolini's urbanity, Landon left the restaurant still angry and bitterly resentful. If it had not been for Ninette Lachaise he would have damned them all to hell and taken the first train back to Rome. He was sick of their intrigues. He hated them heartily for seducing him into friendship and then laying at his door the guilts they blamed on one another.

It was the kind of situation he had avoided sedulously all his life, believing that a man had enough bother compassing his own salvation without acting as judge, jury and wet-nurse to the rest of mankind. But to be trapped like a green boy with his first widow – this was too much! He decided then and there to close his accounts with them and began to walk off his ill-temper by a tramp through the narrow alleys to Ninette's studio.

The moment she was in his arms again, he knew for certain that he loved her. Everything that he had ever dreamed of in a woman seemed to have flowered in this one: simplicity, passion, courage. She had none of the tricks that other women used to evoke tenderness while refusing to return it. What she had she would spend freely and make no usurer's demand for payment. She looked out on the world with an artist's eyes, serene, grateful, compassionate. For the first time in his life, the bachelor's caution deserted him and he told her the truth.

'I had to come. I had to tell you. I love you, Ninette.'

'I love you, too, Peter.' She clung to him for a moment and then withdrew herself gently and walked over to the window to stand, face averted, looking out over the red-tiled roofs of the ancient town. 'Now that it's said, Peter, let's live with it a while. Let's make no contracts, just wait and enjoy what we have. If it grows, it will be good for us both. If it dies, it will not hurt us too much.'

'I want it to grow, Ninette.'

'I, too. But we have both said before what we say now – and it didn't last.'

'I know it will last, for me.'

'Then just keep saying it, *chéri*, all the time, until you believe down to the bottom of your heart that it's true.'

'And you?'

'I'll do the same.'

They stood together at the window, arms laced, bodies close, savouring the first sweets of confession, watching the light pour down, golden and tender, from the Tuscan sky. Then she made him sit down, stripped off her smock and bustled about like a housewife to prepare him coffee. He told her of his lunch with Ascolini and of his anger with Rienzi; told her too of his decision to withdraw, as soon as possible, from the whole shabby business. She listened in silence while the coffee-pot bubbled a comic counterpart to the story. Then she sat down, took his hands between her own, and said, in her frank fashion: 'I know how you feel, Peter. I don't blame you. These are not your people or mine. The pattern of their lives is twisted and distorted in a fashion that neither you nor I could endure. They bear, as we could never do, the burden of old and bitter histories. And yet, in a curious way, they need us – you much more than me.'

'How can you say that, Ninette?'

'Because I need you almost as they do, Peter. You're dissatisfied with yourself, I know; but to us you are the new man from the New World, proof that it is possible to live without history, to start with a clean canvas in a land with new light. It's a symbol, you see, which represents the only solution for these folk and for many others. Someone has to say, "I'm sorry", and begin again. Otherwise the old history corrupts the new and there is, in the end, no hope at all. . . .' She faltered then and broke off as if searching for words to define a troublesome thought. 'It's like ourselves, you see, we've both known other people, loved some and hated the rest. But if we go on living in the past there is no hope for either of us. We have to accept that the present is important and tomorrow is always a question mark. I love you because you are able to do that. Rienzi and Ascolini need you for the same thing. You can afford to be generous with them.'

Landon shook his head. He was troubled by a vague guilt that even then he could not expose to her. 'Don't overrate me, my dear. There are times when I feel very empty.'

'You give more than you know, *chéri*. That's why you're dear to me.'

Then, to his own surprise, a thought which he had concealed from himself found utterance. 'I'm afraid of these people, Ninette. I can't tell you why, but they terrify me with their capacity for malice. They know what they're doing, they confess it, and some of the shame rubs off. It's like listening to a man tell dirty stories about his wife.' He gave a small, harsh laugh. 'I should be used to it – I get it every day from my patients – but here I'm not so well armed.'

'I know,' said Ninette softly. 'I've been here longer than you. They torment themselves because they don't know how to love. But we do. So they can't hurt us – and we may be able to help them.'

'Is that what you really want, Ninette?'

'I'm so rich, Peter, so very rich at this moment, I'd like to spend a little on the rest of the world.'

He took her in his arms and kissed her. The coffee-pot boiled over and they laughed and laughed with the simple, foolish joy of being alive.

In the fall of the afternoon they drove out in Ninette's battered Citröen to San Gimignano – 'San Gimignano of the Wondrous Towers', that miniature town where the Middle Ages are preserved, unenlarged, almost unchanged, in the context of the twentieth century.

The land lay placid under the long shadows of cypress and olive, brown where the ploughshare had turned it, grey under the overhang of the vines, green where hidden springs still watered the young grass. The light was soft, the air calm but warm with the breath of a land still living, still fertile after a lapse of hungry centuries. The peasants, fresh from siesta, were working the terraces and the vegetable plots – men, women and children humped over the mattock or the weeding-fork. The peace of it slid into Landon's soul and he lapsed into that pleasant dichotomy where the body concentrates on the mechanical exercise of progress and the mind ranges free over the timeless panorama of men.

Ninette, too, was silent, absorbed in an artist's contemplation of colour, contour and mass. They were separate but united, private but harmonious, like notes in the same chord, colours in happy complement. They had no needs that were not fulfilled by the simple presence of one to the other, no fears that could not be allayed by a hand's touch or a smile of reassurance. If this were not love, then Landon was ignorant indeed. And if love were a folly, then he was well content to be a fool.

When they came in sight of the grim old monastery which was now the women's house of correction, Ninette shivered as if a goose had walked over her grave. She drew close to Landon and said in a low voice: 'Sometimes, Peter . . . sometimes I, too, am afraid.'

'Of what, dearest?'

'Of all this.' Her gesture took in the sunlit *campagna* and the distant dreaming towers of San Gimignano. 'It is so peaceful, as you see. The peasants are simple folk – narrow like their kind everywhere, but kind and very gentle with their children. Yet every little while something explodes – pam! – and there are violence, hate, and a very animal cruelty.'

'Like the affair at San Stefano?'

'Just like that. That girl, Peter. Before you came, I sketched her face from the photographs in the newspapers. I tried to dissect it as an artist does, and I could find nothing but childhood, yet look what happened.'

'I've had the same thought ever since I read the papers this morning. It's hard to believe in the malice of children, but it exists.'

'They inherit it sometimes, like spirochaetes in the blood. Sometimes they accept it as a substitute for love. Nobody can live with an empty heart.'

'Yet this one was married. She must have known something of love.'

'It doesn't follow, Peter. Sometimes the capacity for love is destroyed. A swamp weed will die in sweet soil. An animal bred in the dark is blind in the sunlight. Look at Ascolini's daughter. Has she ever lacked love?'

'What made you think of her?'

Her answer took him by surprise: 'I dreamed of her last night, Peter – and of you, too. You were holding hands like lovers in a garden. I called out to you, but you would not listen. I tried to go to you but I was held back. I awoke calling your name and crying.'

'Darling, you're jealous.'

'I know. Silly, isn't it?'

'Very silly. Valeria means nothing to me.'

'I keep asking myself whether you may mean something to her.'

'What should I mean?' He felt a pang of shame and embarrassment.

'Kiss and come hither! What do they always mean?' She broke off and gave a little rueful chuckle. 'Bear with me, *chéri*. Every woman has her whims and it's mine to be jealous of the man I love. Let's forget them all and talk about ourselves.'

And talk they did, in the happy, extravagant manner of lovers, while the roof-tops and belfries of San Gimignano hardened themselves against the sky. Finally Landon told her that he would stay in Siena until after the trial and that then he would ask her to marry him.

Oddly, the talk of marriage seemed to trouble her, as if it were asking too much too soon and tempting the old gods of Etruria to a prankish humour. Landon tried to tease her out of it, but the mood persisted. Like many courageous people who accept life on the best terms available, she had a deep, unreasoned fear of demanding too much promise from the future, of counting the crop before the fruit had come to ripeness.

When they came to the city they stopped to drink wine in the old square which was called 'The Place of the Cistern' Landon made a silly ceremony of pouring a libation to placate the deities. Ninette frowned, and said with a touch of irritation: 'Don't do things like that, Peter!'

'It's a joke, sweetheart. It means nothing.'

'I know, Peter, but I don't like making pacts with tomorrow. I want today just as it is, good and bad. I feel safe that way. I don't want to face the great perhaps.'

'Perhaps what?'

'Perhaps I shall die. Perhaps you will grow tired of me and go away. Perhaps I shall go blind and not be able to go on painting.'

'That's nonsense.'

'I know, *chéri*. Everything that hasn't happened is nonsense. But when it does happen, it is better to be prepared. I like to discount the future until I see the sun rise on a new day.'

'But someone has to plan for tomorrow. Life's not just an accident – or a chess game played by an overruling destiny.'

'Then you must plan for both of us, Peter. I'll just try to keep us both happy from one hour to the next.' She stood up and pulled him to his feet. 'Come on, now! There's so much to show you before sunset!'

For the next two hours they explored the tiny city – each step a regression into the violent history of the province. In the twelfth century the citizens had cast out the tyrant,

Volterra. In the fourteenth it had surrendered to Florence, bled dry by the Medici bankers and by the bloody factions within its own gates. Benozzo Gozzoli painted here and Folgore, its poet son, was damned from here to Dante's hell with the eleven great spendthrifts of Siena. When one tower tumbled down, another was built 'furnished with arrows and mangonels and every warlike need'. Nicolò Machiavelli put the trainbands through their paces just outside the walls, and Dante himself led an embassy to the Grand Council from the Guelph League. To the outward aspect, the place was little changed by the centuries, and as the shadows lengthened one almost expected to hear the tramp of men-at-arms and the clatter of horsemen as merchant and knight and wandering friar squeezed themselves in at the gate before sunset.

By the time they had finished their tour they were hot, dusty and panting for a drink. Ninette suggested that they stop at a small roadside restaurant on the way to Siena, which was half eating-house, half rustic wine-shop and, by reputation, a rendezvous for country lovers. They parked the car by the roadside and as they entered the shaded courtyard they saw, five seconds too late, that Valeria Rienzi was seated with a male companion at one of the little marble tables. Landon saw Ninette flush and stiffen, and at the same moment Valeria waved them to her table. There was no option but to be polite. Valeria presented her companion: 'Peter, I should like you to meet a friend of mine, Basilio Lazzaro. Basilio, this is Peter Landon. You know Ninette, of course, Basilio?'

'Of course. We're old friends,' said Lazzaro smoothly. 'And it's a pleasure to meet you, Mr Landon.'

Ninette said nothing. Valeria watched her with feline amusement while Lazzaro and Landon measured each other and decided on instant dislike. There was a stiff little pause and then Valeria said: 'I was trying to telephone you this morning, Peter. I wanted to see you for a little while tomorrow.'

'I've been out most of today,' said Landon awkwardly. 'And I'm not quite sure what goes on tomorrow.'

'May I telephone you then? It is rather important.'

There was nothing to do but to agree. Landon and Ninette disengaged themselves as quickly as possible, took their drinks in silence and hurried back to the car. After a while, Ninette said, irritably: 'I told you, Peter, didn't I? She has interest in you and she will not give it up without a fight.'

'It seemed to me,' said Landon tartly, 'that Basilio what's-his-name had interests in you.'

And there, brusquely, the conversation ended. A small chill wind scurried across the countryside and then dropped. For all their love they could not find words to reassure each other and they drove back to Siena, moody and withdrawn, while the grey dusk settled on the olive groves and the sad funereal cypresses.

In every love-affair, however precipitate, there are moments when the swift, intuitive communion is broken, when the man and the woman are thrust back into that loneliness which first disposed them to each other. The vision that each has of the other is too perfect, the balance of interest is too precarious to sustain the smallest defect or the mildest shock of disappointment. Their first surrender appears so complete that neither can admit the reserves that still exist. They are so tender that they cannot believe themselves intolerant. The resentments flare swiftly into lovers' quarrels. There are anger, separation and withdrawal into privacy which presently becomes intolerable and drives them back, more needy than before, into each other's company.

This is the true anatomy of love: simple and patent to those who have survived it, but complex and painful to those who, like Ninette and Landon, had still to undergo the dissection.

They did not quarrel that night but were reserved with each other. Ninette's jealousy of Valeria Rienzi seemed to Landon petty, childish and contradictory, small compliment to a man who was prepared to sign a marriage contract at the drop of a lace handkerchief. It was Ninette who urged him back into alliance with Rienzi. It was she who had persuaded him that these people had need of his friendship. If now she regretted the decision, there was no good reason to make him pay for it.

For her part, she demanded reassurance, indulgence for her whim. She needed, as women do, a partnership in the apparent folly of the love-game. She resented his raillery as much as his sour disinclination.

There was only one remedy: throw away the book, forget the words and turn to kisses. But they both sheered away from this simplicity. They were afraid of each other that night. They talked contrariwise; they knew that the truth was only a step away – the big Florentine bed with its shadowy drapes and long memories of other loves. Neither of them was innocent of passion, neither lacked experience or inclination, but both of them felt, without being able to put it into words, that the disciplines of continence promised better for them both than the intemperate surrender of other days. It was a folly perhaps. Life is too short to waste so much of it in sterile anger. But everything in love is a folly and they parted, only half-reconciled, with the hope that things would be better in the morning.

Chapter Four

AT TEN-THIRTY the following day Professor Emilio Galuzzi sat in private consultation with his English colleague. There was a subtle change in his manner as if, without witnesses, he were prepared to expose himself more freely to one of the esoteric brotherhood of medicine. He began with a personal apologia.

'You will agree with me, I think, Landon, that we are still the pioneers of an inexact science. Our methods are often fumbling and awkward. Our definitions are sometimes inaccurate. We have had great masters – Freud, Jung, Adler and all the rest – but we know that even their most illuminating researches have often been inhibited by a too dogmatic adherence to unproven hypotheses. For myself, I would like to say that I am an eclectic. I like to reserve to myself the right of choice when one or other of the masters seems to point a clearer way to the truth. From what I have read of your work, I believe that you have a similar attitude.'

'That's true enough.' Landon nodded agreement. 'I think it's true of all sciences that the great leaps of discovery have been made by bold speculators whose very errors have served in the end to elicit another fraction of the truth. The science of the mind is still inexact, but we've come a long way from Bedlam and the primitive notions of diabolical possession or divine madness.'

'Good.' Galuzzi seemed relieved. 'From this point we can begin to co-operate.' He shrugged and made a small, fastidious gesture. 'I have been too often bedevilled by colleagues who seem to think that they hold in their hands the answer to the ultimate riddle of the human mind. We cannot afford to be so arrogant. We are neither gods nor soothsayers. So . . . we come to our patient, this Anna Albertini. I was with her for several hours yesterday. I made a tape-recording of our interview which I should like you to hear. Before we do, however, I should like to make clear to you a point of criminal law as it is presently framed in this country. We have, like you, the normal plea of insanity, whose definition approximates very closely to that currently in use in British courts. We have also another plea, less clearly defined, which is called "*semi-infermità mentale*", or partial mental infirmity. At one end of the scale this definition wears a little of the colour of the American plea of "uncontrollable impulse". At the other, it rests on an acceptance of the principle that certain mental states do diminish the legal responsibility of the individual without entirely destroying it. Do I make myself clear?'

'Admirably,' said Landon with a smile. 'I shouldn't like to face you in court without a well-prepared brief.'

'Rienzi will be facing me,' said Galuzzi dryly, 'and I am guessing that this is the ground on which he will have to stand.'

'You rule out insanity altogether?'

'I do.' His answer was quite emphatic. 'When you have seen the girl I think you will agree with me. I believe that by all the legal norms the girl is quite sane. I see no evidence of mania, schizophrenia or paranoid tendencies. There is no amnesia, no evidence of hysteria. There is some residual shock, but she sleeps calmly, eats normally, takes singularly good care of herself, and seems to accept her situation with reasoned resignation. There is trauma, of course, associated with her mother's death. There is also obsession, reduced but

85

not wholly eliminated by the cathartic effect of the act of revenge. Their degrees and ramifications will need much longer exploration.'

'Do they constitute mental infirmity under the Italian definition?'

Galuzzi laughed and threw out his arms in Latin exuberance. 'Ah! Now we come to the core of it! We are all in difficulty here. The definition is unclear. And too often the judicial mind in this country reacts very strongly against any suggestion that a person legally sane is not fully responsible for his actions. On this point, Landon, you know as well as I that the development of mental science and the evolution of the law do not march at the same pace. Often it is a matter of advocacy to swing the bench to a favourable decision. Often justice is inhibited by the lack of definition in the codex. This is a service that men like you and I can render to the law: to make our findings so clear that they cannot fail to be accepted as a basis for future legislation. But in this case we have to accept the situation as it exists. The best we can do is explore the mind of the accused and determine as clearly as we can the limit of her legal responsibility. Now, before we hear the tape . . . you tell me you have not seen this girl?'

'Not yet. Rienzi saw her and gave me a somewhat colourful description.'

Galuzzi chuckled. 'I shouldn't blame him too much for that. I am older than he is but I confess I, too, was curiously impressed. She has a quite extraordinary beauty, an almost nun-like charm. They dress them like nuns, too, in San Gimignano – drunks, thieves, abortionists and the little whores who sell themselves on street corners. But this one! You could paint an aureole around her head and put her on a pedestal in the church. Anyway, let's listen to her.'

He crossed to the desk and switched on the recorder and a few seconds later Landon was immersed in the dialogue.

Galuzzi's voice took on the cool, informal tone of the trained analyst. The girl's voice was pleasantly pitched, but remote and indifferent; neither dull nor bored, but strangely dissociated, like that of an actor speaking through a Greek mask.

86

'You understand, Anna, that I'm a doctor and that I'm here to help you?'

'Yes, I understand.'

'Tell me, did you sleep well last night?'

'Very well, thank you.'

'You weren't afraid?'

'No. I was very tired because of all the questions. But nobody was unkind to me. I wasn't afraid.'

'How old are you, Anna?'

'Twenty-four.'

'How long have you been married?'

'Four years.'

'What sort of a house do you live in?'

'It's not a house. It's an apartment. It's not very big, but it was enough for Luigi and me.'

'How old is Luigi?'

'Twenty-six.'

'What did you do after you were married?'

'What everyone else does. I cleaned the house and did the shopping and looked after Luigi.'

'This was in Florence?'

'Yes.'

'Did you have any friends in Florence?'

'Luigi had friends from work, and he had his family. I didn't know anyone there.'

'Didn't you feel lonely?'

'No.'

'Was Luigi good to you?'

'Yes. He used to get angry with me sometimes but he was good to me.'

'Why did he get angry?'

'He used to say I didn't love him like I should.'

'And did you?'

'Underneath I did.'

'Underneath what?'

'Inside me. You know, in my head. In my heart.'

'Did you tell Luigi that?'

'Yes. But it didn't stop him getting angry.'

'Why?'

'Because he used to say it wasn't enough. Married people did things to show they loved each other.'

'Did you know what he meant?'

'Oh yes.'

'But you didn't want to do them?'

'No.'

'Why not?'

'I thought he would hurt me.'

'What else did you think?'

'I thought about his gun.'

'Tell me about the gun.'

'He used to take it to work with him every night. That was his job. He had to guard the factory at night. In the morning, when he came home, he would put it away in the drawer of the bureau.'

'Were you afraid of it?'

'Only when I dreamed about it. In the daytime I used to take it out and hold it in my hand and look at it. It was cold and hard.'

'What did you dream about the gun?'

'That Luigi was holding it in his hand and pointing it at my mother. Then it wasn't Luigi. It was someone else. I couldn't see his face, but I knew it was Belloni. Then I would try to get to him, but I couldn't, and I would wake up.'

'Belloni was the man you killed?'

'That's right.'

'Why did you kill him?'

'He shot my mother.'

'Tell me about that, Anna.'

'I'd rather not talk about it. It's over now. Belloni's dead.'

'Does it frighten you to think about it?'

'No, I just don't want to talk about it.'

'All right. Then tell me about your father.'

'I don't remember much about him. He went away in the Army when I was five. Then we heard he was killed. Mother cried a lot. Then she got over it. She moved me into her room and I slept with her.'

'Until the Germans came to the village?'

'No, all the time.'

'When the Germans were there, did you still sleep with her?'

'Yes. She used to lock the bedroom door at night.'

'Where did you go to school?'

'In San Stefano with the Brown Sisters.'

'What did they teach you?'

'Reading and writing and figures. And the Catechism.'

'In the Catechism, Anna, doesn't it say that it's wrong to kill anybody?'

'Yes.'

'But you killed Belloni. Wasn't that a sin?'

'I suppose so.'

'Don't you care?'

'I never thought about it that way. All I knew was I had to kill him because he killed my mother.'

'Did you know it all the time?'

'Yes.'

'How did you know it?'

'I just knew. When I woke up in the morning, when I cooked the dinner or washed the floor or went out shopping, I knew all the time.'

'How did you make up your mind to kill him?'

'It was the gun.'

'But you told me the gun was there all the time. Luigi would take it to work at night and put it in the bureau drawer in the morning. You told me you used to take it out and look at it. Why did you wait all that time?'

'Because it was different. On that morning, Luigi didn't put the gun in the drawer. He emptied his pockets and left the gun on the table beside the bed. When he was asleep I took it and went to San Stefano and killed Belloni. . . . Please, can we stop for a while?'

'Of course.'

Galuzzi got up and switched off the machine. Then he turned to Landon, who was sitting at the desk scribbling notes on the back of an envelope.

'Well, Landon, that's the first part of it. What do you think so far?'

'So far, it's almost classically simple. Shock and trauma caused by the circumstances of her mother's death; the child's incapacity to master the situation, and a consequent blocking of the ego-function; hence the obsession, the nightmares, the sexual incompetence, the transference of symbols.' He shrugged and grinned. 'That's talking off the cuff, of course. I shouldn't commit myself so quickly. One interesting point is the emergence of the vestigial primitive conscience from beneath the overlay of convent education – violence must be purged by violence. It's the archaic attempt to master a situation beyond control by the usual means. You see it again in the acceptance of a magical moment like the discovery of the gun exposed on the table, as a motive for the final act of vengeance. But I'm reading you lectures, Professor. You know all this as well as I do.'

Galuzzi nodded, and said soberly: 'As you say, my friend, it is almost a textbook case. We shall dig further, of course, and we shall come sooner or later to a description of what we are at present refused – the moment of the mother's death. I have no doubt that we shall discover many more complexities than are revealed to us in this first discussion. But even if our first guesses are confirmed, even if we present ourselves with a classic set of symptoms and a perfect pathology of traumatic psychosis, where do we stand then?'

'We're back on the coda,' said Landon grimly: 'the nature and the determining factors of human responsibility. The old moralists had a point, you know, when they refused to surrender too easily the doctrine of free-will.'

Galuzzi nodded and embellished the theme in his pedantic fashion: 'My point exactly, Landon. I cannot believe the determinists who say that there is no real responsibility and that every human act is an inevitable consequence of a thousand others, like a ball bouncing off an unseen wall. The question we have to answer, the question the court will demand to be answered, is whether there remains in this girl enough of free-will, enough of intelligence, to judge the nature of her action and to have been able to choose against it.'

Landon shrugged helplessly. 'Who answers that one, except God Almighty?'

'And yet,' said Galuzzi sombrely, 'every time we set up a court we arrogate to ourselves a divine function, the exercise of the power of life, death and ultimate judgement. Times are when I stand in the witness-box and tremble for my own sanity. Do you want to hear any more or would you rather see the girl first?'

'I'd like to see her with you,' said Landon. 'You can ask the questions, I'll just listen. It's hard enough to conduct an investigation in one's own language without trying to read the colours into another.'

'Let me buy you lunch and a bottle of wine,' said Emilio Galuzzi. 'I think we may have a difficult afternoon.'

Dusk was declining over the old city when Landon returned to the Pensione della Fontana. He felt tired and dispirited, oppressed by the memory of the grim prison and the faces of the unfortunates confined there.

The interview with Anna Albertini had been long and tedious and, for all Galuzzi's skill and Landon's prompting, they had not been able to induce her to reveal anything about the circumstances of her mother's death or her own participation in it. Landon himself had felt frustrated by having to watch another professional in control of a familiar operation.

His depression was increased by the fact that there was no message from Ninette. There were, however, two other messages: a telegram from Carlo in Florence and a request to call Valeria Rienzi at a Siena number before eight that evening.

Carlo's telegram was brief and cryptic: 'It was a joke, but I apologize. Have made progress. Further interviews San Stefano tonight. With client tomorrow morning. Please contact me Hôtel Continentale midday tomorrow.' Landon stuffed the telegram in his pocket and rang for the maid to draw him a bath.

As he soaked himself in the ornate marble tub, he took stock of his situation. For a man on his sabbatical year he had surrendered too much of his freedom, too much of his personal interest, to a group of people in whom he had no stake at all. If the case of Anna Albertini were what it seemed to be – a textbook history – it would add nothing to his experience or his reputation. He could discharge his promise to Carlo Rienzi by writing him a summary of his own and

Galuzzi's conclusions and then indicating lines of questioning for the defence. To Ascolini he owed nothing but the courtesies of a guest. A polite note and a graceful gift would discharge them adequately. To Valeria he owed as much or as little as a summer kiss was worth.

To Ninette? This was a different question. He was in love with her. He had told her he wanted to marry her. She had shied away from an answer. She had told him he was free to wait or to go. So now the question took a different shape. What did Peter Landon want? How much was he prepared to pay? What road would he walk in double harness?

He was still piqued by Ninette's failure to call him. He knew himself unreasonable in demanding so much of her, but when a man had had women at his beck for so many years the habit of demand was hard to break. There were other fears, too. If the lute was rifted so early and so easily, what sort of music would it play after a couple of years of marriage? Perhaps, after all, it was better to pack and go, resigning oneself to the cash guarantee of contentment. Happiness was a doubtful credit in any ledger, and who should know it better than a doctor of sick souls?

Then, by swift reaction, his mood changed from irritation to recklessness. To the devil with them all! He was still free, white and long past the age of consent. He had spent enough of himself; he deserved a night on the town. And if a maid or matron wanted to be kissed, then why not oblige her and himself at the same time? The comic thought came to him that Ascolini would probably approve him heartily at that moment. He stepped out of the tub, dried himself with brisk satisfaction, dressed himself with extra care, and then sat down to telephone Valeria Rienzi.

After a discreet interval she answered, grateful but reserved: 'Peter? It's kind of you to call. Could you spare me a little time this evening?'

'Yes, I can.'

'Could you take me to dinner?'

'Certainly. Where shall we meet?'

She told him she was having cocktails with friends in an apartment on the Via del Capitano. She suggested that he call for her at eight-thirty and then take her to dinner at a near-by restaurant. He liked the idea of company at their first meeting, so he agreed. She thanked him with disarming courtesy and hung up.

Moved by a vague impulse of guilt, he tried to telephone Ninette, but there was no answer from her studio. He felt resentful and then decided, with masculine *naïveté*, that a little separation would be good for both of them. It was still only seven-thirty, so, having an hour to kill, he decided to deal with some of his neglected correspondence.

As he worked through the pile of letters, he found himself bathed in a rosy glow of righteousness. He was a sensible fellow who knew where he was going, a sane citizen in credit with his banker, a professional who did noble service to his fellows. The rest – Ninette Lachaise excepted – was a provincial excursion, a pastoral interlude which would be forgotten as soon as it was ended.

Then, without any warning, he found himself projected into one of those moods in which the terror and the mystery of life became suddenly manifest, when the most trivial actions revealed themselves as matters of cosmic consequence.

He had presented a letter of introduction in Rome and now he was acting as unwilling catalyst in a drama of family intrigue. He had been charmed by a fledgeling lawyer and was now to counsel him on the fate of his client. He had dined with a new woman, as he had done a thousand times before, and now was committed to the resolution of marriage, to the promise of children and the unending chain of human continuity. Now he was to dine with another, reckless but not wholly unaware that this meeting, too, might start another chain of consequences.

It was a curious experience, like standing on a high mountain looking into a valley flooded with darkness. The valley was empty and soundless. One was solitary in eminence, a creature thrust up from nowhere, going to no place. Then a light pricked out, another and another. The moon rose and the valley was abruptly alive with man and all his works and one must, perforce, go down to join the concourse or die, in the cold election of pride, empty and naked.

It was not good for man to be alone. But there was a price to pay for joining the pilgrim train and a tax for every day of the journey. One must break bread with tears and drink thin wine with gratitude. One must submit to be envied and hated as much as to be loved. And if the caravan did not arrive where the master first promised, then one must wear out the sojourn in the desert with resignation, if not with joy. This was the real terror of the human condition, that men were yoked one to another in an ineluctable bondage so that a sickness in one might be a plague upon the whole fraternity and the guilt of a few make scapegoats of all. The small compassion might be a great affirmation and a petty injustice spread to a whole corruption.

A comfortless thought for a summer evening in Tuscany. So he thrust it away and took himself off to dine with Valeria Rienzi.

Give the lady her due, she had a singular charm and could be generous with it when she chose. She flattered him to her friends, but gave him no time to be bored with them. Then she handed him the keys of her car and had him drive her out beyond the walls of the old city to a country restaurant where they ate under a lattice of vines and drank wine pressed in the local vineyard. The wine was potent, there was a trio of sentimental musicians and within twenty minutes Landon was more relaxed and less cautious than he had been for days.

Valeria, too, seemed grateful for the occasion and began to tease him good-humouredly: 'It seems, Peter, that you're beginning at last to enjoy yourself – a little drama, a little comedy, a little romance.'

'It's about time, don't you think?'

'Of course. But until tonight I would never have dared to say it.' She pouted and frowned in comic mime. 'Every time I talked with you I felt like a girl going to her confessor.'

'Not tonight, I hope.' Landon laughed and stretched out a hand to her across the table. 'Let's dance, and I'll make my confession to you.'

It was said lightly, but she held him to it with the same light touch. As they danced close and harmonious, as they sat sipping wine in the pale lamplight, she drew him out so that he talked freely about himself, his family, his career, and of the situation which had brought about his withdrawal from the London scene. Valeria was a good listener, and when she was not playing coquette she dispensed a warmth and a simplicity which he would not have believed in her. Later they talked about Carlo, and she asked him: 'Do you still think he's doing the right thing, Peter?'

'I think it's right for him: though he may win less than he hopes, I think it's good that you and your father have decided to support him.'

She gave him a swift, sidelong glance. 'Do you think he cares at this moment whether we support him or not?'

'I think he cares greatly, though he would not admit it for fear of seeming weak.'

'Have you seen his client – this Anna Albertini?'

'Yes, I had a long session with her this afternoon.'

'What is she like?'

'Young, beautiful – and quite lost, I think.'

She gave a dry little laugh. 'It would be funny if Carlo fell in love with her. Lawyers and doctors do fall in love with their clients, don't they?'

'I think Carlo's in love with you, Valeria.'

She shook her head. 'Not that way, Peter. If I were a lame puppy, perhaps he might be. I know he believes that what he feels for me is love, but I'm afraid it's not my kind. And you, Peter, are you in love with Ninette Lachaise?'

It was as neat as a conjurer's trick. A flick of the silk hand-kerchief and a white rabbit pops out of the empty hat while the conjurer smiles at his innocent audience. And Landon, caught unawares, was as innocent as the moths fluttering around the shaded lamps. He sidled away from the question. 'Don't rush me, Valeria. As you say, I'm just beginning to enjoy myself.'

She reached out and patted his hand with sisterly approval. 'That's good, Peter. And I'm glad for you. It's always best with an experienced woman. If it doesn't work there are no complications, no regrets. Dance with me again. Then we must go.'

After that it was all too easy. The languor of the night took hold of them and when they drove back to Siena she dozed with her head on his shoulder, comfortable as a cat. When they reached the Pensione della Fontana he asked her in for a last drink. She accepted drowsily. But when they were closed in the old room with its high coffered ceiling and its shadows of former loves, passion lifted them like a wave and set them down in darkness and tumult on the tumbled sheets.

In the small morning hours, Landon woke to find her sitting on the edge of the bed fully dressed. She cupped his face in her hands and kissed him on the lips. Then she smiled, and her smile was full of the old wisdom of women. 'I'm happy now, Peter. I wanted you first, you know, and you'll never be able to despise me again. . . . No, don't say anything. It was good for me, and I think it may be good for you. I wanted to hurt you very much. Now I can't. You needn't be afraid of me any more. Carlo will never know, nor Ninette. But you and I won't forget. Goodnight, darling. Sleep well!'

She kissed him again and left him, and he lay wakeful until dawn, fumbling through the dictionary of his trade for words to describe what had happened to him.

He was too old to panic like a youth after his first lapse with a married woman, but he was too experienced not to be honest about its consequences. There was a guilt in what he had done: a personal guilt, an injustice to Ninette, a greater one to Carlo Rienzi. He could blame no one but himself – and he could not afford the luxury of confession. So, with a consummate irony, he was forced back to the prescription which he imposed on all his patients: accept the guilt, know yourself for what you are, wear the knowledge like a Nessus shirt on your own back and bear the pricks and the poison with as much dignity as you can muster.

He wore it all the morning. He tramped the city aimlessly, through sun-parched squares and stinking lanes. He drank too much coffee and smoked too many cigarettes. He cursed himself for a fool but found that he could not curse Valeria. He ended an hour before midday sitting alone in a pavement café, exhausted and humbled by the knowledge that this was a crisis in his life and that he was ill-prepared to meet it.

He had travelled too far and too long not to know that there were twenty agreeable substitutes for the grand passion. One could survive contentedly with any one of them, as most folks survived without truffles for breakfast or champagne for every supper. The parched traveller was happy with a mug of water from the village pump and asked no sweeter or more magical spring. His life could extend itself into a succession of episodes like the one with Valeria, each episode becoming a shade more inconsequent as vitality diminished with the years. And if there were no ecstasy, at least there would be none of the painful commitments of love.

Love was an exotic state, close kin to agony, but when a man had once endured it he was plagued ever after by the memory and the bitter nostalgia for the lost paradise. How many times could the world blow up? And after the one wild splendour, who could clap hands for fireworks and sex in suburbia?

A romantic might make of this moment a tale of spiritual insight and noble resolution. But Landon was deficient in these things as he felt himself to be in so many others. He simply waited, stiff and tired, until calm came over him and he felt ready to face Ninette Lachaise.

His heart was pounding and his hands were clammy as he climbed the stairs and knocked on the door of her studio. Ten seconds later she was in his arms, anxious and reproachful.

'*Chéri!* Where were you all day yesterday? Why didn't you call? I telephoned a dozen times this morning, but nobody knew where you were. We mustn't do these things to each other! Not ever again – promise me!' Then, sensing a strangeness in him, she held him at arm's length and looked into his face. 'Something's happened, Peter. What is it?'

The lie came out more easily than he had hoped. 'Nothing's happened, except that I've been a fool. I'm sorry. I was busy all yesterday. I telephoned you in the evening, but you weren't at home. I went out on the town. I was angry and I shouldn't have been. Forgive me?'

He took her in his arms to kiss her, but she drew away, pale and cold as a statue, and walked over to the window. When at last she spoke, her voice sounded strained and hollow across the big room. 'This is what I have been afraid of, Peter: the moment when what we have been comes to threaten what we want to be. This is why I wanted to wait and give our loving time to grow.'

'Do you still want that?' Studiously, he held himself back from her, held his voice neutral and reserved.

'Yes, Peter, I do, but only if you want it as much as I. And you mustn't lie to me, not ever. If there's something you don't want to tell me, keep it to yourself, but don't lie. I'll make you the same promise.'

'Is there anything else?'

'Yes. I still want time, Peter, before we make up our minds to marry.'

'How much time?'

'Until after the trial.'

'I'd hoped we might leave before then.'

For the first time she turned to face him and he saw that she was fighting to hold control of herself. Her answer was very firm.

'No, Peter. Don't ask me to read you the whole book. But I think you know by now that you owe Carlo a debt and you won't be happy till you pay it. I know I won't either.'

To which he had nothing to say, and he stood, shamed and irresolute, until she came to him and put her arms about him and he felt for the first time the promise of an unspoken absolution.

It was a quarter after noon when Landon reached the Continentale. He found Rienzi in his shirt-sleeves, working through a sheaf of notes at a desk piled high with textbooks. His face was grey, his eyes heavy with fatigue, and he was driving himself through the work with brandy and black coffee – a poisonous combination for a man already half drugged with body-toxin. Landon himself was tired, embarrassed and in no carnival humour, so he decided to share the poison. He poured himself a cup of coffee and two fingers of brandy, then stretched out on the bed while Rienzi talked.

'We make progress, Peter. It's slow, but at least we're going in the right direction. I went to Florence, as you know. I talked to Luigi Albertini. He's an insignificant little character and he'd been well coached by the police. However, as you guessed, he opened up a little when I asked him why his wife was still a virgin after four years of marriage.' Rienzi grinned and mimicked the back-alley dialect of Florence: '"She didn't want to. She thought it would hurt her. I took her to a doctor but he couldn't do anything. What's a fellow to do with a wife like that?" After that he closed up like a shellfish. I had the feeling he was hiding something else, but I couldn't spare the time to find what it was. However, I wanted to keep him worried, so I paid a private investigator to dig up some more information about him. He'll write me if he gets anything.'

'You told me in your telegram you were going to San Stefano. Did you get anything new there?'

'Again, some progress. Fra Bonifacio wanted to see me. One of his penitents had come to him with a trouble of conscience. He wouldn't tell me his name, but apparently it was someone who had been associated with Belloni in the Partisans. Fra Bonifacio told him that he had an obligation in conscience to reveal anything that would help the girl. He wanted time to think about it. If he decides to open up, Fra Bonifacio will get in touch with me immediately. I tried again to talk to Sergeant Fiorello but got nowhere. I've appointed another private investigator to scout the villages and see what he can dig up about Belloni's war-time history. A man like that must have had some enemies. . . . And this morning I saw Anna.'

'I saw her myself yesterday,' said Landon.

'I know. She told me. She was grateful that you and Galuzzi were so gentle with her.'

'Apparently she was more communicative with you than she was with us.' Landon grinned and sipped his brandy. Rienzi came over and sat on the edge of the bed. He asked anxiously: 'What do you think, Peter? What does Galuzzi think?'

'You rule out insanity,' said Landon definitely. 'There is evidence of trauma, obsession and other psychotic symptoms. Galuzzi wants more time to determine how far her condition reduces legal responsibility. I agree with him.'

'Is that all?'

'What more do you want?'

Rienzi began to pace the floor, running his fingers through his hair, talking in sharp, hurried sentences. 'I'm looking for a place to stand, Peter, a position from which to fight. I'm horrified by what has been done to this girl – much more than by what she herself has done. You know what she's like? Like some-one who has lived all her life in one room, looking out of the same window on the same small garden. You know what she said to me today? "Now I can make love. Now I can begin to make Luigi happy." How could she have known what she was doing? She's like someone dropped on to a new planet!'

'The court will have another view, Carlo,' said Landon soberly. 'Best you keep it clearly in your mind. She knew what a gun was. She knew enough to plan a tour by train and taxi. She knew that murder was a police matter. She under-stood its consequences. She lived in a big city. She kept house for her husband. She had a basic education and dressed like a big girl. She was neither crazy nor cretinous and she waited sixteen years to kill a man. I don't say that's the full story – I know it isn't – but that's where the court starts. And you know as well as I do that at the back of their minds are the question of public order and the fear that any clemency will bring back the practice of vendetta to the mountains.'

It was the last thought that sobered Rienzi the quickest. He chewed on it for a moment and then said quietly: 'I know everything you say and more, Peter, but there's something that troubles me deeply and that may possibly give us a start-ing point for the defence. This murder was premeditated for sixteen years. If that is true, then Anna Albertini decided on it at the age of eight, which is not an age of legal responsi-bility. The decision was taken then, Peter, although the act was performed in another time. What happened during those sixteen years? What was the state of this girl during all that time? What was the shock that first projected her into it?'

'You're asking Galuzzi's question and mine, in another form.'

'Then unless you give me the answer, Peter, there will be no justice done.'

Landon put down his coffee cup and swung himself off the bed. Then he in his turn began pacing the floor while he pieced out his argument.

'The law does justice by accident, Carlo. Any law. First and foremost it's a code of public order, a deterrent, a punitive weapon. Justice is still in the hands of God – and He takes a long time to deliver a verdict!'

'Perhaps this time,' said Carlo Rienzi, 'we may be able to persuade Him to work a little faster.' He hesitated a moment and then, moved by a sudden resolution, he swung round to face Landon. 'I have no right to ask this of you, Peter. I can offer you nothing for your services except my gratitude, but I want you to stay in Siena and help me. In spite of Galuzzi, and provided I can get the court to approve, I want to put you in the witness-box for the defence!'

'Just as you like.'

Landon said it so casually that he felt he had betrayed himself; but he had no heart for more acting, and when Carlo gaped at him in surprise and delight he snapped irritably: 'For God's sake, man, you knew all along I'd say yes! Let's not make a drama out of it. And by the same token don't expect miracles. The best I can offer you is an authority to match Galuzzi's.'

Rienzi laughed, a full, boyish laugh of relief and pleasure. 'Miracles, Peter? This is already a miracle.'

'There's another one,' said Landon moodily, anxious to be quit of the subject. 'I lunched with Ascolini, as you know. He wants to help you. He offers you a million lire and a set of notes he has made on the conduct of the case.'

'I can't accept,' said Rienzi with cool emphasis.

'I told him you probably wouldn't, but it might be an idea to send him a note of thanks.'

'I'll do that.' He added quietly: 'You know, Peter, at this moment I am able to feel more kindly to Valeria and her father than I have ever done before. You know why? Because I have you for my friend and because there's someone who needs me more than they do – Anna Albertini. All of a sudden there's a focus for my life, a cause to be anxious about – and it makes me very happy.'

Happy? To Landon he sounded more like a man on the scaffold making a hollow joke while the noose was fitted round his neck. But what was there to say? When you've slept with a man's wife can you rob him of his illusions as well? It was the bitterest draught Landon had ever swallowed in his life. He drank it with a smile, but the taste was sour on his tongue every hour of every day until Anna Albertini was brought to trial.

Chapter Five

THE OPENING of a criminal trial is an oddly theatrical occasion. Tradition and the public instinct demand not only that justice should seem to be done, but that its dispensation should provide a dramatic diversion: a purging by pity and terror of the passions which have been aroused by the criminal act.

There are those who hold that British court procedure makes better theatre than its continental equivalents; but let no unwary delinquent underrate either of them. The British tradition derives directly from the old Germanic system of trial by combat. The court is a place of contest and disputation, arbitrated by a judge and a jury. Prosecution and defence elicit their evidence by examination and cross-examination. They dispute fact and interpretation. They engage in wordy battles like knights in the ancient lists.

The Latin mode, by contrast, is one of inquisition, based on Roman law and modified by the method of the Canonists. It consists of a preliminary inquiry by a magistrate into all available evidence, which is then summarized and submitted to the court in the form of a prepared brief, on whose merits the case is heard. The prisoner does not plead guilty or not guilty. There is no contest, simply a public revelation of facts, a plea on the basis of facts by the defence and the prosecution, and then a decision – not a verdict – delivered by the president on the votes of five judges: two from the judiciary and three representing the people.

For one bred in the British tradition, there is always something a trifle sinister in the inquisitorial method since it seems to deny the accepted principle that the onus of proof rests on the Crown and that a man is innocent until he is proven guilty. The Latin method assumes in practice, if not in fact, that truth is at the bottom of a deep well and that the accused is guilty until the inquisition has enough facts to prove him innocent. In the end it seems that justice is as well or ill served by the one method as by the other.

Every court has something of the aspect of a theatre. There is a stage where the personages act out the rituals of revelation, conflict and resolution. There is a symbolic montage: the arms of the republic over the judges' dais, the carved chair which sets the president above his assisting judges, the rostrum which sets them apart from the officials of the court. There are stalls for the audience, who must conduct themselves decorously while transferring their partisan sentiments to the actors on the stage. There is a gallery for the critics and the censors of the Press. The principals are in costume. The movement is stylized. The dialogue is formal and traditional, so that, as in all theatres, reality is revealed through unreality and truth is exposed by a mummer's fiction.

Landon and Ninette arrived early, to find the antechamber choked with a press of people: reporters, photographers, witnesses, spectators, harassed officials, all talking at once, all making their own buskers' drama before the official programme began.

Old Ascolini pushed his way through the crowd to greet them. He looked tired, Landon thought. His pink cheeks were paler, his skin transparent, as though the lively spirit were burning through the tissues of his body; but he greeted them with the old quirky humour: 'So the love-birds show themselves at last! Let me look at you, young woman. Good! So far, love is an agreeable pastime, eh? Maybe soon you will be able to finish my portrait. And you, Landon, you are to be the expert witness, eh? You're a stubborn fellow, aren't you? You surprised us, Valeria most of all, I think!'

'Is she here today?' It was Ninette who asked the question.

'Over there, sulking in a corner. I've seen very little of her

103

these last weeks. She has troubles of her own, I think. And I am afraid I cannot reach her.'

It was a touchy subject. Landon tried to talk him away from it. 'How's Carlo this morning?'

'Feeling the strain.' Ascolini gave him a crooked, sardonic smile. 'You should know better than I, Landon. You've been working with him.'

Landon chose to ignore the barb and asked quietly: 'What's your feeling about the trial, Doctor?'

Ascolini spread his hands in a rueful gesture. 'What I expected. A hostile climate and a vague rumour of surprises. Carlo has told me little. But if you are free at any time, Landon, I should like to drink a glass of wine with you both.'

'Any time, *dottore*,' said Ninette with a smile. 'Just knock on the door.'

'With young lovers it is usually safer to telephone. But I shall see you.'

There was a flurry in the crowd as the door opened and they were thrust forward, willy-nilly, into the court-room. It took ten minutes to subdue the rabble into a whispering audience; then the actors began to drift on to the set.

First came the Public Minister, who would conduct the prosecution: a tall, hawk-faced official with iron-grey hair. He took his place at a table on the right of the judges' rostrum and began a whispered discussion with his assistants. Next came the Chancellor and the Clerk of the Court, detached, faintly pompous fellows who sat at a table near the prisoner s dock facing the Prosecutor across the floor.

Carlo Rienzi came in next with two seedy, middle-aged colleagues and they settled themselves at a table facing the rostrum. Carlo had aged much in the last few weeks. He had lost a great deal of weight. His clothes hung baggily on his thin shoulders. His face was drawn and yellow. There were deep lines scored around his mouth and at the corners of his eyes. In his black gown, with the white, starched jabot, he looked like a monk harried by conscience and ascetic practice.

Ninette touched Landon's arm and whispered: 'We must look after him, Peter. He looks so dreadfully alone.'

Landon nodded absently. She had not meant it so, but it

was a sharp reminder that even after weeks of common labour his debt to Rienzi was still unpaid.

Suddenly there was a gasp and a flutter of talk as Anna Albertini was brought in and led to the prisoner's dock. The noise was quickly hushed by the Clerk, but the girl gave no sign that she had heard it. She stood stock-still, hands gripping the brass rail of the dock, eyes downcast, her face bloodless but still beautiful under the harsh, yellow light.

Finally the court was called to order for the entrance of the judges and the President and the crowd stood in silence until they had settled themselves on the rostrum and spread out their papers.

The President was an imposing figure: a tall, stooping man with white hair and an old, wise face in which understanding and the impersonal majesty of the law seemed constantly at war with one another. He frowned at the rustle as the crowd sat down, but he offered no comment. Then the Chancellor stepped forward and announced: 'May it please the President and members of the court – the Republic against Anna Albertini; the charge, premeditated murder.'

Landon felt Ninette's hand tighten on his arm. There was a small flutter of fear at the pit of his belly. The flails of the law were beginning to beat on the threshing-floor and they would not cease until the chaff had been winnowed and the last grains of truth had been piled for the mills.

The President's first words were addressed to the girl in the dock: 'You are Anna Albertini, born Anna Moschetti in the village of San Stefano, lately resident in Florence?'

Her answer was firm, flat and colourless: 'I am.'

'Anna Albertini, you are charged in this court with the wilful and premeditated murder of Gianbattista Belloni, Mayor of San Stefano, on the fourteenth day of August this year. Are you represented by counsel or do you require the assistance of a public advocate?'

Carlo Rienzi rose and made the formal announcement: 'The accused is represented, Mr President. . . . Carlo Rienzi, advocate.'

He sat down and the President bent for a moment over the papers on his desk. Again he addressed the prisoner: 'According to the indictment before me, you, Anna Albertini, arrived by taxi-cab in San Stefano at midday on the date named. You walked to the Mayor's house and asked to see him. You were invited to enter, but you refused and waited at the door. When the Mayor came out, you shot him five times and walked to the police station, where you surrendered the weapon, were taken into custody and later charged. You made a statement: "He shot my mother in the war. I promised I would kill him. I have done it." Do you now wish to withdraw or challenge this statement?'

Carlo Rienzi answered for her. 'We do not wish to withdraw or challenge the statement made by the prisoner. We are satisfied that it was made freely and without coercion.'

The President gave him a puzzled, frowning look. 'Counsel has read the statement?'

'Yes, Mr President.'

'You understand fully its incriminating character?'

'Fully, Mr President. But it is our submission that for justice's sake this statement must be read in the light of evidence still to be presented in this court.'

'The submission is valid, Mr Rienzi. My colleagues and I will take note of it at the proper time.' He turned to the prosecution. 'The Public Minister may present his case.'

The tall, hawk-faced fellow stood up and announced, quite mildly: 'Mr President, gentlemen of the court, the events in this crime are so simple, so clear and brutal, that they require no oratory from me to bring you to condemn them. With the permission of the President, I propose simply to present my witnesses.'

'Permission granted.'

The first witness was the burly Sergeant Fiorello. In spite of his rugged face and his country accent, he cut a notable figure in the box. His answers were concise, his narrative fluent. He identified himself as Enzo Fiorello, rank of sergeant in the service of Public Security. He had spent twenty-five years in San Stefano and was now in charge of its station. He identified the prisoner and the weapon she had used. He sketched the circumstances and the aftermath of the murder and earned a word of commendation from the President for his expert handling of the situation. He earned another for his moderate interrogation of the accused and his swift suppression of disorder in the village. By the time the prosecution had finished with him, he stood up like some local Hampden – a champion of order but a sympathetic guardian of his people.

Then Carlo Rienzi produced his first minor surprise. He declined to examine the witness but requested that he be recalled later for questioning by the defence. The President raised a dubious eyebrow. 'This is an unusual request, Mr Rienzi. I feel it must be justified to the court.'

'It is a question of clarity in our presentation, Mr President. We propose to elicit certain information from later witnesses and on some of it we shall need to re-examine Sergeant Fiorello. If we examine him now, the questions will have no relevance.' He bowed formally to the Prosecutor. 'At this moment we are in the hands of the Public Minister and we must follow his sequence of witnesses.'

There was a moment of whispered conference on the rostrum, then the President agreed. Rienzi thanked him and sat down.

Landon looked across the court to see what Ascolini had made of the tactic, but his face was hidden and Landon saw only the serene, classic profile of Valeria.

It was as hard to read malice in her as it was to read murder in the white virginal face of the girl in the dock. Landon was reminded of the Japanese legend of those beautiful mask-faced women who changed by malignant magic into foxes when the moon was full. And yet she had kept her bargain. Whatever Ninette had guessed, Valeria had told her nothing. When, during the past weeks, he had met her in Carlo's absence, she had maintained discretion. Once only, coming on him in an empty room, she had rumpled his hair and whispered: 'I miss you, Peter. Why do girls like me always pick the wrong ones?'

For the rest, Landon trusted her and was forced to a reluctant respect.

Now a new witness was being led to the stand: Maria Belloni, wife of the dead man, the stout motherly woman who had stood in the doorway of the Mayor's house and greeted Anna Albertini. Now, dressed in widow's weeds, she seemed shrunken and old, burdened beyond endurance by loneliness and grief. When the oath was administered, the Prosecutor approached her, gentle as an undertaker. His fine voice intoned the words like the syllables of a psalm: 'Signora Belloni, we share your grief with you. We regret that you should be exposed to the pain of a new questioning, but I want you to try to compose yourself and answer the questions of the President.'

'I'll – I'll try.'

'You are a very courageous woman. Thank you.'

He remained near her while the President worked through the formal gambits.

'Your name is Maria Alessandra Belloni and you are the wife of the deceased?'

'Yes.'

'The court would like to hear in your own words what happened just before your husband was killed.'

For a moment, it seemed that she might break down completely. Then she recovered herself and began her testimony, hesitantly at first, then on a rising note of passion and hysteria. 'We were sitting down to eat like we always do . . . my husband, the boys, me. There was wine and *pasta* and a special *risotto*. It was a feast, you see: my husband's birthday. We were happy like a family should be. Then there is the ring at the door. I go out. This one is standing there.' She flung an accusing hand towards Anna Albertini. 'She says she wants to see my husband. She looks so small and lonely I think to do her a charity. I ask her to come and eat with us. She says no; it is a private matter, it will take only a moment. I . . . I go back and call my husband. He gets up from the table. He still has the napkin round his neck and a little sauce at the corner of his mouth. . . . I . . . I remember that still . . . the sauce at the corner of his mouth. He goes out. Then . . . then we hear the shots. We rush out, we find him lying in the doorway with blood all over his chest. She killed him!' The words came out in a wild scream. 'She killed him like an animal . . . she killed him . . .' The scream broke off and she buried her face in her hands, sobbing.

Landon looked across at Anna Albertini. Her eyes were closed and she was rocking on her feet as though she was going to crumple in a faint. Rienzi was on his feet in an instant. His voice was sharp with protest. 'Mr President, my client is under a great strain. I must ask that she be given a chair and a glass of water.'

The President nodded. 'The accused may sit during the evidence. Bring her a drink.'

One of the guards went out and brought in a chair. The Clerk of the Court offered a glass of water from his own table. The girl drank it, gratefully, and then sat down. All the while, the Prosecutor stood by Maria Belloni, comforting her with practised gentleness. It was, perhaps, three minutes before the President was able to resume his questioning.

'Signora Belloni, had you ever seen the prisoner before she came to your house?'

'Not since she was a little girl during the war.'

'Did you recognize her?'

'Not then. Only later.'

'Do you know why she killed your husband?'

'Because he did his duty.'

'Will you explain that, please?'

'During the war, my husband was the leader of the Partisans in this area. There were lives in his hands, many lives. There were also traitors who sold information to the Germans and to the *Fascisti*. This girl's mother was one of them. Because of her, some of our boys were taken, tortured and then killed. So she was arrested. There was a trial and she was condemned to death. My husband presided at the court and later at the execution. But this was war. He had to protect his men – and their women, too.' Quite suddenly, she seemed to become vague and dissociated, as if she were lapsing out of the reality of the court into a privacy of grief and terror. 'But that was long ago, it was finished, done, like all the other things that happened in the war. Then . . . this happens. . . . It is all crazy like a nightmare. I keep thinking that I must wake up and find my man beside me. But he doesn't come . . . he doesn't come!'

Her voice trailed off and she lapsed into low, broken

sobbing. A whisper of pity went round the court like a breeze in a wheatfield, but the President silenced it instantly. He said: 'Does the defence have any questions for this witness?'

'We have three questions, Mr President. The first is this: how did Signora Belloni know of the charges against Anna Albertini's mother, of the trial and execution?'

'Will you answer that, please?'

Maria Belloni raised her head and stared vaguely at the rostrum. 'My husband told me, of course, and the others who were there. How else would I know? I had children to care for, a house to keep.'

'Thank you. The next questions, Mr Rienzi?'

'With the permission of the court, I should like to put them directly to the witness.'

'Permission granted.'

Rienzi got up and walked slowly across to the witness-box. His manner matched that of the Prosecutor for mildness and compassion. 'Signora Belloni, was your husband a good husband?'

Her answer came back, swift and bitter: 'A good husband! A good father! He loved us – took care of us. Even in the worst days, we were always fed and warm. He never did anyone any harm. The President of the Republic sent him a gold medal and called him a hero. That's the sort of man he was. Then she came along and killed him like a dog!'

Rienzi waited a moment until she relaxed, and then asked her with deceptive mildness: 'Was your husband always faithful to you?'

The Prosecutor jumped to his feet. 'Mr President, I object!'

The President shook his head. 'We find the question relevant to the summary before us. The witness is required to answer it.'

'I repeat the question, *signora*,' said Rienzi, patiently. 'Was your husband always faithful to you?'

'Of course he was! A woman always knows, doesn't she? He was a good husband and a good father. There was nobody else.'

'Thank you, *signora*. That is all.'

For the life of him, Landon could see small relevance in the question. The spectators in the court saw no drama in it either. Landon felt, with vague disappointment, that Carlo was fumbling badly against unchallengeable witnesses.

As Maria Belloni was led from the witness-box, there was a whispered consultation between the President and the other judges. Then the President addressed himself to the Prosecutor: 'My colleagues point out, quite rightly, that, given the evidence of the witnesses so far called, given also the signed statement of the accused which the defence accepts as true and voluntary, there is no doubt in their minds as to the fact and material circumstances of the murder of Gianbattista Belloni. They point out, however, that the second part of the charge must be sustained by the Public Minister: namely, that the murder was wilful and premeditated.'

The hawk-faced Prosecutor smiled. He could afford to be indulgent with a watertight brief that was already half proven. He said genially: 'We have established fact and motive, Mr President. We submit that premeditation will be proven by the testimony of our next witnesses. The first of these is Giorgio Belloni, son of the dead man.'

Giorgio Belloni proved to be a thin, narrow-faced youth with restless hands and a strident country accent. His testimony was simple and damning. He had been confronted twice with Anna Albertini – first on the day of the murder, later at the preliminary examination. They had been schoolchildren together and he had recognized her instantly. Both times he had challenged her to tell him why she had killed his father and on each occasion she had given, before witnesses, the same answer: 'I have no quarrel with you, Giorgio, only with him. I had to wait a long time, but it's finished now.'

When Rienzi declined either to challenge the testimony or to examine the witness, the President frowned and the judges on the rostrum leant towards each other whispering. Ninette turned to Peter and asked anxiously: 'What's he doing, Peter? How can he possibly fight now?'

'Give him time, sweetheart. This is only the first round.'

'Look at Doctor Ascolini.'

He glanced across the room and saw the old man leaning forward with his head in his hands, while Valeria sat erect beside him, a small, ironic smile on her lips. The Prosecutor announced his next witness with unctuous satisfaction: 'Luigi Albertini, husband of the accused.'

All heads were turned at a stifled cry from Anna.

'No, Luigi . . . no!'

It was the first sign of emotion she had shown since the trial began. Her eyes stared, one hand holding a crumpled handkerchief went to her mouth and it seemed for a moment as if she wanted to rush from the dock to the pale, handsome youth who was taking the stand. Then one of the guards placed a restraining hand on her shoulder and she sat rigid again, closing her eyes as if to blot out an impending horror. The young man was sworn and the President questioned him in a level voice: 'Your name is Luigi Albertini and you are the husband of the accused?'

'Yes.'

The reply was barely audible and the President admonished him sharply: 'This is a painful occasion, young man, but you are here to be heard by the court. Please speak up! How long have you been married?'

'Four years.'

'You have lived with your wife all that time?'

'Yes.'

'What work do you do?'

'I'm a night-watchman in the Elena textile factory in Florence.'

'What are your hours of work?'

'From nine in the evening until six in the morning.'

'In the course of your work, do you carry a gun?'

'I do.'

At a sign from the President, the Clerk of the Court walked across to the witness-box and held out the weapon.

The President asked again: 'Do you recognize the weapon?'

'Yes, it's mine.'

'When did you last see it?'

'After I came off duty on the morning of the fourteenth of August. I put it on the bedside table. I usually put it in the bureau drawer, but this time I was tired and I forgot.'

'The gun was loaded?'

'Yes.'

'What do you usually do when you come off duty?'

'I have a meal and go to bed.'

'You did that on the morning of the fourteenth of August?'

'Yes.'

'What time did you wake up?'

'Three in the afternoon.'

'Was your wife at home?'

'No.'

'Where was she?'

'I didn't know. She left a note saying not to worry about her and that she would be back in a couple of days.'

'When did you discover your gun was missing?'

'As soon as I found the note.'

'When did you see it again?'

'When the police brought me to Siena to see my wife.'

'Thank you.'

The President looked up questioningly at Rienzi.

He stood up slowly and said: 'Once again, Mr President, we must ask the indulgence of the court. I should like this witness recalled for defence examination at a later time.'

The President frowned and said, tartly: 'I would advise Counsel for the Defence that the judgement of the court will be given on the facts contained in our brief and interpreted in evidence. He would be strongly advised not to rely upon tactical manœuvres.'

'With respect, Mr President,' said Rienzi, firmly, 'this court exists to dispense justice and it would be a sorry day if too rigid a procedure were to inhibit such dispensation.'

Even to untutored observation, it was a risky move. The assisting judges looked up, displeased, and then turned to the President for a direction. The old man sat silent for a moment, toying with a pen. Finally, he frowned and said: 'In view of the dubious situation of the defence, we are inclined to grant his request. The witness is excused but he will be recalled later.'

'Thank you, Mr President.'

Rienzi sat down and the Public Minister took the floor with placid triumph.

'May it please the President and members of the court, it is the submission of the Republic that without further testimony murder is proved and premeditation as well. However, in order to anticipate any submission that may be made by the defence on the grounds of insanity or mental incapacity, I should like to call as my last witness Professor Emilio Galuzzi.'

Professor Galuzzi made an impressive progress to the stand. He spoke slowly and pedantically, but there was no doubting either his authority or his competence. With the consent of the President, the Prosecutor led him personally through the examination.

'Professor Galuzzi, what are your official appointments?'

'I hold the Chair of Psychiatric Medicine at the University of Siena. I'm the Director of Psychiatric Treatment at the Santa Caterina Hospital in this city. I act as adviser to the Department of Justice on Mental Health and Criminal Psychology.'

'Have you examined the prisoner Anna Albertini?'

'Yes. Acting under instructions from the Chancellor of this court, I made a series of psychiatric and medical examinations of the accused.'

'Will you tell the court your findings, please?'

'I found no evidence of any physical disorder or of any hysteric symptoms. There was evidence of residual shock, but this was consonant with a normal reaction after a crime of this nature and with the processes of arrest, imprisonment and interrogation to which the accused had been subjected. I did note, however, strong evidence of psychic trauma directly related to the circumstances of her mother's death. This was revealed by the classic symptoms of obsession, emotional incapacity and an apparent perversion of moral sense in respect of the crime.'

'Would you say, Professor, that the accused was, in the legal sense, a sane person?'

'Yes.'

'For this reason you agreed that she was fit to stand trial in this court?'

'Yes.'

'Again in the legal sense, Professor, she is to your view a responsible person?'

'You're asking me to repeat myself,' said Galuzzi, mildly. 'Legal sanity implies legal responsibility.'

The Prosecutor acknowledged the reproof with a thin smile. 'I have one more question. In your view, and in the same legal sense, was Anna Albertini a responsible person at the moment of the crime?'

'I would say so, yes.'

'That is all. Thank you.'

Carlo Rienzi stood up. 'With the permission of the President, I should like to ask the witness some questions.'

The President looked up at the clock, which showed five minutes to midday. He said, with tart humour: 'The court welcomes any display of activity on the part of the defence, but we are coming close to the midday recess. Will Counsel's questioning take long?'

'It may take some time, Mr President.'

'In that case it would be better to take the recess now. Counsel may begin his examination when we resume sitting. The court is adjourned until three o'clock this afternoon.'

He gathered up his papers and walked out, followed by his colleagues. The guard led Anna Albertini from the dock and the court broke into a hubbub of talk. Landon and Ninette pushed forward to speak to Carlo, but before they reached him Valeria was already there and they were close enough to catch the first terse exchanges. Valeria asked irritably: 'Are you coming to lunch, Carlo? I don't want to hang around here too long.'

Carlo stared at her vaguely. 'No, don't wait for me. I want to talk to Anna. I've ordered lunch in her cell.'

'Charming!' said Valeria with contempt. 'Charming, if a trifle bizarre! Then you won't mind if Basilio takes me to lunch?'

Rienzi shrugged wearily and turned away. 'You must do whatever you want, Valeria. I can't fight two battles at once.'

'You're not doing very well in this one, are you, darling?'

'I'm doing my best,' said Carlo moodily, 'and there's a long way to go yet.'

'A lifetime for your little white virgin!'

She turned away to follow the crowd from the court, but Landon, bitterly angry, blocked her retreat. 'Drop it, Valeria! Stop acting like a bitch! No man deserves what you're trying to do to Carlo.'

'You should be more polite, darling. I can do worse things if I want to.'

She gave him a little indulgent pat on the cheek and left him, flushed and impotent, counting once more the cost of a night's indiscretion. He turned back to the defence table, where Ninette, mercifully, was talking with Carlo: 'You're looking tired, Carlo. You must take care of yourself.'

Rienzi smiled ruefully. 'It's been a rough time. Except for Peter here I've been much alone. And Valeria is playing games to make it harder.' He turned to Landon. 'How does it sound from the front, Peter?'

'As we planned it – a preliminary skirmish.'

A brief, boyish grin lit up Rienzi's drawn face. 'I think we may do a little better this afternoon. Now, if you'll excuse me, I want to see my client. She needs a great deal of support just now.'

'Why not dine with us this evening?'

He hesitated, but Ninette gave him her most winning smile. 'Please, Carlo! You owe us a little of your company. We'll wait for you after the next session and then we'll dine at my apartment. You can relax there and perhaps play us a little music.'

'I'd like that. Thank you.'

He gathered his papers and walked, a stooping, tired figure, towards the door that led to the remand cells. Landon and Ninette watched him go and were touched by a common pity for so much lonely talent and so much genuine good will. Ninette exploded angrily: 'Valeria's a monster! If she can't break him one way she'll try another. What did you say to her, Peter?'

'I told her she was a bitch – and to leave Carlo alone.'

'You're not afraid of her, are you, Peter?' The question took him unawares and for a moment he had no answer. To his surprise, Ninette laughed quietly. 'Never let a woman blackmail you, Peter. Not even me. I love you, *chéri*, and I too can fight for what I want. Come on! You can buy me a drink and something to eat.'

The ante-room of the court was almost empty, but Dr Ascolini was waiting for them near the outer door. Without so much as a by-your-leave, he linked arms with Ninette and said, positively: 'I refuse to eat alone. You will both have lunch with me at Luca's. I want to talk with you.'

There was little time to talk as they threaded their way along the narrow, crowded pavements. But when they were settled in the baroque comfort of Luca's, Ascolini challenged Landon: 'Well, my friend, what do you think of Carlo's chances?'

'It's too early to say.'

'And you, Ninette?'

'Frankly, *dottore*, I don't know what to think. I cannot believe that he is so inept as he has seemed to this point. But he has made no impression on me, and I think very little on the members of the court.'

The old man chuckled with satisfaction. 'So now perhaps you are prepared to agree that I might have been wise to dissuade him from this case?'

Ninette Lachaise shook her head. 'Not wholly. Even if he fails, and Peter thinks the odds are that he will, he will have tried his strength. He cannot fail to make some profit.'

'Even if he wrecks his career?'

'A career is less important than self-respect, *dottore*. You know that.'

'*Touché!*' said Ascolini with a grin. 'You have a formidable prize in this woman of yours, Landon. Now I should tell you both something which may surprise you: I think Carlo is doing remarkably well.' He waited a moment, savouring their surprise. 'You, my dear Landon, are bred to the forensic fireworks of a British court. You think in terms of a duel between opposing Counsel. You want one fact balanced against another, one argument qualified by an opposite one. You demand the sway of sympathy and the clash of personality. So you miss the strategy which our system demands.' He sipped his drink and wiped his lips fastidiously with a silk handkerchief. 'Consider what Carlo has done so far. He has reduced himself in the eyes of the judges so that they are concerned whether adequate justice is being done to the accused. Therefore they are inclined to allow him more latitude than they would otherwise do. He has permitted the prosecution to expend its whole argument in one morning's session. His timing allows him to examine a key prosecution witness at the beginning of a fresh session and to re-examine others in the light of defence evidence. This is sound campaigning – most sound with an unpromising brief.'

'Carlo would be encouraged to hear you say that.'

The old man frowned and answered unhappily: 'I doubt it. The climate between us is less favourable than ever. Valeria is now flaunting this Lazzaro fellow under Carlo's nose. He cannot fail to believe that I approve it.'

'She's destroying herself,' said Ninette with sudden anger. 'Can't she see that?'

'More clearly than you, I think,' said the old man sombrely. 'But there are matters that have no aptitude for contentment. I am one, she is another. Our sole satisfaction is to wrest from each moment whatever it holds of sweet or bitter. It is, if you want, an impulse of conquest and not of enjoyment. We seek to dominate and, if we cannot, we are happier to destroy. Carlo has withdrawn himself from us. All his interest is centred in this case – and, I'm afraid, in his client.'

'I'm afraid of that too,' said Landon with sharp interest. 'I've watched it happening these last weeks. I've tried to show him where it leads. I've pointed out the dangers to him and his client, but I'm afraid he's in no condition to measure them. I'm worried about him. In this profession, as in any other, a man needs a line of retreat from the demands which are made on him. If he doesn't find it at home, then he may attempt either an impossible dedication or a dangerous identification with his client.'

Ascolini nodded agreement, and asked with grave interest: 'Which way is Carlo leaning?'

'He thinks it is to dedication. I'm afraid it's the other way. He makes no secret of his compassion for Anna Albertini. He spends himself to ensure her comfort and to offer her reassurance. For her part, she is coming to lean on him for everything. Which makes a double danger.'

'I know,' said Ascolini. 'Valeria makes sordid jokes about it, and this is bad for any man working on the edge of his nerves. But he fights back now. He will not let us play games with him as we once did. The boy has become a man, and there is a fund of anger in him.'

He broke off, as if weary of so much unhappiness, and signalled a waiter to attend them. While they ate, they talked of more amiable matters, but by the time the coffee was brought they were back to the trial again, and the old man was expounding in sober, legal fashion his views on the problems of the defence.

'. . . In a case of this kind, where the facts and circumstances of a crime are beyond doubt, there is no hope of acquittal. No society can condone a murder. Between you and Carlo you have framed a plea of mitigation on the grounds of provocation and partial mental infirmity. Your problem is, of course, that you are brought immediately into areas of dubious definition where success depends as much on the skill of the advocate as on the legality of his plea. This is where experience comes in – and Carlo is deficient in experience.'

'I think you still underrate him, *dottore*,' said Ninette gently.

'Perhaps.' Ascolini smiled wryly. 'Even so, child, I'm afraid this court will be more stringent than you think, since too liberal a decision may lead to public disorders.'

'The vendetta?'

'The vendetta, the crime of passion – any circumstance where the law has failed to prevent or punish injustice, and the individual takes redress into his own hands. No society can permit this, however great the original wrong, because society dares not take liberties with its own survival.' His fine hands dismissed the subject as a riddle beyond solution. 'This is why justice is represented by a woman. She is fickle, paradoxical, relentless, but she has always an eye to the main chance.'

They laughed at his cynicism and he was pleased. Yet Landon felt in the same moment a pang of pity for him: a man with a touch of greatness, a cool analyst, a doughty fighter, a stoic humorist, yet robbed of the repose of age by the passions he had indulged in himself and others. It was not their place to judge him, but Landon understood all too clearly the dilemma in which he found himself. He had derided too long the man he now needed as a son. He had loved too selfishly the daughter who now used love as a weapon against him. Ambition was satisfied and passion spent. All that was left to him was the fierce peasant pride – weak buttress against the siege of years and solitude.

Landon was glad when Ninette said to him in her quiet, percipient fashion: 'Carlo's having dinner with us tonight. Why don't you come, too, *dottore*? It would give you both a chance to relax together.'

He smiled and shook his head. 'You have a gentle heart, young woman, but don't let it run away with you. It is Carlo who needs your company. And I'm a crooked old devil who will say the wrong thing from sheer perversity.' He pushed back his chair and stood up. 'Let's get a little fresh air before the next session.'

Twenty paces from the court-room, in the narrow, white-washed remand cell, Advocate Carlo Rienzi was serving luncheon to his client. He had ordered the meal from a neighbouring restaurant, complete with wine, silvery cutlery and fresh linen napery. Now he was busy as a housewife, spreading the cloth, laying the places and serving the food while the girl stood looking out of the single barred window towards a patch of blue sky.

The cell was austere as a monk's hole – with a truckle-bed, a crucifix on one wall, a pair of stools and a rough wooden table – but to Carlo Rienzi it wore for the moment an air of comfort and intimacy.

For the past weeks he had visited Anna Albertini almost daily, but had never once been private with her. There was always a guard within earshot whose menacing presence imposed a formality on their exchanges. Here, for the first time, they were truly alone. The heavy door was bolted, the Judas shutter was closed, and the languid guard was eating his lunch and washing it down with the wine Rienzi had brought for him.

Anna Albertini, however, showed no sign of pleasure or surprise at the new situation. She had thanked him gravely when the meal was brought in, and then had left him to serve it. When he was finished, he called her: 'Come and eat something, Anna.'

'I don't want anything, thank you.' She did not turn to answer him but spoke to the sky in a flat, toneless voice.

'It's a good meal,' said Rienzi with forced brightness. 'I ordered it myself.'

She turned then, and there was a hint of warmth in her reply: 'You shouldn't have taken all this trouble.'

Rienzi smiled, poured two glasses of wine and handed one to her. 'If you're not hungry, I am. Won't you join me?'

'If you want me to.'

Remote and placid, she moved to the table and sat down facing him. Rienzi began eating immediately, questioning her between mouthfuls.

'How do you feel, Anna?'

'Quite well, thank you.'

'It was rough this morning. I'm afraid it's going to be worse this afternoon.'

'I'm not afraid.'

'You should be,' said Rienzi roughly. 'Now stop being silly and eat your lunch.'

Obedient as a child, the girl began picking at her food while Rienzi sipped his wine and watched her, wondering as he always did at her uncanny air of innocence and detachment. After a while, she asked him: 'Why should I be afraid?'

For all his experience with her, Rienzi was staggered. 'Don't you understand, Anna? Even now? You saw the court, you heard the evidence. If the Prosecutor has his way you'll be in prison for twenty years. Doesn't that scare you?'

Her small, waxen hand pointed round the room. 'Isn't this prison?'

'Yes.'

'This doesn't scare me.' She was wide-eyed at his obtuseness. 'People are kind and considerate. I'm happy here. I'm happy at San Gimignano, happier than I've ever been in my life.'

'Because you killed a man?' Rienzi's tone was sharp with irritation.

'No, not really. Because I sleep quietly, don't you see? I don't have nightmares. I wake in the morning and I feel new, a new person in a new world. There's nothing to hate, nothing to fear. For the first time I feel that I am myself.'

Rienzi stared at her, caught between pity and wonder and a little wordless fear. 'What were you before, Anna?'

Her face clouded, and her eyes became suddenly vague. 'I never knew. That was the trouble: I never knew.'

Then, as always, he was shaken with pity for her. He bent over his plate and ate a while in silence. Then, more genially, he told her: 'We do have a chance, you know, Anna. It's a slim one. But we may be able to get you off with a very light sentence.'

'I hope so,' said Anna Albertini placidly, 'for your sake.'

Rienzi gaped at her, startled. 'For my sake?'

'Yes. I know this case means a great deal to you. If you win it, it will make your reputation. You'll be the great advocate you've always wanted to be.'

'How do you know that?'

'I'm not a child, you know,' said Anna Albertini.

Rienzi digested the wry morsel for a few moments and then tried another line of questioning: 'Tell me, Anna, if we do succeed and you get a light sentence, what will you do when you come out of prison?'

'What I've always wanted to do – go back to my husband, be a good wife, bear him children.'

'Are you sure you could?'

'Why not? I told you, I'm a new person. The nightmares are over.'

'You may find worse ones waiting for you,' said Rienzi harshly. He pushed back his chair and walked away from the table, to stand as Anna had stood, looking through iron bars at a pocket-handkerchief sky. The girl watched him with childish puzzlement. She said, unhappily: 'I don't understand you at all.'

Rienzi swung round, stared at her for a moment, and then launched into a simple, passionate appeal: 'Anna, I'm trying to make you understand something. At this moment, and until the end of your trial, you are in my hands. I act for you, think for you, plead for you. But afterwards, whichever way it goes, you will have to do all these things for yourself. You will have to build a new life – inside the four walls of the prison or outside in the world of men and women. You have to begin preparing yourself now for whatever may happen. You will be alone, do you understand?'

'How can I be alone? I'm married to Luigi. Besides, you'll help me, won't you?'

Rienzi hedged his answer: 'A wise advocate interests himself only in the case, Anna, not in the private life of his client.'

'But you're interested in me, aren't you – privately, I mean?'

'What makes you say that?'

'I feel it, that's all. When I'm standing there in the court, I tell myself that as long as I think of you everything will be all right.'

'That's not true, Anna. I'm just an ordinary lawyer with a bad brief. I can't work miracles. You mustn't expect them.'

It was almost as if she had not heard him, could not even see him. She went on with the pathetic earnestness of a child trying to explain herself: 'So far as I'm concerned, you are the only one in the court. I hardly see the others. I hardly hear them or know what they say. It's as if . . . as if . . .'

Rienzi prompted her sharply. 'As if what?'

'As if you were holding my hand, as my mother used to do.'

'God Almighty, no!'

The girl stared at him in distress. 'Did I say something wrong?'

'Eat your dinner, Anna,' said Rienzi dully. 'It's getting cold.'

He turned away from her and began pacing thoughtfully up and down the narrow room while the girl picked listlessly at the meal. After a few moments, a new thought seemed to strike her. and she asked: 'Where's Luigi? Why hasn't he come to see me?'

'I don't know, Anna.'

In her odd, absent fashion she seemed to accept the answer. Rienzi hesitated a moment and then asked her: 'Tell me, Anna, why did you marry Luigi?'

'My aunt said it was time for me to settle down. I wanted it, too. Luigi was a nice boy, gentle and kind. It seemed we could be happy together.'

'But you weren't?'

'When we were courting, yes. I was proud of him and he seemed to be proud of me. We would walk and talk and hold hands and kiss. We would make plans about what we were going to do – about names for our children, the sort of apartment we'd like. . . .'

'But afterwards?'

Anna Albertini looked at him strangely, and for the first time he saw the hint of a break in her composure. 'Afterwards was my fault. I just couldn't help myself. Every time he took me in his arms I . . .' She broke off and threw out her hands in a gesture of appeal. 'Please! I don't want to talk about it. It's all over now. I'm changed. I know I'll make him a good wife.'

'Does he still mean so much to you?'

'He's the only one I have.'

'What did he say to you when they brought him to see you in the prison?'

'Nothing. He just looked at me. I tried to explain to him, but they wouldn't let me talk. And then he went away. I don't blame him. I'm sure he'll understand in the end. Don't you agree?'

'I hope so,' said Rienzi deliberately, 'but I wouldn't count on it.'

For the first time, the real point of his interrogation made itself clear to her. Her hand went to her mouth and her face crumpled into a mask of horror. 'He doesn't love me any more?'

'No, Anna. And I'm going to put him in the witness-box again this afternoon. You may not like what you hear.'

She did not weep or cry out, but got up slowly from the table and walked to the window, where she stood, tight and trembling, the palms of her hands pressed against the white stone wall. Rienzi asked her: 'Were you really in love with him, Anna?'

'I don't know.' Her voice was dull and toneless. 'That's the point. Until now I've really never known about anything – even myself. So long as Belloni was alive things seemed to make sense, there was just a long, straight road, with me at one end of it and Belloni at the other. So long as I kept walking, I knew I must meet him sooner or later. Now he's dead, and there's nothing . . . no road, nothing!'

'Then you must find a new road, Anna.'

There was an infinite pathos in her reply: 'But a road always goes somewhere. I don't know where I want to go. I don't even know if there's a me. There's just my name, Anna Albertini, but no me. Can you see one?'

'I can, Anna.' He went to her and took her cold hands in his own. 'I can see one, touch one. She is made to have children of her own and hold them in her arms. She is very beautiful. She can love and be loved.'

'The only one who ever loved me was my mother.'

'She is dead, Anna.'

'I know.'

He pleaded with her passionately: 'But you're alive, Anna. You will go on living. You have to have something to live for.'

'I used to have Belloni. Now he's dead, too.'

'That was hate, Anna. You can't go on hating a dead man!'

'I wanted to love Luigi, but he doesn't love me. Where do I start? Where do I go?'

Sombrely, he told her again: 'If we lose our case, you'll go to prison for twenty years.'

'You know I'm not afraid of that. In a way it's been quite good. They tell me what to do, how to do it, where to go.'

'But this is not living.' He was angry now, and vehement. 'This is death! This is like the princess in the enchanted wood. You will have no nightmares, but you will have no life either! You will be led this way and that, like a clockwork figure, until beauty dies and love dies and there is no hope for you any more!'

'Please don't be angry with me.'

He caught her shoulders in a savage grip and shook her. 'Why not? You're a woman, not a rag-doll. You can't go on any longer shifting the responsibility for your life to someone else. It was you who broke Luigi. He wanted love and you couldn't give it to him. I want something from you now – help, co-operation! You're giving me nothing!' He released her and she stood rubbing her bruised shoulders, her eyes filled with the first tears he had ever seen in her. Instantly his anger was gone and he was overwhelmed by tenderness. He put his arm about her and drew her dark head against his breast. 'I'm not blaming you, Anna. I'm not God. I'm trying to get you to blame yourself.'

Then, for the first time, she began to weep, clinging to him desperately while her body shook with sobbing. 'Don't leave me. Don't leave me, please. I feel safe with you!'

Brutally, he thrust her away and blazed at her again: 'You can't feel safe! You've got to feel naked and alone and scared! You've got to want something so badly that it breaks your heart. You're a woman, Anna, not a child!'

Pitifully, she pleaded with him: 'I want to be a woman. Can't you see I want to be, but I don't know how? Help me! For God's sake help me!'

She clung to him again, her dark head on his shoulder, her hair brushing his lips, Rienzi tried awkwardly to comfort her while he stared, unseeingly, beyond her towards all the bleak implications of her dependence on him. Then he disengaged himself gently.

'I'll have to go now, Anna. We're due in court in a few minutes.'

'Don't go. Don't leave me!'

'I must, Anna,' said Rienzi with sober pity, 'I must.'

He turned away, walked to the door and called the guard to let him out. When it slammed behind him Anna Albertini stared blank-faced at the Judas window, then, seized with sudden terror, she flung herself on the bed, weeping like a lost child.

Chapter Six

THE AFTERNOON session opened tamely, on a note of academic calm. Professor Galuzzi took the stand and Carlo Rienzi led him through a short résumé of the testimony he had given in the morning. Then Rienzi began to ask for definitions.

'Professor, I wonder if you will be good enough to explain to the court the meaning of the words "trauma" and "traumatic psychosis".'

Galuzzi smiled, coughed, adjusted his pince-nez, and explained: 'Literally, the word "trauma" means a wound. In the medical sense, it signifies a morbid condition of the body caused by some external disorder. In the psychiatric sense, it means much the same thing – a scar caused by emotional or mental shock. The words "traumatic psychosis" describe a disordered state of mind induced by the trauma. If I may explain more clearly, a scar on the finger is a trauma – not a very serious one. The scars left by major surgery are also traumas. There are similar degrees of scarring to the human psyche.'

'And the more serious traumas are always persistent?'

'Always. Though time and treatment may diminish their effects.'

'Correct me if I am wrong, Professor, but does not the word "psychosis" describe a deep-seated, grave and more or less permanent mental disorder?'

'In general terms, that's true.'

'So that a psychotic patient is always, in greater or lesser degree, handicapped?'

'Yes,'

'Let us take some simple examples, Professor.' Rienzi's tone was mild, almost deferential. 'A child loses a beloved parent. Would you call this an emotional shock?'

'Most certainly.'

'It would leave a scar?'

'Yes.'

'Which might reveal itself through some psychic infirmity in later life?'

'It might – yes.'

There was a small silence in the court. All eyes were on Rienzi as he walked back to his table, picked up some papers and then returned to Galuzzi. There was a change in him now. His shoulders straightened, his tone became crisper, the tempo of his questions grew faster.

'Let us take the case of Anna Albertini. She had lost both her parents by the age of eight. According to the evidence of the prosecution, her mother was executed by a firing-squad. How would you judge the scar inflicted on her young mind?'

'A very grave one.'

'Another question, Professor. You say you carried out tests on the prisoner. What was the nature of these tests?'

'In general terms, they consisted of a medical examination, a neurological survey and a modified form of analysis.'

'You know, then, that although she has been married for four years she is still a virgin?'

'Yes.'

'You would agree that this indicated an abnormality in her relations with her husband?'

'Yes.'

'How did you diagnose the abnormality?'

'As a condition of sexual incapacity in the accused related to and probably induced by her childhood experiences.'

'In other words, by the trauma, or scar, we have been talking about? Would you describe Anna Albertini as a psychotic subject?'

'Yes.'

'In other words, Professor, what you are saying is that she is mentally infirm?'

The Prosecutor stood up, protesting: 'I object, Mr President. The question leads the witness to a conclusion which is properly the function of the Bench.'

'The objection is upheld. Counsel for the Defence must confine himself to eliciting information in terms of the brief before us.'

'With respect, Mr President,' said Carlo Rienzi firmly, 'I am concerned to define clearly to the court the nature of the information elicited. However, in deference to the President's wishes, I will re-frame the question. Tell us, Professor, is it or is it not true that a psychotic patient is mentally infirm?'

'It is true.'

'No more questions.'

'You are excused, Professor,' said the President.

There was a moment of whispered consultation on the rostrum and Ascolini turned to Landon and Ninette with a grin of triumph. 'You see? I told you he had cards in his sleeve! This is good – very good!'

To judge from the murmur that ran through the court, most of the spectators had taken the point too. The Pressmen were scribbling notes and the Prosecutor was conferring with his associates. Alone of all the people in the court Anna Albertini sat calm and unmoved, like a priestess presiding over some ancient rite which had long since lost relevance or meaning.

The President rapped with his gavel and there was silence again while the Prosecutor stood up and addressed himself to the panel of judges: 'Mr President, gentlemen of the court, the indictment which is in your hands is so clear and simple, the testimony of the witnesses so concise and unanimous, that I hesitate to waste any more of the court's time by calling other testimony which is available to us. We have submitted proof of the crime, we have submitted proof of premeditation. Both are confirmed by the voluntary statement of the accused. It is not for me to comment on the new line opened by the defence, but we would point out that it has accepted or left unchallenged all our testimony. We should appreciate a direction, Mr President.'

For a reason which Landon did not understand, the President seemed piqued by the suggestion. He said, acidly: 'I fail to see any reason for new direction in this case. If the prosecution has no more witnesses to call, then the defence may present its own testimony. Mr Rienzi?'

'With the permission of the court, I should like first to re-call Luigi Albertini.'

At the mention of the name, the girl in the dock seemed to waken. Her hands fumbled restlessly on the brass railing and her eyes, wide and troubled, followed every step of the weak, puzzled youth towards the witness-stand. Rienzi let him stand there a few moments, then began to question him with cool deliberation.

'Mr Albertini, how long have you been married?'

The boy looked up, startled and irritated. 'I said it before: four years.'

'Has your marriage always been a happy one?'

There was a pause, a shamed look towards his wife and then a mumbling, sullen answer: 'It's never been happy.'

'Why not?'

'I – I'd rather not say.'

'You must say,' Rienzi told him, flatly. 'Your wife is on trial for murder.'

Albertini flushed and stammered unhappily: 'I – I don't know how to say it.'

'Say it as you know it – simply, bluntly. Why was your marriage not happy?'

'We – we never made love together as married people should.'

'Why not?'

'Because whenever I took Anna in my arms she would start screaming: "They're killing her! They're killing my mother!"'

'Do you understand why she did this?'

'Of course I do!' A sudden feeble anger flared out of him, and then died. 'Anna understood it, too. But it didn't help either of us. Four years that went on.'

'During those four years – difficult years, I admit – did you ever seek medical advice?'

'Many times and with many doctors. They all said the same thing.'

'What did they say?'

'"Give her time and patience and she might get better."' He burst out, bitterly: 'But she never did! What kind of life is that?'

'And now, Mr Albertini?'

The boy looked puzzled. 'I don't know what you mean.'

Cold as a swordsman, Rienzi moved in for the kill. 'I think you do. Is it not a fact that ten days after your wife's arrest you made application, first to the Archbishop of Florence and then to the civil authorities, for the annulment of your marriage on the grounds of non-consummation?'

There was a moment of dead silence and then a scream of pure horror from the girl in the dock. 'No, Luigi, no!' The next instant, she was grappling with the guards and crying in a long, moaning ululation: 'Don't do it, Luigi! Don't leave me! Don't! Don't!'

The President's voice cut across the tumult: 'Remove the prisoner.'

In the body of the court, Professor Galuzzi jumped to his feet. 'With respect, Mr President, I suggest the prisoner be given immediate medical attention.'

'Thank you, Professor. The court would appreciate your attendance on the accused and your later advice on her fitness to continue the hearing.'

As Anna was wrestled out, moaning and struggling, her husband stood, downcast, in the dock and Carlo Rienzi turned a pale, composed face to the judges. 'I am finished with my witness, Mr President. I regret the disturbance, but I had no choice.'

For the first time, a wintry smile of approval showed on the old man's face. 'You are new to this court, Mr Rienzi. I hope we may see more of you.' He picked up his gavel. 'The court is adjourned for thirty minutes or until such time as the prisoner is fit to attend.'

In the disorder that followed his exit, Ninette and Landon sat with Doctor Ascolini and waited for the chattering crowd to disperse. Carlo picked up his papers and walked out of the court towards the remand cells.

Ascolini was as excited as a schoolboy, bouncing in his chair and making a whirlwind pantomime for Ninette's benefit. 'You see where the instinct shows, child? The method, the dramatic sense? This is the talent of great advocacy. You saw what he did. First he takes a hostile witness and borrows straw from him for his own bricks. He takes the specialist word "trauma" and all of a sudden it is a new one – "mental infirmity". We have the first brick laid. But Carlo knows and we all know that each of us is infirm in one fashion or another.

So he stages a big drama, tears, shrieks and disorder, to show what infirmity may mean – a pretty girl who can't enjoy a tumble in bed. This is another brick: sympathy. And we all ask the same question: "How can this happen to a pretty girl that we'd all like to sleep with?" For the moment we forget that she has killed a man and that another woman sleeps lonely because of her. Two bricks! They are not yet a foundation for any defence. But the promise, girl! The promise in the man! I'm proud of him!'

'Then go and tell him so, *dottore*,' said Ninette firmly. 'A dozen steps and a dozen words and it is done. Go on now.'

'It's not time yet.'

'There will never be a better time, *dottore*. Swallow your pride.'

For a moment he hesitated, then he stood up, smoothed down his coat and walked with firm steps towards the far door of the court-room. Landon was dubious and said as much, but Ninette was jubilant over the success of her manœuvre. 'It's important, don't you see, Peter? To Carlo, if he can call on Ascolini's support and advice for the rest of the case. To Ascolini, who has come to his own crisis. The best things we do are done quickly, from the heart.'

'We know what's in our own hearts, darling: I'm not sure we understand what's in theirs.'

'You make mysteries, Peter, where none exist. These two are ready for friendship. There is a respect on both sides. Let a good moment pass and there may not be another for a long time.'

To which he had no adequate reply, and besides it was easier to kiss her than argue with her. He surrendered with a shrug and a smile and they walked out hand in hand to the babble of the anteroom. The talk was deafening. It rose on high waves of emphasis and tumbled into frothing troughs of confusion. Words, phrases, scraps of interpretation were tossed up like spume-flakes and blown away. Women laughed, men looked subtle and knowing. Secrets were touted as freely as backstage gossip at an opera.

It was a bitter little commentary on the need of human nature to make a circus out of death and spectacle out of the scapegoat driven into the desert. Pity is a comforting indulgence, easily turned to contempt or ribaldry, but compassion is a rare virtue, founded on the admission that each hides in his own heart the weakness that he damns in his fellows, and that pain or thwarted desire may drive him to greater excesses than they have committed. The cruelty of a crowd is less terrifying than the fear which it hides, the despair of personal forgiveness which inhibits the forgiveness of others.

'Peter, look!'

Ninette's fingers dug into his palm and he glanced up to see Valeria Rienzi pushing her way through the crowd towards them. Her face was white and strained and she accosted them abruptly: 'I want to talk to you two. Come and have a cup of coffee with me.'

Without waiting for an answer, she linked arms with them and hurried them to a little bar a hundred yards down the street. They had hardly settled themselves at the table before she burst out: 'I thought you'd both like to know. Basilio's left me. He told me so at lunch. Just like that . . . the comedy's over!' She gave a sharp, hysterical laugh. 'Oh, I know what you're thinking! He would have done it sooner or later, just like he did it to you, Ninette. But it wasn't like that . . . it wasn't like that at all. You know who organized it? My wise, loving father. He likes people of breeding, you know. Only the best stallions come to the Ascolini stud! So he telephoned Basilio and threatened to make trouble in his business if he didn't stop seeing me. Clever, isn't it? Everybody's mated now except me and Father. Carlo has his little virgin, you have each other. That leaves Father and me. What do I do now, Peter? Where do I look?' Her voice rose higher and heads were turned in their direction. 'You know how I am in bed. What's your prescription?'

Under the astonished eyes of the drinkers at the bar, Landon leaned across the table and slapped her hard on both cheeks so that the rising wave of hysteria broke into weeping. Ninette said nothing, but sat, shamed and blushing, while Landon fished a handkerchief from his pocket and pushed it across the table to Valeria. He said calmly: 'Dry your eyes, girl. You're making a fool of yourself!'

His tone sobered her and she began dabbing at her cheeks while Ninette and Landon looked at each other and at the stark revelation between them. Landon was the first to speak. He said quietly: 'I think you'd already guessed it, Ninette. I'm sorry you had to hear it this way.'

She shook her head, not trusting herself to speak. But she stretched out an impulsive hand and laid it over Landon's. In the same calm voice Landon spoke again to Valeria: 'Why don't you say the rest of it? You want revenge. You know the way to get it. Tell the story to your father. Then tell Carlo. This is the best time, isn't it, right in the middle of this case?'

'I want to.' Valeria's voice was almost a whisper. 'You don't know how much I want to.'

'But you won't,' said Ninette sharply.

'Why not?'

They faced each other like duellists across the table and Landon felt himself as far excluded as if he stood on the moon. Ninette Lachaise said quietly: 'You won't do it, Valeria, because, whether you know it or not, Carlo's your last hope. I know it because I've been part of the way you've gone. You can't survive too many men like Lazzaro. And after a while that's all we get, any of us. It doesn't really matter whether Carlo wins or loses, but if you break him before he has had his chance, you break yourself too.' In the same breath she turned to Landon, and said with a twisted little smile: 'You go back to the court, Peter. It's women's business from here on.'

When he walked out into the flare of the midday sun, he felt like a man reprieved from the noose. Five minutes later he was back in the court with Ascolini at his side, waiting for the prisoner to be brought in and the judges to make their entrance. The old man was curiously subdued. When Landon questioned him about his meeting with Carlo, he answered absently: 'We talked a while. He was quite friendly. I made some suggestions. He seemed grateful.'

'But it was a progress?'

'Oh, yes. I should call it a progress.' After a moment he added: 'Carlo took me into the cell to see the girl. I talked with her and with Galuzzi.'

'How did she impress you?'

'A pathetic child – a tragic woman. What else can one say?'

Landon would have said that the old man had matters on his mind that he was not prepared to discuss, but he made no comment and a few moments later Anna Albertini was brought into the dock and the judges filed in to continue the hearing.

The girl was a pitiful sight. She was sitting bolt upright in the chair, her hands gripping the brass rail of the dock. Her face was pinched and elongated, her eyes ringed with deep shadows, her hair no longer sleek but damp and clinging about her cheeks and temples. But when the President asked her whether she felt well enough to continue, she answered in a firm, flat voice: 'Yes, thank you.'

Rienzi confirmed her assent and then called his first witness for the defence: a countrywoman in her late thirties with a faded, sensual charm that contrasted vaguely with the dress of a peasant matron. She took the stand serenely and smiled self-consciously as the Clerk administered the oath. The President's method with her was brisk and businesslike.

'Tell the court your name, please.'

'Maddalena Barone.'

'Where do you live?'

'Pietradura. Ten kilometres north of San Stefano.'

'Are you married?'

'No.'

'Have you any children?'

'Yes. One son.'

'How old is he?'

'Sixteen.'

'Who was his father?'

'Gianbattista Belloni.'

There was an anguished cry from Maria Belloni: 'It's a lie – a dirty lie!'

The President slammed the gavel on the bench. 'If there is any more disturbance, I shall have you removed from the court!'

The Prosecutor jumped to his feet. 'Mr President, I protest! A man is dead – murdered! His past sins can have no relevance in this court.'

The President shook his head. 'We must overrule the objection. The Public Minister has been at pains to elicit facts about the character and reputation of the dead man. The defence must have the same latitude.' He went on questioning the witness. 'Did the father of your child ever make any contribution to his maintenance?'

'Yes. He paid every month. It wasn't much, but it helped.'

'How was this money paid to you?'

'By Sergeant Fiorello.'

'Did he deliver it personally?'

'No. It came through the post.'

'How do you know it came from Sergeant Fiorello?'

'After my boy was born, I wrote to his father asking him to help me. He didn't answer, but then Sergeant Fiorello came to see me.'

'What did he say?'

'He said I would get regular money. He would post it to me every month. But it would stop if I opened my mouth about who the father was.'

'Why are you now prepared to reveal this fact to the court?'

'Fra Bonifacio came to see me and told me it was my duty to tell the truth.'

'Thank you. You may step down.'

In the brief, tense pause that followed, the only sound was the muffled weeping of Maria Belloni. The Prosecutor made another, more restrained appeal: 'Mr President, I should like to call to the court's attention the fact that payment of maintenance through an official and confidential channel reflects credit and not dishonour on the memory of Gianbattista Belloni.'

The President assented, urbanely. 'No doubt my colleagues will take this fact into consideration at the proper time. Mr Rienzi?'

'With the permission of the court, I should like to re-examine Sergeant Fiorello.'

'Permission granted.'

The burly sergeant took the stand and again Landon was struck by his air of competence and composure. He blinked a little when Carlo requested permission to conduct the interrogation himself, but otherwise he showed no sign of emotion. Carlo's examination began in a flat, prosy style: 'Sergeant Fiorello, I want to recall to you some of the details of your service as a police officer. You entered the service twenty years ago under the Fascist administration and after training you were posted to San Stefano. You remained there all through the war. And after the war you were promoted to the rank of sergeant and given charge of the post. Is that correct?'

'Yes.'

'After the war many of your colleagues in the service were dismissed on the grounds of Fascist sympathies or on charges of oppression and cruelty?'

'That's right.'

'And during the war some of them had been shot by the Partisans for the same reason?'

'Yes.'

'How did you escape? How did you achieve promotion?'

'The official inquiry showed that I had been active in the underground movement and had worked in secret with local Partisan leaders.'

'Especially with Gianbattista Belloni?'

'Yes.'

'And the records of the inquiry contain an official letter of commendation from Belloni?'

'That's true.'

'What was your opinion of him?'

'A patriot and a brave man.'

'You have since had no reason to change that opinion?'

'No.'

'I call your attention, Sergeant – and I call the attention of the court – to item number 75 in the summary of evidence handed down to this court from the judicial inquiry.' He waited a moment while the judges leafed through their papers and then went on: 'This item is a photostatic copy of an entry annexed to the Records and Charges Book of the Public Security Division in San Stefano. The entry is in fact an account of the trial, sentence and execution of Agnese

Moschetti, mother of Anna Moschetti, in November 1944. The account is attested by Gianbattista Belloni and five other participants in the military court. You will note that the date of the statement is 16 November 1944 – three days after the death of Agnese Moschetti. But it was not annexed to the police record until 25 October 1946, long after the armistice, a month after the appointment of Sergeant Fiorello to command the post. Can you explain these dates to the court, Sergeant?'

'I can. The account of the trial was made and attested while the Fascist administration was still in power and the Germans were in occupation of the country. It was, therefore, an incriminating document. Belloni kept it until after the war and then handed it to me for inclusion in the official record.'

'Would you regard it as an unusual document?'

'In what way?'

'In the context of the times and the local conditions, the trial and execution of Agnese Moschetti were acts of war. Why did Belloni feel it necessary to record them? Can you tell me of any other Partisan proceedings that were similarly recorded?'

'No, I can't.'

'Then why did Belloni take this unusual step?'

'As he explained it to me, the execution of a woman was a bitter business – those were his words, "a bitter business" – and he wanted the facts recorded and known.'

'And that was the only reason?'

'I don't know of any others.'

'There had not been, for instance, any demand for public inquiry?'

'Not that I know of.'

'No rumours or doubts or questions about the real nature of the Moschetti affair?'

'None.'

'As a matter of interest, Sergeant, where did the trial take place?'

'That's in the statement. Anna Moschetti's house in San Stefano.'

'Where were the police on that night – and, specifically, where were you?'

'We were out on patrol, miles away. Belloni had faked a telephone call and a report of a Partisan attempt to blow up the railway line.'

'Did you know what was being planned?'

'No.'

'But I thought you had his confidence and that you co-operated with him?'

'It was the method – nobody knew more than he had to. It was safer that way. I did what I was told and asked no questions.'

'Sergeant, you understand that you are testifying under oath?'

'I do.'

'Then let me repeat an earlier question. After you were appointed to command the post, did anybody at any time ask you to open an inquiry into the circumstances of Agnese Moschetti's death?'

'No!'

Rienzi's finger stabbed at him like a scalpel. 'You lie, Sergeant! You lie under solemn oath – and I shall prove it to this court!' He turned and made a small, apologetic bow to the judges. 'I am finished with this witness, Mr President.'

'But the court is not finished with him!' The President turned a cold eye on the burly, impassive fellow on the stand. 'You still have time to amend your testimony, Sergeant. If later testimony proves you guilty of perjury, you may face grave punishment.'

For a moment, Landon thought he would brazen it out, but at the last moment he wavered and stammered: 'I – I answered the questions as put to me. There was no demand for an inquiry, but – but there was talk about having one. It didn't come to anything.'

Carlo leapt to his feet. 'Please, Mr President, I should like to have the Clerk read a transcript of my earlier question which specified "rumours, doubts or questions".'

'We may dispense with the transcript,' said the President firmly. 'The question is still fresh in our minds. The Chancellor

139

and the Public Minister will take note of the conduct of this witness and that charges may eventually lie against him for perjury, obstruction of justice and conspiracy. Step down, please.'

As Fiorello walked back to his place, he seemed to have shrunk six inches in height and girth. Rienzi, on the other hand, seemed to take on new stature with every moment. For all his grey, insomniac complexion and his drawn, peaked face, strength went out from him and authority increased in him. In the intervals of interrogation or while the judges conferred, as they were conferring now, he seemed able to efface himself from one's attention, so that each new appearance had a new impact and each interrogation a new aspect of drama. After the short discussion on the rostrum, the President recalled the court to order and put a new question to Rienzi: 'My colleagues point out, with some justice, that the testimony of the defence seems to be placing considerable emphasis on the character of the deceased and on an event which took place sixteen years ago – the execution of Agnese Moschetti. They feel, and I feel too, that the defence should help us by establishing the relevance of such testimony.'

'It is our submission, Mr President, that the testimony is relevant to every issue in this case: to the nature of the crime, to motive, provocation, premeditation, to the moral and legal responsibility of the accused and to the question which is paramount in the mind of every member of the judiciary and every member of the body politic: how justice may be done within the limitation of the law.'

A faint smile of approval twitched the thin lips of the old jurist. 'If the evidence of the Counsel for Defence matches his eloquence, the court will be well served. Your next witness, please.'

'I call Fra Bonifacio of the Order of Friars Minor, parish priest of San Stefano.'

There was a curious pathos in the spectacle of the stooped, weather-beaten cleric padding across the court in his sandalled feet. In spite of his tonsure and habit of an ancient Order, he looked exactly what he was – an ageing shepherd of an unruly flock who had found the world too big for him.

The Clerk stepped forward to administer the oath: 'Do you swear before God to tell the whole simple truth without concealment or addition?'

The friar hesitated a moment and then turned to the judge. 'May it please the President?'

'Yes, Father, what is it?'

'I cannot swear to tell the whole truth – only that part of it which lies outside the seal of confession and which comes within my knowledge as a public citizen.'

'We will accept your oath on those terms.'

'Subject to the seal, then, I swear.'

'Defence may question the witness.'

Rienzi's method with the old priest was deferent and almost humble. Once more, Landon was struck by his chameleon talent for adaptation to a situation and a person. He asked quietly: 'How long have you lived in San Stefano?'

'Thirty-two years.'

'You know everybody in the town?'

'Everybody.'

'You knew the mother of the accused, Agnese Moschetti?'

'I did.'

'And you knew the accused as a child?'

'Yes.'

'After her mother's death, you were the one who took care of her and later made arrangements to send her to relatives in Florence?'

'That is correct.'

'During the war you were a member of a Partisan band fighting against the *Fascisti* and the Germans?'

'That is not quite correct. My first duty was always that of a priest ministering to the spiritual needs of my flock. I did, however, on many occasions work with local Partisans.'

'Specifically, you worked with Gianbattista Belloni?'

'I did.'

'What did this work entail?'

'Carrying information, hiding fugitives, looking after the wounded, sometimes transporting guns, food and ammunition.'

'You did all these things right up to the armistice?'

'No.'

'Will you explain that to the court, please?'

'In the last stages of the war and immediately afterwards, I felt bound in conscience to withdraw from Belloni and in fact to reprove him openly.'

'Why?'

'I believed that many of his actions were dictated not by the needs of war but by a desire for private vengeance or private gain.'

'Can you give the court any examples?'

'Belloni and his men took away our local doctor and shot him, simply because he had given medical care to a wounded German. He ordered the execution of a peasant and his wife whose land adjoined his own property. Later he bought this land at a trifling price. Immediately after the armistice he directed the summary trial and execution of seven towns-people. Continued complaints were made to me by women and girls who had been molested by him or by members of his band.'

A flutter of comment broke out in the court and the Prosecutor leapt to his feet. 'Mr President! I must protest in the strongest terms against the irregularity of these proceedings. Belloni is dead and beyond the jurisdiction of this court. We are concerned only with a charge of murder against Anna Albertini, which I submit we have proved beyond question. Belloni is not here to answer for himself. We are not trying him but Anna Albertini.'

For the first time, Rienzi made his own emphatic rebuttal: 'Mr President, gentlemen of the court! Our concern is justice, an assessment of guilt. Our judicial system defines and graduates the crime of murder, not only in terms of the act, not only in terms of premeditation or provocation, but in terms of motive and mitigation. I submit with all respect that you cannot arrive at a just decision without knowing all the circumstances and all the characters concerned in it, including the character of the dead man.'

The President nodded assent. 'The Counsel for the Defence may continue his examination.'

'Thank you, Mr President.' He turned back to the

witness. 'Now, Father, the court would like to hear what you know of the death of Agnese Moschetti, mother of the accused.'

'I'm sorry.' The old man drew himself up and answered firmly: 'I cannot answer that question. I was not an eye-witness. Much of the knowledge I have came to me first under the seal of confession. I do not feel free, therefore, to give any evidence on the point.'

'Would it be true to say, Father, that people gave you this information in the confessional because they were afraid to give it publicly?'

'I cannot answer that, either.'

Rienzi accepted the answer respectfully. He waited a moment and then moved off on to another tack. 'Let me ask you a personal question, Fra Bonifacio. Did you yourself make any public protests about the trial and execution of Agnese Moschetti?'

'I did. I condemned it in the strongest terms from my pulpit. I made mention of other acts of violence committed not only by the Partisans but by those in power. I tried to initiate punitive action through the former police representative, Sergeant Lopinto.'

'But after the armistice, when Sergeant Lopinto was dead and Sergeant Fiorello was in charge, and Belloni was back as Mayor and master of the village – did you take any action then?'

'Yes. I asked Sergeant Fiorello to reopen the case and insti-tute a public inquiry. He refused.'

'Did he give any reason?'

'Yes. He said many things had been done during the war which were better forgotten. People had to start living normally again. There was no point in continuing old hates.'

'And you agreed with that?' asked Rienzi, softly.

For the first time the old man hesitated. His face clouded, his lips trembled and he seemed to stoop a little more as though weighed down by the burdens of guilt and memory. 'I – I was not sure. There was much to recommend the thought. This is the tragedy of war, that men of goodwill are committed to evil courses and wicked things are done in the name of good. Besides, we had to rebuild our lives and we could not rebuild them on bitterness.'

'So you did nothing more about the inquiry?'

'Until the death of Gianbattista Belloni – no.'

'So, in fact, Father,' said Rienzi, with cold precision, 'you too lent yourself to a conspiracy of silence on this matter?'

'A man can only take the path he sees at his feet. It appears I chose the wrong path. I am sorry for it now. A priest has so much more to answer for.'

There was no one in court who did not feel for the old man in this moment of bitter avowal. But Rienzi was not finished with him yet. He walked back to his table and unwrapped, with theatrical deliberation, a small, brown-paper parcel. Then he walked back to the witness-stand, holding in his hands what appeared to be a piece of broken masonry. He held it out to the friar. 'Do you recognize this?'

'I do. It's a piece of stone from the wall of the churchyard at San Stefano.'

'There are words written on it. I do not ask you to read them, only to tell me by whom they were written.'

'By Anna Albertini, the accused.'

'Do you know when they were written?'

'The day after her mother's death.'

'Did you see them written?'

'I did. I came on her scratching them into the wall with a piece of tin.'

'Thank you, Father, that is all.'

As the friar stepped down from the box, a bowed, shambling man, Rienzi turned to the judges' rostrum. 'With the permission of the court, I propose to return to this object in later evidence and to identify it more fully for the court. For the present, I would direct the attention of the court to the condition of my client. She has been, as you know, under grave strain. She is, as you see, very much reduced and in need of rest and medical attention. I beg the clemency of the court and request that this hearing be adjourned until tomorrow, when we shall present the final evidence for the defence.'

The President looked up, sharply. 'The court has already allowed a great deal of latitude to Counsel in the presentation of his case. I must warn him against leaning too much on tactic and stratagem.'

'This is not a stratagem, Mr President,' said Rienzi hotly. 'It is a request made out of consideration for my client, who is on trial on the gravest possible charge. We are content to abide by the decision of the Bench, but we submit that medical advice may be indicated.'

The President bent down to talk with his judicial associates and then with the people's judges. After a moment, he said: 'Will Professor Galuzzi step forward, please?'

The whispering in the court went on unchecked as Galuzzi conferred with the President and the other members of the Bench. Finally, the President announced, formally:

'In compliance with the request of the defence, this court is adjourned until ten o'clock tomorrow morning.'

'Thank you, Mr President,' said Carlo Rienzi, and walked back to his table like a man who had just staked his life's savings on the last roll of the dice.

'I hope' – muttered Ascolini, 'I hope he has good cards for tomorrow. If not, they will crucify him.' Then, abruptly, he said: 'Carlo's dining with you tonight. I want to talk with you before you see him.'

Landon frowned dubiously. 'I doubt I'll have time. Ninette's not here, and I promised to wait for him after the session.'

'Then send him a note.' The old man's tone was testy. 'Tell him to go directly to the apartment an hour from now.'

'But why, Doctor?' There was a note of irritation in his voice. His patience was frayed thin by the exactions of these people.

Ascolini was subtle enough to take the point. He spread his hands in apology: 'I know! I know! We ask too much and give too little. We draw you into our intrigues and wound you because you are our friend. I'm sorry. I promise you this will be the last time.' He fished out a small notebook and a silver pencil. 'Please indulge me this time. Write a note to Carlo and have one of the clerks take it to him.'

Reluctantly, Landon scribbled the note and the old man

handed it to an official to deliver to Rienzi. Then he steered Landon out of the court-room, through the clamour of the dispersing spectators and into the pale, late sunlight of the city.

Three minutes' devious walking brought them to a small square with a time-scarred fountain in the centre of a surprising little café that offered iced tea and sweet pastries. The square was still hot and humid, but inside there were deep shadows and a grateful cool. They were served quickly, and Ascolini began, brusque and unsmiling, to set down his thoughts.

'Carlo has done much, much better than I expected. He cannot win, of course. Tomorrow will be a dangerous day for him, but if he survives it he will have scored a professional triumph. There will be twenty briefs on his desk before the week is out. And this will be only a small presage of what is to come. His first battle will have been won, as indeed it is won already – to prove himself a good advocate and an independent spirit. But one battle is not a campaign and there are others, more bitter, still to be fought. For this one he has been armed with education and training. For the others I'm afraid he is quite unprepared.'

'I advised him weeks ago,' said Landon bluntly. 'He can win them only by walking away. Valeria is no good to him. She'll take everything and give nothing. He'll spend the rest of his life trying to tame her – and end an old man living with a shrew.' Then he added, regretfully: 'I'm sorry, Doctor. I have a great respect for you and she's your daughter. But I can't be polite any more.'

'You don't have to be polite,' said Ascolini mildly. 'I know she's jealous of you and Ninette and that she wants to make trouble between you. But you did make some of it yourself when you slept with her.'

Shamed and shocked, Landon gaped at him. 'How did you know that?'

Ascolini waved an inconsequential hand. 'She told me the day after your little escapade.' He chuckled with sour amusement. 'Oh, I imagine she promised discretion and secrecy but you should have known better than to be taken in by such protestations.'

'I should,' said Landon, 'but I didn't. What was the point
in telling you?'

'A threat,' said Ascolini quietly. 'An assertion of power by
jealous woman. If I interfered any more in her relations with
Lazzaro she would tell Carlo and she would tell Ninette.'

'She told Ninette at lunch.'

Ascolini nodded sagely. 'I expected she might. How did
Ninette take it?'

'Better than I deserved,' said Landon. 'I left them together.
What happens now I wouldn't know. When you knew,
Doctor, why didn't you come to me?'

Ascolini gave one of his eloquent shrugs. 'I saw a profit in
not telling you. I thought, and thought rightly, that you
would feel obliged to Carlo and would stay to help him. For
the rest,' he chuckled again in self-mockery, 'I could understand it. I've done it myself with other men's daughters and
other men's wives. And there was a satisfaction in watching a
man like you squirm a little. I shock you, I know, Landon.
But I told you a long time ago this is the kind of people we
are. My only credit is that I am honest enough to admit it.
I'm not a noble father putting a virgin daughter on the
auction block. I've connived at too many follies not to wear
this small one with equanimity.'

Landon burst out, bitterly: 'Then why the hell did you
make such a fuss about Basilio Lazzaro?'

Ascolini answered in the same equable tone: 'Even in a
society like ours, Landon, old, sophisticated and often corrupt,
there are limits beyond which a woman cannot go and still
preserve her place. We are amused by the diversions of convenient marriage. We object to vulgarities like Lazzaro. This
affair had to stop or Valeria could have no retreat at all.'

'Do you think she has now?'

'Just one – Carlo.'

'Ninette said the same thing. I'm not sure that I agree. The
road may be closed already.'

'Do you think I don't know that?' For the first time, there
was a flash of anger from the old advocate. 'Why else do you
think I give you so much confidence? I want to use you,
Landon. . . . Look! I saw Carlo this morning. I spoke with

147

him and with Galuzzi. I am too old not to understand how matters stand between him and his client. You're a professional. You know what this means. Carlo has affection for this girl. I read the signs. I've had clients of my own to whom I have been drawn in circumstances much less favourable. I was cynical enough to enjoy the opportunity. But Carlo is no cynic, and he has been starved of love too long.'

Landon shook his head and leaned back wearily from his untasted coffee. 'I'm sorry, Doctor. I can prescribe for Carlo – and I've already done it – but I can't make him drink the medicine. Besides I don't think it can go too far. The girl is mentally infirm!'

'And have you, my dear Landon, never met those who need an infirmity in the beloved?'

'Sometimes.' Landon's impatience was rising. 'But what the devil do you expect me to do? Read him a little lecture and send him back to the loving Valeria?'

'I'm sorry, Landon,' said Ascolini with grave dignity. 'We have spun webs for you and now you are as enmeshed as we are. One day, perhaps, we may have grace enough to make amends, but you've asked me a question and this is my answer.' He paused a moment and then laid it down with an almost touching simplicity. 'Tell Carlo, from one who knows, that it is sometimes better to be content with a small, sour apple than to eat strange fruit in an alien country.'

When Landon reached the apartment, he found Ninette alone, bustling about the preparation of Carlo Rienzi's dinner. They embraced, but without passion, and then Ninette told him: 'I had a long talk with Valeria. I understand her, Peter, and I'm sorry for her. All her supports have been knocked away with one stroke – and Ascolini is responsible. I'm fond of him, as you know, but he has been brutally selfish in this matter, as in so many others. All his life he has tried to centre Valeria's affection on himself. Now, because he wants children, because Carlo suddenly begins to look like the son he wanted, he turns away from Valeria. She's lost, Peter, lost and bitter and jealous. So she tried to strike at anyone within reach.'

'She still has Carlo to strike at,' said Landon unhappily. 'I think I should tell him before she does.'

'No, Peter!' Ninette was firm. 'So long as there's a chance that he won't know I think we have to take it. After my talk with Valeria I think there is that chance. She knows at least that I feel no malice towards her – and that you don't either.'

'I think I'd feel better if I talked it out with Carlo.'

'Would he, Peter?'

'I don't know.'

Then she faced him with the question he had been dreading all the afternoon: 'And how do you feel now, Peter – about us?'

'I'm ashamed of myself, if that's any help.'

'Why are you ashamed, Peter? Because you're not the man you thought you were?'

'Partly. We all have our pride, you know. And partly because you deserve better from me.'

'Do you mean that, Peter? Even though you know about Lazzaro and me?'

'Lazzaro was an old episode for you. Mine was something different. There was no excuse for it.'

'There's always an excuse, Peter. That's what worries me. I'm not perfect, God knows. If we were married I'd probably give you twenty more excuses in a month, but if you took them I would hate you. I don't want that kind of marriage, Peter. I don't want a union that flowers inevitably into the kind of cruelty we've seen practised in the last few weeks. I'm not built to endure it. I'd wither under it very quickly. I love you, *chéri*, but I want to see you content. I love you enough to want you gone if you can't be content with me.'

'I love you too, Ninette, more desperately than I ever thought possible.' He moved towards her, but she drew away. He went on, slowly, piecing out the thought with difficulty: 'All my life, for a thousand reasons and one, I've tried to be self-sufficient, self-dependent, beyond the touch of the pain that other people can inflict. That's the way they know me in my profession – the driving man, the ambitious fellow they'd like to trip but can't because he knows too much and feels too little. I can go back to that, but I can't be content

with it any more. I know what I need. I know that I nee[d]
you. I want to tell you something, sweetheart. I've never sa[id]
this to another person in my life. At this moment I'm almo[st]
like Carlo Rienzi. You can put any price on yourself. I thin[k]
I'd pay it.'

For a long moment she stood slack and irresolute, measu[r]-
ing him, measuring the risk to herself. Then she shook h[er]
head and said in a whisper: 'There's no price, Peter. Just lo[ve]
me. For God's sake, just love me.'

Then she came to him running and clung to him and the[y]
kissed and were glad and it seemed almost possible that you[th]
and all its illusions might be reborn again.

When Carlo came he found them happy as birds in [a]
apple tree. They hustled him into the studio and settled dow[n]
to lay the foundations of a convivial evening. Chianti an[d]
Barolo and Tuscan brandy are rough remedies for t[he]
megrims, but they worked for them that night. They dra[n]k
deeply and laughed immoderately and made a lavish produ[c]-
tion of Ninette's dinner and then lapsed by degrees in[to]
drowsy contentment, while Carlo sat at the piano and play[ed]
Scarlatti and Brahms and old plaintive melodies from the fo[lk]
music of the mountains.

It was a good time, a gentle time: a recall of youth and t[he]
high untarnished hopes of innocence. Their doors we[re]
locked against intrusion. Their windows opened on silv[er]
roof-tops and a sky rich with stars. Harsh memories we[re]
muted to mezzotint. The music laid a balm to new woun[ds]
and was lenitive to old regrets. When it was done, they s[at]
quiet in the half-dark, the talk floating between like stra[w]
in slack water. Carlo said softly: 'I am grateful for tonight
more grateful than I can tell you. Tomorrow is a critical d[ay]
for me, and you have made me ready to face it.'

'How will it go, Carlo?' asked Ninette.

'Who knows? We are on the knees of the Blind Godde[ss]
I dare not hope too much.'

'Are you satisfied so far?'

'For myself, yes. I think we have done better than anyo[ne]
believed possible. I can look at myself in a mirror and kno[w]
that I have proved what I set out to do. At the beginning

ought this would be enough. Now, it is all too little.' He broke off to light a cigarette and the flare of the match lit up his face, peaked and pale, but endowed with the new maturity of experience. 'It is Anna who troubles me now. She trusts me so far. She has so little fear, so little understanding of what my failure may mean to her. This is a nightmare to me.'

'Perhaps to her it is a mercy,' suggested Ninette.

'Oh no!' His reaction was swift and passionate. 'You don't understand. In the beginning it was a mercy – but not now. How can I explain it? When I first met her, she was like a child – no – like a woman who had wakened out of one world into another, strange but much more beautiful, in which there was nothing to hate, nothing to fear, nothing to desire. Even the prison seemed to her a comfortable place. I thought at first that she did not understand her situation, but she understood it very well and could look forward to twenty years of confinement without a single terror. Her only interest in her defence seemed to be that she should not disgrace me. I spoke to you about it, Peter, and you explained it to me as the euphoria of shock, the well-being of those who have survived a massive onslaught on the tissue of mind and body and have lapsed into the anaesthesia which nature provides beyond the powers of the physician. Then, slowly, awareness began to grow in her. She began to talk to me of her husband, of the failure of their life together, of her hope to come now to the consummation of love and bear him children. I did a brutal thing when I put him in the witness-box, but it was necessary. And it has had a strange effect. For the first time, she has begun to be aware not only of tragedy but of hope. If she is robbed of it now, God knows what may happen to her!'

His voice trailed off and they sat smoking in silence while the shadows closed in on them and the cigarette smoke drifted up, grey and ghostly, into the darkness of the ceiling. After a while, Ninette asked: 'How do you see her, Peter? What kind of a person is she?'

Landon thought about it for a moment and then said, judicially: 'The answer is, I think, that she's not yet a person at all. She's twenty-four years of age, familiar as any of us with the motions of a work-a-day world, but still a child with a child's innocence and a child's wonder and a child dependence.'

'That's it, Peter!' Carlo's voice was eager. 'Valeria and he father think I'm in love with Anna. Perhaps I am, but no as they imagine. Valeria has never given me a child, but think I have the same feeling for Anna as I should have for daughter: a care, a tenderness, and a pity for so much sim plicity.'

'Will she ever grow up?' It was Ninette who asked th question and Landon who answered it.

'It's possible, but it will be a slow process. Carlo has alread seen some of the signs. The act of murder was, in effect, a attempt by violent means to shake off the burden of her pas The next step is the one we see now: she is groping, children grope, for an affirmation of identity.'

'Like this afternoon.' Carlo took up the thread of the argu ment. 'For the first time, she was angry with me because told her she must be afraid for herself, instead of leaving me t carry the burden of her fears.'

There was a moment's pause, and then Landon spoke quiet and shrewd, out of the shadows. 'What did she say t that, Carlo?'

'That I was impatient with her, that I asked too much too soon, that she wanted to be a woman, but could not grow alone.'

'Poor child!' said Ninette softly. 'Poor lost child!'

'But don't you see!' Rienzi's voice took on a new, vibran urgency. 'She is looking for herself now, she is looking for new road. If we lose our case and she is sent to prison fo twenty years, she will sink back into the absolute calm of despair. She will end like those poor creatures who sit at their lives in one corner, seeing nothing, hearing nothing saying nothing, without even the thought of death to comfor them. But if we can win, if we give her hope of release withi a reasonable time, then she may continue the search, and given a little love, she may well succeed. Even the care which she senses in me has done much for her. A little more – an who knows?'

In spite of himself, Landon gave voice to the final question: 'Can you spare so much, Carlo, and have you the right?'

His answer came back, sharp and strong: 'I think I have. I have spent so much for no return – why should I not spend a little on this lost one?'

'The time may come,' said Landon deliberately, 'when your child is a woman and will ask more than you have to give.'

'I cannot think of that,' said Carlo Rienzi. 'I cannot think past tomorrow.'

Chapter Seven

THE FOLLOWING morning Landon and Ninette arrived at the court forty minutes before the session was due to open but the anteroom and the pavement were already choked with people clamouring for entrance. It took twenty minutes of argument with a harassed official before they were admitted into the court-room, where other privileged visitors were already seated.

Ascolini was there with Valeria. She was dressed more soberly than usual. Her face was pale, her eyes heavy and her manner was oddly absent and distracted. Landon and Ascolini sat side by side between the two women. The old advocate, too, was tense and preoccupied. He answered Landon's questions vaguely and summed up the morning's prospects in short, irritable phrases: 'So far, it has been a matter of tactics. Carlo has gained ground. The main lines of his plea have clarified themselves. The dispositions of the court seem slightly in his favour. From this point, everything depends on the testimony he has to offer and on the use he makes of it in his final summation. I'd have liked to discuss it with him, but he, too, has a hard head. I feel old this morning. It is time I thought of retirement. . . .'

The doors each side of the court opened and the personages began filtering on to the stage for the final act of the legal drama. The Chancellor and his clerks settled themselves at their table. The Prosecutor talked in low tones to his assistants. Carlo Rienzi came in with his two seedy colleagues trailing behind him. He sat down at his table and began leafing through his briefs and making notes on a scratch-pad beside him. There was a burst of excited talk as Anna Albertini was brought in by her gaolers. Then, as if to forestall any more discussion, the President and his assisting judges filed in briskly and took their places on the rostrum. There was whispering and scuffling as the spectators settled themselves and then the dry clatter of the gavel reduced the crowded room to deathly silence.

Carlo Rienzi stood up. His voice was cool, clear and impersonal. 'Mr President, gentlemen of the court, we have two more witnesses to offer and then our testimony is complete. With the permission of the court, I should like to examine Ignazio Carrese.'

'Permission granted.'

The man who approached the witness-stand was a short, stocky peasant nearing fifty, with gnarled hands and a shuffling gait and a dark, sun-tanned face, seamed and scored like the weathered rocks of his own countryside. When the oath was read, he mumbled an assent and stood, arms limp, shoulders humped, eyes downcast to the floor in front of him.

Rienzi let him sweat a moment and then stood a pace away from him until the peasant lifted his head and faced him with frightened eyes.

'Tell the court your name, please.'

'Ignazio Carrese.'

'What do you do for a living?'

'I'm a farmer in San Stefano.'

'Do you own your own land?'

'Yes.'

'Have you always owned it?'

'No. I bought it after the war.'

'Where did you get the money?'

'Belloni lent it to me.'

'What interest did he charge you?'

'None at all.'

'Was he always as generous as that?'

Carrese dropped his eyes, hesitated, and then mumbled his answer: 'I – don't know. He was to me, anyway. I – I was his number two in the Partisans.'

'Do you understand that by answering some of the questions I am going to put to you, you may do yourself harm?'

The witness looked up and then straightened himself as if to meet a destiny long deferred. His voice took on a new, firmer tone. 'I – I understand that.'

'Why have you agreed to give evidence?'

'I talked to Father Bonifacio. He told me . . .' His mouth trembled and it seemed for a moment as if he were about to break down.

Rienzi checked him sharply: 'Told you what?'

'That it wasn't enough to be sorry. I had to make amends.'

'A tardy wisdom,' commented Rienzi dryly, 'which I hope may commend itself to this court.' His silence challenged them for a moment, then he went on, more quietly: 'Ignazio Carrese, I want you to take your mind back to a day in 1944. It was a Saturday, I believe.'

As if anxious to purge himself as swiftly as possible, the witness stumbled on, lapsing occasionally into the raw country dialect. 'That's right, it was a Saturday night. We were all at the hideout in the hills . . . me . . . the other boys. We were waiting for Belloni. When he got in, we saw he was hopping mad. He had that crazy look he used to get when someone crossed him. He said: "That's it! Nobody slaps Belloni and gets away with it! There's a job tomorrow, a big job!"'

'Did he tell you what this big job was?'

'Yes, he did.'

'What did he say?'

'He said . . . he said . . .' Beads of sweat broke out on his lined forehead and he wiped them away with a grubby handkerchief.

Rienzi pressed him, firmly. 'What did he say?'

He said: 'It's the Moschetti bitch. Her husband's a bloody Fascist and she's no better. She's got to go!'

There was a low moan from the dock and all heads were turned to see Anna Albertini swaying in her chair, eyes closed, her face chalk-white.

Rienzi's words rang across the court like a pistol crack: 'Control yourself, Anna.'

There was a gasp of surprise in the court.

The President looked up, startled and displeased, but the effect on Anna Albertini was instantaneous. She opened her eyes, sat bolt upright and steadied herself on the edge of the dock. She said in a low voice: 'I'm sorry. I'll be all right now.'

Rienzi turned back to his witness. 'Belloni said: "Her husband's a bloody Fascist and she's no better." Did you understand what he meant?'

The old peasant seemed to shrink again and his voice lapsed into a low undertone. 'Sure. Everybody knew. He'd been trying to get her to sleep with him for weeks, but she wouldn't have him.'

'He was prepared to kill her for that?'

'Yes.'

'Didn't any of you protest?'

'Sure! Sure!' He tried with feeble animation to justify himself. 'I tried . . . and a couple of the others . . . but Belloni did the same thing as always – he pulled out a gun and said: "You know the rules. You do as you're told or you get shot. Take your pick."'

'And the next day,' said Rienzi softly, 'you killed the mother of Anna Albertini?'

'We didn't kill her! Belloni did. We . . . we just went along like we had to.'

There was a long rigid silence in the court. All eyes were turned to the shabby, stooping countryman on the stand. Then, as if by common impulse, they turned to the girl, who sat like a stone woman, staring sightlessly into the distance. Very calmly, Rienzi took up his examination again. 'Will you tell us, please, how the killing took place?'

The old peasant took a deep breath and began struggling through the last revelation. 'It was Sunday night . . . we . . . we all went along to the Moschetti house. We found Agnese Moschetti with the girl. . . .'

'This girl?' Rienzi's outflung hand pointed to Anna Albertini.

'Yes . . . she was only a kid then, of course – eight or nine, I

hink. We – we held her, while Belloni took the mother into
he bedroom. The kid screamed and kicked like a wild thing
ntil we heard the shots. . . . Then . . . then she stopped . . .
lidn't say another word, just stood there, staring . . . staring
ike she was dead. . . .' His voice broke and the last words
ame tumbling out of him in tearful agony: 'Oh God, I'm
orry! But I couldn't stop it . . . I couldn't!' He buried his
ace in his gnarled hands and sobbed uncontrollably while
Anna Albertini sąt motionless, caught in the old, cataleptic
norror.

Slowly Rienzi walked back to his desk and picked up the
piece of masonry which he had shown to Fra Bonifacio. He
held it out to the old peasant, who stared at it dumbly.

'Have you ever seen this before?'

Carrese nodded, unable to speak.

Rienzi pressed him quietly: 'Can you read?'

'Yes.'

'Will you please read the words written on this stone?'

Carrese turned away, his face contorted. 'Please . . . please,
lon't ask me.'

Rienzi shrugged and turned to face the President. 'With the
permission of the court, I shall read them. They are simple
words, gentlemen, scratched deep with a piece of tin. They
are weathered by sixteen years of wind and rain, but they are
still legible. They say: "Belloni, one day I will kill you!"'
He handed the stone to the President, who glanced at it
briefly, then passed it down for the scrutiny of his colleagues.

Slack and exhausted, Rienzi stood in the clear space before
the judges' rostrum. He waited while the stone was passed
from hand to hand, then he took it back and crossed the court
to the prosecution table. He laid the stone down in front of
the Public Minister and announced 'I should like the prosecution to read the words, too: words written by a child of
eight the day after her mother's death, three days before a
kindly relative came and took her away to live in Florence.'
His voice rose on a note of sharp anger. 'They prove his case!
Premeditation! Premeditation by a child of eight, who saw
her mother raped and murdered by a hero of the Partisans!
I am finished with this witness, Mr President.'

The countryman shuffled back to his place in the hushed court. The President scribbled a note on his pad and passed it down to his senior assistant. Then he said, in a flat, tired voice: 'Call your next witness, please, Mr Rienzi.'

'I call Mr Peter Landon!' After the dramatic testimony of Carrese, Landon felt that his own entrance was an anti-climax; but his appearance and the English sound of his name caused a buzz of comment in the court. He took the stand, assented to the oath and identified himself. Rienzi elaborated a moment on his qualifications and appointments, and then asked the court to accept him as an expert witness of equal status with Galuzzi.

As if to detract even further from the dramatic impact of the previous testimony, Rienzi then called on the Clerk of the Court to re-read the transcript of Professor Galuzzi's testimony. The Clerk shuffled his papers, coughed, adjusted his spectacles, and then read, parrot-fashion, the long, definitive passages. While they were being read, the crowd shifted and stirred uneasily. Landon threw a cautious glance at Rienzi, but there was no response from the pale, drawn face and the bleak inquisitor's eyes. When the Clerk had finished the transcript, Rienzi thanked him formally and then began to interrogate Landon: 'You would agree, Mr Landon, with Professor Galuzzi's definitions?'

'I would – yes.'

'You would agree, in general terms, that psychic traumas reveal themselves in various forms of mental infirmity, often long after the event which has caused them?'

'In general terms – yes.'

'You heard the testimony of the last witness. You heard how this accused, as a child of eight, was witness to the brutal circumstances of her mother's rape and murder. You would agree that this would be sufficient to cause a psychic wound of the gravest possible kind?'

'I would.'

'Mr Landon, how would you define the word "obsession"?'

'In psychiatric terms, it means a persistent or recurrent idea usually strongly tinged with emotion and frequently involv-

158

ing an urge towards some form of action, the whole mental situation being pathological in character.'

'"Pathological" meaning, in this case, diseased or infirm?'

'That's correct.'

'Could you make your definition a little clearer to the court?'

'Well, some patients have obsessions of guilt, so that they are prepared to accuse themselves of crimes they have never committed. Others are obsessed by unreasonable anxieties, so that they will not cross a street for fear of being killed. There are some people who will go round the house twenty times at night to assure themselves that the doors and windows are locked. This, too, is an obsessive condition.'

'Is this condition curable?'

'Sometimes it can be alleviated by analysis, which reveals to the patient the roots of his disorder. Sometimes, however, the idea and the emotional pattern become so fixed as to be incurable – except perhaps by that type of surgery known as prefrontal lobotomy.'

'From your examination of the accused and from the evidence elicited in this court, would you say she was the victim of an obsessive condition?'

'Undoubtedly.'

'Which began with the psychic shock inflicted on her by her mother's death?'

'Yes. Her failure to consummate marriage, for instance, is an obsessional symptom directly associated with the violence done to her mother.'

'Now. Mr Landon, I want you to be very clear on the import of my next question. I want the court to be clear on it, too, lest I should seem to be leading this witness away from fact and into the domain of speculation. This is, I hasten to assure the President, no part of my intention. The testimony of Dr Galuzzi raised the crucial question of moral sense and moral responsibility. I should like to be more specific on this point.' He turned to Landon and asked with great deliberation: 'Does the obsession which we have been discussing – the fixed idea, the fixed emotional pattern – deprive the patient of moral responsibility? Does it diminish this responsibility so that the patient cannot help what he does, but is compelled to it by forces outside his control?'

It was a loaded issue and Landon knew it. He took time to digest the question and his answer was studiously exact. 'Modern psychology points to many states in which the subject is or seems to be deprived of responsibility for his actions, or in which his moral sense and therefore his moral responsibility are diminished. However, it must be said that such states are not yet matters of legal definition, and the patient who commits a criminal act may still be amenable to the law as it is now framed.'

'Would you say that the infirmity of the accused would diminish her moral responsibility?'

'Most certainly.'

'Would it retard in any fashion her growth as a person?'

'It's elementary, I think. The human psyche develops, as the body does, by organic growth, environmental influence and education. Its development may be inhibited by bodily infirmity, by trauma or maleducation.'

'And, as in the case of the body, one psychic function may be inhibited while all the others are normal?'

'That's true. A brilliant mathematician, for instance, may have the emotional responses of a child.'

'Would it be true to say, Mr Landon, that in certain psychic shocks, not only is normal growth inhibited, but the sufferer is left, shall we say, fixed and anchored at the moment when the shock took place?'

'This is one mode of obsession – not an uncommon one.'

'An act committed under such an obsession would, therefore, have the same moral character, the same emotional pattern, as if it were committed at the time of the first shock?'

Landon frowned and pursed his lips. 'It might. You must not ask me to go further than that. One could only establish the fact by long, controlled clinical analysis.'

'But you would admit at least the possibility?'

'Any psychiatrist must admit that much.'

'Remembering what happened to Anna Albertini, remembering the evidence of her later incapacity, remembering your own clinical examinations, would you admit the possibility in her case?'

'One could not discount it.'

'Let us be clear on this, Mr Landon. You admit, without any doubt, grave shock, grave psychic damage?'

'That's right.'

'You admit an obsessional state with diminished moral responsibility?'

'Yes.'

'You admit at least the possibility that the murder of Gianbattista Belloni might have, in the mind of the accused, the same character as if it had taken place immediately after her mother's death?'

'On this point I am not prepared to go further than I have gone already.'

'Thank you, Mr Landon.' Rienzi turned away. 'The defence rests at this point, Mr President.'

'The witness may step down.'

Although they had planned the questionnaire together, Landon had the uneasy feeling that Rienzi had mistimed it and treated it in a fashion altogether too casual. To the spectators also, it was a tame, almost pathetic conclusion. The storm which Rienzi had seemed to promise them had blown out in a single squall. Landon said as much to Ascolini, but the old man shook his white mane and muttered testily: 'It is not you who are trying the case but the fellows on the rostrum. The boy did well. He gave them their moment of drama – then a draught of cool reason. Besides, there is more to come. Listen!'

The tall, hawk-faced Prosecutor had taken the floor and, in grave, measured tones, was addressing the judges: 'Mr President, gentlemen of the court, no one has been more deeply moved than I by the evidence of the defence. No one has greater sympathy than I for the burden which has lain, all these years, on the shoulders of this unfortunate young woman. But . . .' An orator's pause, well-timed and pregnant with admonition. 'But I must take my stand, as you, the members of the judiciary, must take yours, on the law. The law is a wall between order and chaos. There is a sense in which the law is more important than justice. Suspend the law – as it was suspended in this country for too many years – and you let in violence and disorder of every kind. Try to bend the law even in favour of the deserving, try to modify it because of your own sympathies, and you create a precedent for new and greater crimes; you say that violent revenge is lawful, that political assassination is allowable; you bring back to this country the vendetta, in which a tradition of murder is handed down from generation to generation. You dare not do this! On the evidence submitted to you, you must convict this woman. The crime itself is proven beyond a shadow of doubt; premeditation is proven – sixteen years of premeditation, the record of which was written first on a cemetery stone and then in the blood of Gianbattista Belloni. Much has been said in this court of the dubious character of this man. We challenge none of it. But we take our stand on the most primitive principle of the law: that murder, for whatever motive, is an immoral and illegal act. You may, at your discretion, consider a merciful punishment for the unfortunate girl who stands in the dock. But you must recognize her crime for what it is – wilful and premeditated murder! I am the servant of the law, gentlemen, as you are. I need say no more than this – I submit that you cannot do less.'

It was so simply done that one almost missed the talent behind it: the nice judgement, the meticulous timing, the actor's verve and the gambler's shrewdness that made him refuse even to skirmish round the outer edge of his phalanx. Sympathy might run against him, but the currents of interest, precedent and judicial responsibility ran strongly in his favour. He had a pat case, and a gratuitous plea for leniency would dent it not at all. He sat down, sober and a trifle smug, as the President called Carlo Rienzi to present his plea and summation.

Carlo got up slowly, twitching his gown up on his shoulders and gathering himself for the final moments of his first forensic adventure. He glanced briefly at Anna Albertini and then, in quiet, persuasive fashion, addressed himself to the judges: 'Mr President, gentlemen of the court, my learned friend has spoken to you of the law. To hear him, you would believe that the law is something fixed, immutable, beyond dispute or interpretation. This is not so. The law is a body of traditions, precedents and ordinances, some good, some bad, but all dedicated in principle, if not in fact, to the security of the subject, the maintenance of public order and the dispensation of moral justice. Sometimes these ends accord with one another. Sometimes they are in contradiction, so that justice may be ill served while order is most securely maintained. Sometimes the ordinance is too simple, sometimes it is too detailed, so that there is always need for gloss and annotation and the conflict of opinions to arrive at its true intent. The decalogue says bluntly: "Thou shalt not kill". Is this the end of it? You know it is not. You put a uniform on a man's back and a gun in his hands and you say: "It is a holy and blessed thing to kill for one's country," and you pin a medal on his chest when he does it. Let us be clear on this issue, gentlemen. The law is an instrument and not an end. It is not, and never can be, a perfect instrument of justice.

'It is not merely the law which is imperfect. There is imperfection also in its ministers – the police and the judiciary. If these fail in their duty, if their power is perverted, as it was perverted during the war in San Stefano, so that evil men flourish and the innocent are left defenceless, what then? If, at the moment when Belloni dragged this girl's mother away to be raped, Anna Albertini had shot him dead, would you then have charged her with murder? No! You would have commended her as a brave child defending her mother's honour. You might even have pinned on her breast the medal which a grateful country gave to Gianbattista Belloni!

'I do not say this, Mr President, to claim for the defence a ground of argument outside the law. I say it in affirmation of a principle to which great jurists in this country and elsewhere have subscribed: that it is the duty of a court not merely to uphold the law, but to ensure that the greatest justice possible is done within its imperfect framework.

'I know and you know that you will never be able to give justice to my client. You cannot bring back her dead mother. You cannot draw back the veil and hide from her young eyes the horror of rape and murder. You cannot restore to her the years which she has spent in the syncope of obsession. You cannot bring back the husband who has withdrawn himself from her, nor the capacity to enter even the elementary relationship of marriage. All you can do is lay new burdens upon her, of guilt, punishment and reparation.

'You are in dilemma in this matter, gentlemen. We are all in dilemma. We are obliged to that which we cannot perform. We believe that which we cannot affirm in this court, because the vocabulary of the codex lacks words to define it. We are committed to that which we condemn in the accused – the *lex talionis*, an eye for an eye, a tooth for a tooth!

'You will, because you must, find Anna Albertini guilty, *de facto*, of an act of homicide. Yet you know and I know that had the act been committed in another time – though in the same context of shock and provocation – you would have praised it as an act of virtue. You know that this act might never have been committed, had not a guardian of the law conspired many years ago to deny to Anna Albertini a legal redress. But when you retire to reach your decision, you will not be able to take effective cognizance of that fact. You will consider, and I believe you will decide favourably on, the defence plea of mitigation on the grounds of partial mental infirmity. You will reject out of hand the prosecution's case for premeditation, understanding that the evidence of trauma and obsession puts it completely out of court.

'But the tragedy, gentlemen, the bitter tragedy of your situation is that you will fail to dispense justice; not for want of knowledge or good will, but because our law has never adequately defined the nature of moral responsibility, because its evolution has not kept pace with the findings of modern psychiatry on the intricate ills of the human mind.

'What can you do, being dedicated to truth and to justice but knowing them beyond your noblest reach? I submit that you must define this act in the most lenient terms sanctioned by the law. You must mete out a minimum penalty, not only in terms of duration, but also in terms of place and condition. If you must confine this girl, who is still only a child, let it not be in a house of correction, but in a place where she may find

ve and care and a hope of cure for the infirmities which have
een laid upon her. . . .'

For the first time, he faltered. His shoulders shook and he
ood with head bowed, fighting to recover himself. Then he
raightened up and flung out his arms in a final impassioned
lea: 'What more can I say, gentlemen? How else can I show
ou how to conform the cold unreason of legality with the
uth and the justice to which the human instinct points with
nerring finger? Like you, I am a servant of the law, and, like
ou, I am this moment ashamed of my servitude. God help us
ll!'

Without another word, he turned away, walked to his table
nd sat down, burying his face in his hands.

It was a magnificent moment, an instant of vision such as
reat preachers sometimes impose on their audience. The
aradox of the human estate was suddenly laid bare, the pathos
f it and the pity and the massive terror that attend the most
anal imperfection. In the court a woman sobbed brokenly.
Ninette dabbed at her eyes and old Ascolini blew his nose in a
reat trumpet blast. The white-haired President wiped his
pectacles and his assistants tried vainly to mask the emotions
hat this youthful advocate had stirred in them. Only Anna
Albertini sat, wraithlike and withdrawn, oblivious of the high
limax of the scene.

The President bent forward in his chair. 'Mr Rienzi. . . .'

Rienzi looked up, vaguely, and all saw that his face was wet
with tears. 'I – I beg your pardon, Mr President.'

The President nodded sympathetically. 'The court under-
ands that Counsel is under a great strain, but it is customary
fter the pleas of both prosecution and defence to give the
ccused the opportunity of making a personal statement.'

Rienzi glanced across at Anna Albertini and then shook his
ead. 'We waive the privilege, Mr President. There is nothing
o add to our defence.'

'Then the court is adjourned while my colleagues and I
onsider our decision.'

He was hardly on his feet before a woman's hysterical voice
houted from the back of the court: 'Let her go! Hasn't she
ad enough? Free her!'

A couple of officials rushed towards the woman, but before they reached her the whole audience had taken up the cry, stamping and shouting: 'Free her! Free her!' in a fury of shame and pity and frustration.

In the disorder that followed, the judges made a hurried exit, Anna was whisked back to the cells and Ascolini hurried Valeria, Ninette and Landon into the enclosure of the court where the four of them stood with Rienzi and his colleagues watching with slack amazement as the policemen herded the people like sheep through the anteroom and into the street and the cries went up more loudly and fiercely, 'Free her! Let her go!'

The doors slammed shut and they were left with their own private drama of confusion and wonder. For a moment, no one said a word, then old Ascolini threw his arms round Carlo and embraced him in the ardent fashion of the South. 'Wonderful, my boy, wonderful! I'm proud of you! You will do great things, but you may never have another moment like this for twenty years! Look at him, Valeria! Look at the man you married! Aren't you proud of him?'

'Very proud, Father.' With the practised charm of an actress, she put her arm round Carlo and pressed her cool lips to his cheek. Landon was standing near enough to catch her words: 'You win, Carlo! I won't fight you any more. I promise that.'

There was an infinite weariness in his whispered reply: 'Did it need so much, Valeria? Did it need all this?'

Then he kissed her lightly on the cheek and came forward with a tired smile to receive their congratulations. The Prosecutor gathered up his papers and strolled across with casual professional friendliness. 'My compliments, Rienzi! The best handling of a bad brief I've seen in many a long day!' He turned to smile at Ascolini. 'A star pupil, eh, *dottore*? We old dogs will have to learn new tricks to match this one!'

Rienzi flushed and murmured vaguely: 'Kind of you to say so!'

'Not at all, my dear fellow, you deserve it. And you'll do very well out of the case. The Press will give you a very good un. The President's not a man to throw compliments round ither. Give it a week or two and you'll have more briefs than ou can handle!'

Rienzi grinned ruefully. 'We still haven't got the decision.'

'Nonsense, my dear fellow!' The Prosecutor smiled and atted him genially on the shoulder. 'The decision is unmportant. It's your performance that counts, and you made a tartling début.'

As he drifted away, Ascolini snorted irritably: 'The fellow's fool! Take no notice of him.'

Rienzi shrugged abstractedly. 'He meant to be kind. Tell ne, *dottore*, how do you think it will go?'

Ascolini pursed his thin lips and then said, carefully: 'I hink you have a good chance. Medical evidence works trongly in your favour. You did well to underline in your olea the judicial dilemma. This always disposes to sympathy or the accused. On the other hand, the judiciary is always concerned with legal precedent. It cannot lend itself, or appear o lend itself, to condonation of the vendetta. I should not like o be in their shoes at this moment. But you, my boy, you have lone as well as any man.' He smiled a little self-consciously nd said: 'If you haven't pawned the watch, I'd like to have it ack.'

'You make me very happy, *dottore*,' said Carlo gravely. 'But n fact I did sell the watch.' He grinned boyishly. 'This has een an expensive venture for me.'

'It will pay you back a hundred times over,' said Ascolini warmly, 'and then you will buy me another watch.'

Rienzi turned to Ninette and Landon. 'I owe you a great leal, Peter – and Ninette also. You've been more patient than – than any of us – deserve.'

Landon flushed and said in a low voice: 'Let's keep that art of it for later, Carlo. I have things to say, too.'

There was a small, embarrassed pause, but before anyone ound words to bridge it, Professor Galuzzi came in from the emand cell and walked across to join them. Rienzi asked him nxiously: 'How is Anna, Professor?'

'Better than I expected. I've given her a light sedative and tranquillizer. We'll get her through the rest of the day without any trouble. I'd like you to join me in her cell in a few moments. You made a remarkable plea, young man. I found myself deeply moved by it.'

'Did you agree with it, Professor?'

'In the main, yes. The definition of criminal responsibility is one of our great problems in forensic medicine. Your examination of Mr Landon here brought it in very clear focus. With your permission, I should like to quote from it in a paper which I am preparing for the *Medical Record*.'

'That's a great compliment, Professor.'

'Not at all. You have done us all a service.'

Rienzi hesitated a moment and then put the blunt question: 'You will naturally be asked to make a report on this case and recommendations for treatment of my client. Would it be an indiscretion to ask how you will frame it?'

'Not at all,' said Galuzzi, amiably. 'I shall suggest minimum confinement, preferably in one of our more modern psychiatric institutions where patients have a large degree of freedom, comfort and constructive activity. In addition to this, I shall recommend regular observation, analysis and therapy.'

'You will recommend this, even if we lose our plea?'

'Certainly. I must point out, of course, that the final decision rests with the court.'

'I understand that. I'm sure you will understand that I have a personal interest in the girl's future.'

'I'll be happy to keep you in touch with her progress. Now, if you'll excuse me, I'm likely to be called at any moment to consult with the magistrates.'

He made a little formal bow and left them. Rienzi looked after him with anxious eyes. Valeria watched her husband shrewdly but said nothing. Ascolini said gently: 'Each to his own profession, my boy. Your client will be in good hands.'

'I know,' said Carlo moodily. 'I know.'

Valeria's voice, tinged faintly with irritation, cut across the talk: 'How long will the judges be out? We can't just stand around here all the morning.'

'They'll be some time, I think,' said Carlo. 'Why don't you all go out and get some coffee? If I know where you are, I'll send a clerk round to call you when they're ready.'

'Why not come with us, Carlo?'

'No, my dear. I'll wait around here. I want to talk with Anna. There may be very little time – afterwards.'

'Send word to the Caffè Angelo,' said Ascolini briskly. 'It's the nearest place. We'll be there. Relax, my boy, it will soon be over.'

When they were leaving the court, Valeria said, with a curious touch of pity: 'He'll be lonely without his little virgin.'

'He's been lonely so long,' said Ascolini harshly, 'he's probably accustomed to it. You're a fool, Valeria. He's survived his crisis. Yours is still to come.'

Ninette said tactfully: 'It's a nervous time, *dottore*. We all need to be patient with each other. Why don't you two men take a stroll and meet Valeria and myself later at Angelo's?'

It was Landon's cue and he took it gratefully. 'Let's do that, *dottore*. I could use something stronger than coffee.'

The two girls left them and they began to stroll in leisurely fashion round the sunlit perimeter of the Campo. Ascolini seemed tired. He leant heavily on Landon's arm and talked in halting, meditative fashion as if all his trenchant confidence had deserted him.

'Valeria is beginning to be jealous, which is a good thing. But it is not enough. She will need to be generous as well. When this is over, Carlo will be spent and lonely; he will need gentleness and consideration.'

'Will Valeria be able to give them?'

'I hope so. But they need practice and – and a certain humility. She, like me, is deficient in both. I am troubled, Landon. I am old enough to see the magnitude of my mistakes, too old to avert their consequences. I have lived a long time without belief. Now . . . I begin to be afraid of death and judgement. Strange!'

'Valeria's afraid too, isn't she?'

'Of other things. Of losing me. Of being forced to submit herself to other standards than mine. Of losing the easy absolution which she has had from me.'

'Of losing Carlo?'

'Of having him reject her – which is not quite the same thing.'

'Reject her for what? A mistress?'

'No. This would not trouble her too much, I think. It would justify her own follies. His guilt would preserve her power over him. And Carlo is not a man to find happiness in a back-stairs liaison. The danger for both of them is more subtle – that Carlo will borrow dignity and satisfaction from apparently noble aims, while Valeria is left with no dignity and diversions already stale.'

'You're thinking of Anna Albertini?'

'This is the beginning of it, though not necessarily the end. It is a worthy enterprise, you see: a lost one to be rescued and guided to safe harbour; innocence to be protected; the unloved to be cherished back to normal growth. There will be others, more and more as he gets older: cheats, murderers, violent husbands, unhappy wives, with all of whom he will become involved in greater or less degree. I can understand it.' He chuckled grimly. 'I have played the merry lecher with too many women; yet there have been one or two for whom I have been the white and gallant knight, who took them home to mama instead of taking them to bed. This is how we justify ourselves, Landon. You know it as well as I.'

Landon knew it only too well, but he did not know what he could do about it. Marriage was an uneasy bargain at the best of times, and stiff-necked virtue could often destroy it more quickly than amiable sin. Mutual dependence was a habit, mutual care was a grace of rare cultivation, but both must begin from a moment of common need, and Rienzi and his wife seemed to have missed it by a long, long way. He said as much to Ascolini, and he nodded, gravely: 'The need is there, Landon, but Carlo has grown tired of telling and Valeria has never learnt the words. I tried last night to teach them to her, but I'm not sure that she understood. Perhaps Ninette will do better.'

'I hope so.'

'The trouble is, there's not much time. Carlo's career was begun today. Soon it will begin to roll like a railway train. After that, there will be no leisure for lovers' games.'

170

After which melancholy summary, there was little to be said, so they turned into a bar and drank a glass of brandy together. Then they walked back slowly to the Caffé Angelo to meet the womenfolk.

To Landon's relief, they found them talking companionably over the coffee-cups. Valeria was pale and subdued and it seemed that she had been crying, but she smiled wanly and said: 'Ninette has been kind to me, Peter. I've treated you both very badly but I hope we may be friends from now on.'

'We won't talk about it any more,' said Ninette firmly. 'It's finished – done! And tonight there will be a celebration.'

'A celebration?' Ascolini cocked a shrewd eye at his daughter. 'Where?'

'At the villa,' Valeria told him quietly. 'A homecoming for Carlo. There will be Peter and Ninette, and you, Father, will bring Professor Galuzzi and anyone else you think Carlo might like. I've telephoned and Sabina has everything in hand. We need something like this, Father.'

Ascolini chuckled happily. 'Child, we shall make a *festa* to end all *festas*. Leave the guest-list to me. Are you sure they'll be ready for us at home?'

'I'm sure of it, Father.'

'Good. Now, let's write down the names. Then I'll borrow Angelo's telephone and we'll be organized.'

Ten minutes later, he was perched like a cheerful gnome on a high stool summoning the worthies of Siena to attend him at the family triumph.

In the white conventual cell, Anna Albertini lay tranquil in a drugged sleep while Carlo Rienzi kept vigil beside her. Her face was waxen but relaxed in a strange, empty beauty. Her hands, outflung on the grey blanket, were slack and undemanding as those of a sleeping baby. Her hair, tumbled on the pillow, was like a dark halo around her ivory brow. Her small, virginal breast rose and lapsed in the languid rhythm of repose. Passion and guilt and terror were strangers at such a sleeping, and Carlo Rienzi, at this penultimate moment of the battle, felt himself floating like a straw in the backwater calm of the narrow room.

All that he could do had been done. All that he had promised had been fulfilled. The outcome lay now in the lap of the Blind Goddess. For himself, he felt spent, empty and parched as a summer brook; but as he looked down at the pale, innocent face, he felt the first grateful runnel of tenderness break out inside him like a spring bursting out of dry sand. It was a kind of refreshment after the arid discipline he had imposed upon himself and, moved by a sudden impulse, he stretched out a tentative hand to brush away a trailing hair from the girl's forehead.

He drew it back with a guilty start when he heard the rattle of bolts, the creak of the opening door, as Professor Galuzzi was admitted into the cell.

Galuzzi surveyed him for a moment with a shrewd, scholarly eye, and asked: 'How is she, Mr Rienzi?'

'Sleeping quietly.' Rienzi stood up and moved away from the bed. Galuzzi picked up one slack hand, took a short pulse-count and then laid the hand back on the blanket. 'Good. We can let her sleep a while. I think the judges will be out some time. You've given them a great deal to think about, Rienzi.'

'Have you consulted with them yet?'

'I have. I've given them my opinion in the same terms as I gave it to you.'

'I'm grateful,' said Carlo Rienzi.

Galuzzi looked at him for a moment, hesitating over the lines of fatigue and strain in his young, handsome face. Then he said, in meditative fashion: 'One day, Mr Rienzi, I think you will be a very great advocate. You have the mind for it: the dramatic quality, the single-mindedness amounting almost to obsession. All the great ones have it – surgeons, philosophers, inventors, jurists. But, like all greatness, it requires discipline.'

'What are you trying to tell me, Professor?' asked Rienzi quietly. 'Has it something to do with my client?'

'A great deal, I think,' said Galuzzi in the same thoughtful vein. 'You're not content with what you've done in court – and I doubt whether any other advocate could have done half as much. You want to go further. You want to reshape her life after the trial.'

Rienzi was nettled. He said sharply: 'Someone would have to do it.'

'Why you?'

Rienzi made a small, shrugging gesture of puzzlement. 'Put it that way and I hardly know how to answer. But, don't you understand, until this point I've held the life of this girl in my hands. She has depended on me utterly. I can't just drop her like a stone in a pool and forget her. Surely you see that?'

Galuzzi ignored the question and asked another of his own: 'This is your first big case, isn't it?'

'Yes.'

For a moment Galuzzi said nothing more, but walked back to the bed and stood looking down at the sleeping girl. Then, very softly, he began again: 'There will be so many others, Mr Rienzi. Can you carry them all as you propose to carry Anna Albertini?'

'No, I suppose not.'

'Take the surgeon – and I myself practised surgery for a long time. How often does he stand with a human life held literally in his own two hands? Sometimes it slips away. Sometimes, mercifully, he holds it safe. Can he regret what he has lost, or carry for the rest of his life the burden of what he has saved?' He swung round and faced Rienzi with the sharp challenge: 'Are you in love with this girl, Mr Rienzi?'

'I – I don't think so.'

'But you're not sure?'

For a long moment Rienzi did not answer. Finally, he made the reluctant admission: 'No, I'm not sure.'

Galuzzi turned away and walked to the window. After a while he came back to face Rienzi. His eyes were touched with pity and his voice was gentle: 'I should have guessed it. No one could have made the case you did without a touch of passion.'

'I told you I'm not sure.' Rienzi's voice was edged with anger.

'I know. But she is sure.'

Rienzi stared at him, startled. 'You mean she's in love with me?'

'I didn't say that. I don't think she knows what love is. But

173

the only objects of passion in her life – her mother, her husband, even Belloni – have dropped out of it. Her obsession has fixed itself on you.'

Rienzi took a deep breath. 'I was afraid of that.'

Galuzzi looked at him with a half-smile on his thin, fastidious lips. 'But flattered too, eh?' He gave a little, humourless chuckle. 'If I have learnt one thing in twenty years of psychiatric medicine it is this, Mr Rienzi: the human mind never works simply. When it appears to do so, then it is at its most complex. It is like those ivory balls which the Chinese carve so skilfully, one inside the other. No matter how deep you probe there is always something else to surprise you.'

To Galuzzi's surprise, Rienzi smiled and quoted lightly: '"I went to my uncle the Mandarin to question him about love. He told me to ask my wayward heart." Don't worry too much, Professor, it may never happen.'

'If it does happen,' said Galuzzi in his grave, academic fashion, 'if you do commit yourself to any involvement, the consequences for both of you may be more terrible than you can imagine.'

He turned on his heel and left, and when the door closed behind him Carlo Rienzi sat down by the bed and took the hand of the sleeping girl in his own.

The police were taking no chances of a disturbance at the close of the trial of Anna Albertini. The approaches to the court were picketed with motor-cycle police. There were guards on every door, stocky, tough fellows with short batons and pistols in holsters of black leather. Justice was about to be done and folk could either like it or lump it; but either way they would keep their mouths shut or have their heads broken.

The court was full of whispers. Even the character of the light seemed to have changed so that every feature of every personage was etched sharply, like mountains under a storm sky. Rienzi was standing by the dock, talking in low tones with Anna Albertini. When the judges came in, he gave her an encouraging smile, patted her hand and walked back to his table. Silence, tense and explosive, settled on the room as the President sat down and began, with maddening deliberation to arrange his papers. Then he began to speak:

'I have presided over many cases in this court, but I say now that none of them has laid so heavy a burden on me and on my colleagues. We are not monsters. We are men of average understanding, pity and sympathy. But, as the prosecution has so justly stated, we are also the representatives of the law – its keepers, its interpreters, its arbitrators. Upon our decisions later discussions will be based. The precedents we create will influence the course of justice long after we are dead. If we judge falsely or foolishly, we may pervert justice for many, many others.'

He paused and looked around the court, a white-haired image of temperance and orderly reason.

'If you want an example of how this may happen, you have it in the present proceedings. There was a time when the law no longer functioned in this country. There was a time when men were confused by what were called "the necessities of war" – when the only court was the drumhead, when those who claimed to mete out summary justice were, in fact, using their accidental power for revenge or private gain. The law was perverted by politics, by power, by deliberate conspiracy. The crime for which Anna Albertini has been tried began in this time of disorder, but . . .' he waited a moment, and then went on firmly: '. . . it ended in another when the rule of law had been re-established. Now, Anna Albertini must be judged according to the codex.'

No word was spoken, but one felt the ripple of interest moving through the room like a shock-wave through water. The President turned over a page of his notes and continued soberly: 'However, as Counsel for the Defence pointed out in his most eloquent plea, the law takes consideration not only of the act itself, but of the intention, the provocation, the responsibility of the person committing it. To all these things my colleagues and I have given the greatest reflection. The intention, in this case, was quite clear: murder for revenge. The provocation was great – greater than any of us might care to sustain. But to say that provocation excuses the act is to open the door to every sort of violence, to bring back to

175

this country the ancient and horrible practice of traditional vengeance.

'The question of responsibility is much more complex and on this we have debated long and studiously. At no time has the defence suggested that Anna Albertini was insane at the time of the act. At no time was it intimated that she was incompetent to stand trial in this court. Counsel has argued with considerable weight that the traumatic shock of her mother's death left her in a state of mind in which time and the change of circumstances did not exist for her. His view is supported, at least in part, by expert medical testimony.

'From this point he developed – with considerable forensic skill – a double plea. His first submission was that the act of murder committed by Anna Albertini had the same character in law and morals as if it were committed at the time of her mother's death. A psychiatrist might build a feasible hypothesis on this point, but,' he laid it down with singular deliberation, 'it is my view and the view of my colleagues that this hypothesis has no value in law.

'His second argument, that the state of the accused represented a mental infirmity and that her criminal responsibility was diminished thereby, was much more cogent and, in arriving at our decision, we have given full weight to it. We have taken note also of the terrible provocation which preceded the act, albeit by many years. We have taken into account also the many years of mental torment which this young woman has suffered, the wreck of her marriage and the dubious future which she now faces.'

He turned over the last page of his notes, gathered himself for a moment and then, more dispassionately, began to deliver his decision.

'The prosecution has requested a verdict of premeditated murder. It is our view that this charge is too grave to be sustained. We have, therefore, found on a lesser one.'

He turned towards the dock and made the cold official pronouncement: 'Anna Albertini, the decision of this court is that you are guilty of the lesser charge of homicide while in a state of partial mental infirmity, for which the law prescribes a sentence of imprisonment from three to seven years.

In view of all the mitigating circumstances, we have decided to award the minimum penalty of three years, which you will spend in such a place or places as may be determined from time to time by our medical advisers.'

The words were hardly out of his mouth before Carlo Rienzi slumped forward in his chair and buried his face in his arms. Anna Albertini sat in the dock, pale, cold and virginal, while the court broke out into a tumult of cheering that even the scurrying police were powerless to stop.

Chapter Eight

'TOMORROW,' said Ninette firmly, 'tomorrow we pack and go. We'll get ourselves married in Rome and find ourselves a villa out near Frascati, a place with a garden and a view where you can study and I can paint. We need it, *chéri*! We've spent too much of ourselves in this place. It's time to go!'

They were walking in the garden of Ascolini's villa, watching the light spread westward over the valley, while the cicadas made their crepitant chorus and a languid bird chirped in the shrubbery. Carlo was asleep. Ascolini was drowsing in his library, and Valeria was playing the diligent *châtelaine*, arranging flowers, bustling the servants about the kitchen in preparation for the evening's entertainment.

In spite of protests from Landon and Ninette, Ascolini had insisted that they come directly from the court to the villa. Valeria, too, had pleaded urgently for their presence. It was as if they were afraid of being alone with one another, as if they needed a catalyst to start the slow process of restoration and reunion. Landon and Ninette were tired and resentful, but they comforted themselves with the thought that on the morrow they should be quit of courtesies and free to address themselves to their private affairs.

After the drama of the court and the confusion of the aftermath, the countryside imposed a welcome calm on them all. Valeria drove, Carlo sat beside her, spent and taciturn, while

Ascolini sat in the back seat rehearsing the morning's triumph. Then he, too, lapsed into silence while the vineyards and the cornfields swept past and the olive leaves drooped, dusty and listless, on the hillside.

They lunched on the terrace, chatted vaguely for a little while and then dispersed. Carlo was in the grip of a fierce reaction. Valeria was conducting herself with self-conscious discretion and Ascolini was simply watching the gambits like a wary old campaigner. Landon's own position was summed up in Ninette's verdict: '*Finita la commedia!* Time to be quit of all others but ourselves. Let them play out their own epilogue. We mustn't wait for the curtain call.'

So, in the long decline of the afternoon, they strolled in the pleasances of the villa and talked in the happy, inconsequent fashion of new lovers. They talked of Frascati and how they should live there: not penned in the town, not among the princely villas of the Conti and the Borghese and the Lancellotti, but in some small estate in the folds of the Alban hills, with a vineyard, perhaps, and a tenant farm with a green garden to walk in and watch the sun go down on the distant sprawl of imperial Rome. They talked of an exhibition for Ninette, of friends who would come to share their pastoral, of how their children might be born citizens of the Old World and of the New.

Then, as the shadows lengthened, Ascolini came out to join them, chirpy as a cricket after his siesta. 'A great day, my friends! A great day! And we owe you a debt for your part in it. You know what we need now.' He jerked an emphatic thumb in the direction of the house. 'A love-philtre for those two. Don't laugh. The grandmothers in these parts still make them for peasant lovers. We, of course, are too civilized for such nonsense, but . . . it has its uses.'

Ninette laughed and patted the old man's arm. 'Patience, *dottore!* No matter how much you prod him, that little donkey will trot at his own pace!'

Ascolini grinned and tossed a pebble at a scuttling lizard. 'It is not I who am impatient, but Valeria. She is eager now for reunion. She demands proofs of forgiveness. But I tell the same thing: "*Piano, piano!* Soft words, soft hands, when a man is tired like this one." ' He chuckled happily. 'With me, it was different. After every big case, I was wild and roaring for a woman! Maybe Carlo will come to it, too – when he gets Anna out of his blood.'

'Where will they put her, do you know?'

'It's not fixed yet. They've taken her back to San Gimignano, but I understand Galuzzi has hopes of transferring her to the Samaritan Sisters at Castel Gandolfo. They have a big hospice there for mental cases. It's very beautiful, I believe. Very efficient, too.' He shrugged off the subject and asked: 'What will you two do now?'

'We're going to Rome,' Landon told him, 'just as soon as we can pack and close Ninette's studio.'

'I hope we may see you there. We, too, will be leaving in a few days. I want Carlo to begin taking over my practice.'

'How does he like the idea?'

'It appeals to him, I think, now that we can meet on equal terms. For my part, I need leisure to set my life in order. If these two can content themselves together, then I, too, can begin to be happy.' He plucked a twig from an overhanging bush, sat down on a stone bench and began drawing slow cursive patterns in the gravel. 'Life is a twisted comedy, my friends. Had you told me six weeks ago that I should come to this – that I should be playing cupid and dreaming of grand-children and even thinking of going to confession – I should have spat in your eye! But this is what has happened. I wonder, sometimes, whether it is not too easy, and whether there is not a fellow waiting round the corner with a bill of reckoning in his hand.'

'Why should there be, *dottore?*' asked Ninette warmly. 'Life is not all debit and credit. Sometimes there are gifts for which the only price is gratitude.'

'Sometimes,' said Ascolini, dryly. 'Perhaps I'm a suspicious fellow who doesn't deserve his good fortune.'

'Then let me tell you ours,' said Ninette with a smile. 'We're going to be married.'

Ascolini stared at her for an instant. Then his shrewd old face lit up with genuine delight. He threw his arm around her and waltzed her up and down the path. '*Maraviglioso!*

Wonderful! And you will have a sack of children, all beautiful. And you will be the most beautiful mother in the world! All this and talent, too! Landon, you are a fortunate fellow! *Fortunatissimo!* And you owe it all to us. If we hadn't sent you back to Siena with a flea in your ear, you'd still be playing kiss-me-quick with the models and the telephone girls. But what an omen! There is double reason for a *festa* tonight.' Breathless and excited, he grasped their arms and trotted them both up the gravelled path towards the house. 'You must tell Valeria, child. And you, Landon, will read Carlo a little sermon on marriage and the joys of fatherhood and all the fun you have arriving there. When the first baby comes, we'll have a great christening and I'll guarantee a cardinal in a red hat to do the job for you. Then you must make me godfather so that I can look after his faith and morals!'

'We'll have to reform you first, *dottore!*'

'By that time, child, I shall probably be wearing a hair shirt and beating my chest with a brick, like San Geronimo!'

It was a comic picture and it made them laugh. They were still laughing when they reached the terrace and Ascolini shouted for a servant to bring wine and glasses. Valeria came out to join them, and when Ascolini told her the news her eyes filled up with tears and she embraced Ninette ardently.

Her friendliness surprised Landon. Ascolini's conversion was easier to accept. He was getting old and, faced with the great 'perhaps', he was clinging to the simple certainties of life: pride and irony were too thin a diet for the winter years. Passion was being disciplined by the sheer diminution of age; native shrewdness and perverse experience were maturing into wisdom. But Valeria was a different case. She was still young, still wayward, initiated too early to the taste of truffles for breakfast, and Landon could see no good reason for so swift a reform.

Then, slowly, understanding began to dawn. This was the whole nature of these people. This was the essential paradox of their character and history. Old Cardinal du Bellay had called them *'peuple de grands enfants. . . . C'est une terrible beste, que cette ville-là, et sont estranges cerveaulx'* a terrible beast of a city . . . great children . . . strange brains. . . . Their own San Bernardino, a very modern psychologist in the fifteenth century, had characterized them even better: 'I understand the weakness of your character. You leave a thing and then return to the same thing; and seeing you now in so many divisions with so many hatreds, I believe that, had it not been that you are very, very human, you would have ended in doing yourself some great harm. However, I say that your condition and you yourselves are very changeable. And how very changeable you are, also with evil, for you soon return to good.'

They were very human people: too human for colder spirits to live with in comfort. They were violent by nature, incapable of compromise. The same mould produced the mystic and the murderer, the political assassin and the ascetic who took the Kingdom of Heaven by storm.

The valley below was filling with shadow, but the place where they stood was still bathed in sunlight, a symbol, Landon thought, of the gentler feelings which seemed to pervade the Ascolini household. He asked himself whether he had discovered, at last, the root of Carlo's problem: that he understood Valeria and her father too little and demanded too much – a Roman constancy, an urban rectitude – when all they had to offer was courage, a fluent passion, and the high, visionary folly of an older day.

The wine was brought and they drank a toast to mutual happiness. They talked a while of simple things. Then Valeria took Ninette inside to find her a dress while Landon went in search of Carlo to borrow a clean shirt for dinner.

He found him rubbing the sleep out of his eyes in a small room that must have been his retreat when the marital chamber was too cold for comfort. Rienzi greeted him cheerfully, lit a cigarette and then said, laughing: 'There's a commentary for you, Peter! I stage a great triumph. My name will be in every newspaper and I end like this – sleeping in my underpants in the spare room!'

'Just as well, laddy. You have a big night ahead of you.'

'I know.' He frowned in distaste. 'I'm not sure I want to face it.'

'Nonsense, man! It'll do you good. And besides it's a grace-ful gesture and you've got to accept it gracefully.'

'It was the old man's idea, of course.'

'No, it wasn't. It was Valeria's.'

He gave Landon a sharp look. 'Are you sure of that?'

'Of course I'm sure. She and Ninette cooked it up between them. Ascolini simply telephoned the invitations. I was there. I should know.'

'She means it then,' he muttered, moodily.

'Means what?'

'A new start. An attempt to patch up our marriage.'

'Yes, she does mean it. I hold no brief for her, as you know, but I'm convinced that she's sincere in this. How do you feel about it?'

Rienzi chewed on the question a moment, then lay back on the bed and blew smokerings towards the ceiling. He said, slowly: 'That's a big question, Peter – and I don't know how to answer it. Something's happened to me and I don't know how to explain it, even to myself.'

'It's simple enough, for God's sake! You're tired, played out. You've fought a big case at a critical time in your life. Now you need rest and a little readjustment.'

'No, Peter. It's more than that. Look!' He heaved himself up on his elbow and talked eagerly. 'You know the way I used to imagine this day – the day of my first success? I'll tell you: just as it happened in the court. The decision, the acclamation, the congratulations of my colleagues, Ascolini's surrender. Then? Then I would come to Valeria and take her in my arms and say: "There it is! I've tumbled the stars in your lap. Now stop being a child and come to bed and let's make love and start a baby!" And she would come happily and there would be no more fighting – except lovers' quarrels that would still end in bed.'

'That's exactly as she wants it at this moment. If you don't believe me, try it!'

'I know,' said Rienzi, flatly. 'I don't need you to tell me. But don't you see? I don't want it any more! I don't have the feeling. You know what it's like.'

Landon knew, but he could not find words to tell Rienzi

who hurried on, explaining himself in an urgent tumble of words: 'When I was a student in the first year of law, we had a great party. It was the night when the results were posted and I had passed. We got drunk and sang songs and felt twice as large as life. Then we all decided to finish the evening at a house of appointment, the biggest and most luxurious in Rome. Wonderful! We were young, full of sap, puffed with success. Then, when we got there, eh! It was nothing. I wasn't afraid, I wasn't innocent, but the thing was a cold transaction. Too many feet had walked over the doorstep. Too many fools had walked up the same stairs.'

'Did you go to bed?'

He laughed wryly. 'No. I walked home and held hands with the landlady's daughter, who was so innocent she thought a kiss would make her pregnant.' His face clouded again. 'But seriously, Peter, that's how I feel now with Valeria. I just don't care. I have no interest. What do I do?'

'Lie a little. Give it time. Blow on the coals long enough and you have fire again.'

'But if there are no coals, Peter – only charcoal and ashes?'

'Then you are in a bad way, brother! There's no divorce in the Church or in this country, and you've got no talent for a double life. So give it a try, man, for pity's sake! You're not a baby. You know the words. And women are happy to believe what they want to hear.'

'You're right, of course.' He jerked himself off the bed and stubbed out his cigarette. 'Except that I'm a bad liar and Valeria knows the words backwards. Still . . . *vesti la giubba*! On with the motley and see what sort of a play we make! Now, let's see if we can find you a shirt.' He burrowed in a drawer and came up with a beautiful creation in cream silk which he tossed to Landon with a grin. 'Wear it to the wedding, *amico*, and drink a toast to the reluctant groom!'

It was a bad joke, but Landon let it pass. This was no time to read Rienzi a lecture on marriage and the joys of fatherhood, so he let that pass, too. He thanked Rienzi for the shirt and walked back towards the guest-room to get ready for dinner. He wondered why Rienzi had said no word of Anna Albertini, and he asked himself, cynically, whether the boyhood history were not repeating itself in fantasy: the shamed man and the little white virgin holding hands at the top of the stairs while the big lusty world rolled on about its business.

The first act of Ascolini's dinner party was a formal success. More than twenty people sat down in the big dining-room: local pundits and their wives, a member of the Chamber of Deputies, a brace of legal eminences, the doyen of the Siena Press, Professor Galuzzi, and an astonishing marchesa, fragile as a Dresden doll, who scolded Ascolini with the frankness of an old lover.

Ascolini gave one of his bravura performances. Valeria smiled and directed the whole affair with a deft hand. Carlo walked through his part with a vague charm that disarmed the men and left the women crooning with satisfaction. Ninette was radiant and besieged by elderly gentlemen who had discovered all too late an interest in art. Landon had small talent for this kind of social charade and he was rescued from complete boredom only by Professor Galuzzi, who proved himself an urbane and witty talker and a satirist of formidable dimension.

When the meal was over, they took their brandies out on to the terrace and watched the moon climb slowly over the distant ridges of Amiata. Valeria's nightingales were not singing yet, but Galuzzi was a diverting story-teller and Landon did not miss them at all. Inevitably, Galuzzi worked his way round to the Albertini affair and, after a cautious glance to assure himself that they were still alone, he delivered himself of some disturbing reflections.

'One day, Landon, this young Rienzi will be a very great jurist. But there's a flaw in him somewhere and I cannot put my finger on it.'

'What kind of flaw?'

'How shall I define it? A confusion, a conflict still unresolved.'

'The conflict's clear enough, I think. It's not a very happy marriage.'

'I've heard this before. It's common talk. One observes the incompatibility, but this is not what I mean. I've watched him closely with this client of his, a curious relationship, to say the least.'

'How – curious?'

'On the girl's part,' said Galuzzi carefully, 'it is, shall we say, normally abnormal. The mind in disorder seeks a focus for its dissociated faculties, a relief from the burden of its fears and frustrations and infirmities. It demands a scapegoat for its guilts, a protector for its weakness, an object for its ailing love. This is what Rienzi has become for the girl. You know as well as I how this kind of transference works.'

Landon said uneasily: 'Carlo's quite aware of that part, I think.'

'I know he's aware of it,' said Galuzzi tartly. 'I warned him.'

'How did he take the warning?'

'Very well. And I must say that his conduct has been professionally impeccable. But it is precisely at this point that the flaw begins to show: an arrogance, an attitude of possession, a subtle conviction that he exercises a benign influence over this girl, a too great readiness to assume responsibilities beyond his function.'

Everything that Galuzzi said Landon was prepared to echo and affirm. But the nagging sense of guilt made him attempt at least a token defence of Rienzi. 'Isn't this a fairly normal reaction – the first client, the first big case?'

'On the face of it, yes. But there is another element which I find hard to define.' Galuzzi sipped his brandy in meditative fashion, and then lit a cigarette. He went on, slowly: 'You know what I think it is, Landon? A tale of innocence and the lost paradise . . . I see you smile – and well you may! We are cynics, you and I. In our profession we have to be. We lose innocence early and seldom regret it until we are old. It's a wasteful way to live, because we spend a whole lifetime getting back to the first point of departure. But it's a very human way – and for most of us it's the only way we learn to tolerate ourselves and tolerate others. We come in the end to forgive because we cannot endure without forgiveness for ourselves. We learn to be glad of half a loaf and not too proud when we achieve half a virtue.' He laughed and threw out his arms in a spacious gesture. 'Why should I read you a lecture on innocence, Landon? You have as much experience as I have. Fellows like you and me can pick a virgin at twenty paces and an honest man blindfolded. There aren't too many of either! The world is full of half-virgins and near-liars.' His face clouded again and he went on: 'Rienzi is no more innocent than most, but he has never been able to forgive the lack in himself or in the world. He wants the moon and the sixpence too. He wants to be loved by a virgin and solaced by a whore, because each in her own way gives him the illusion of virtue. His ambition is nourished, his whole career is built on other men's sins. But this is not enough. He must play the little priest and read sweet lectures to his client in prison. A fellow like this is impregnable! Nothing can touch him because everything is food for his delusions.'

'By the same token,' said Landon sombrely, 'nothing can make him happy.'

'I agree. Nothing can make him happy because he judges everything in the light of the lost paradise.'

Abruptly, Landon faced him with a new question: 'Do you propose to let Rienzi keep in touch with the girl?'

Galuzzi smoked for a moment in silence and then answered slowly: 'I've thought about that a great deal. I doubt whether I could prevent what is a reasonable contact between lawyer and client. I doubt also whether I would want to. To this point, Rienzi has been good for the girl. He may continue to help her for a long time. So I have decided to compromise.'

'How will you do that?'

'I'm trying to have Anna Albertini transferred to an institution at Castel Gandolfo, just near Rome. That may take a little time. For the present, she will be placed in the care of the Sisters of the Good Shepherd who run a similar, but smaller, mental home near Siena. I've told Rienzi he can visit her there immediately after she has been admitted. Then I want her left alone for a while so that I can keep her under my control and devise a regimen of analysis and treatment.'

'How did Rienzi take the idea?'

'He had to take it, but he didn't like it.' Galuzzi shrugged, flipped away his cigarette, and stood, a dark, imposing figure against the rising moon. 'How does one draw pictures for the blind? How does one fight the potent magic of self-deception?'

Bluntly, Landon faced him with the last question: 'Do you think Rienzi's in love with the girl?'

'Love is a chameleon word,' said Galuzzi, absently. 'Its colour matches a gamut of diverse experiences. Who can say that, even when we protest it most nobly, we are not loving ourselves?'

On that comfortless thought they left it and walked inside to join the other guests.

The party was tapering off now, fragmenting itself into little groups which, having exhausted their stock of civilities, were busy with local gossip and provincial reminiscence. Landon rescued Ninette from a too talkative politician and suggested that they arrange a ride back to Siena with the first party to leave. Carlo wandered up at the same moment with a glass in his hand and waved away the suggestion: 'Nonsense! You can't leave yet! Let's get rid of this stuffy bunch and we'll finish the evening together. Then I'll drive you back myself.'

His eyes were glazed, his voice slurred, and Landon had no intention of letting him get within fifty feet of a car, so he grinned and said: 'Not tonight, Carlo! You're tired and you're tipsy and it's time you went to bed!'

'To bed?' He gave a drunken chuckle and gagged on another mouthful of liquor. 'Everybody wants me to go to bed! Valeria, the old man, and now you! Nobody asks me what I want. I'm just a stallion, that's all! A noble sire led out to service. You know what they want me to do?' His voice rose higher and the liquor slopped from the glass on to the polished floor. 'People the place with advocates – great advocates, like Ascolini and me!'

It was time to do something. Landon took his arm firmly and steered him towards the door, humouring him as best he could. 'That's fine, Carlo! Nobody wants you to do anything that doesn't suit you. Ninette and I will stay around, but you've got to sober up a little.'

'Who wants to be sober? This is a great day. I'm a success! And I'm going to be married again!' Landon had him out of the *salone* now and was working him up the stairs, out of ear-shot, when Valeria appeared on the landing above them. Rienzi raised his hand in a maudlin salute: 'There she is! The little bride who wants to be the mother of the Gracchi. How many children do you want, darling? Shall we have them all at once or in easy stages?'

'Get him to bed, for God's sake!' said Valeria bitterly, and tried to hurry past them down the stairs.

Rienzi reached for her, but Landon fended him away and wrestled him back against the banisters. He surrendered with a drunken laugh.

'You see, my friend, she despises me! You don't despise me, do you, Peter? You know I'm a great man! Little Anna doesn't despise me either. I saved her, you know that! Nobody believed I could do it, but I saved her. Poor little Anna! Nobody's giving her a party tonight.'

He leaned against the banisters and began to cry. Half-pushing, half-carrying, Landon got him up the stairs and into the small bedroom, laid him on the bed and took off his jacket, shoes and tie. He was still mourning and mumbling when Landon closed the door and went downstairs. Ninette signalled to him from the door of the library and he went in to join her while Ascolini and his daughter farewelled the last of their guests. She kissed him and said: 'Thanks, *chéri*. You did that very neatly. I don't think anybody saw too much. Valeria's going to drive us back to town. Poor girl, I feel very sorry for her.'

'It's a bloody mess, sweetheart. But this one they'll have to clean up for themselves.'

'What's the matter with Carlo?'

'He's tired. He drank too much. And he's all mixed up, like a country omelette.'

He told her of his talk with Carlo and of Galuzzi's uneasy diagnosis. She sighed and made a shrugging Gallic gesture of despair. 'What more can one do, Peter? What is there to say? Is there any hope for these people?'

'None at all!' said Ascolini from the doorway. He was leaning against the door-jamb – a white-haired, grey-faced old man in a dinner-jacket that seemed suddenly too large or him. 'We never forget anything and we never forgive anything. There's a blight on us. Worms in the fruit and weevils in the wheat! Go home, my friends, and forget us.'

He crossed the room with a slow, tottering step and slumped into a chair. Landon poured him a glass of brandy and he drank it at a gulp, then sat, slack and listless, staring at the floor. Valeria came hurrying in with a coat thrown over her dinner-frock and a small suitcase in her hand. She was white with anger.

'We're going now, Father. Don't wait up for me. If Carlo wants to know where I am, tell him I've gone to ask Lazzaro to have me back. He's no great prize – God knows – but at least he's a man!'

'Please, child, don't do it!' A last flush of anger and animation galvanized the old man. 'Let our friends take the car. You stay here and wait out one more day with me.'

'With you, Father?' Her voice was high, harsh and bitter. 'You told me last night I must stand alone now; you had your own life, you said, and I must live mine and take the consequences! Well, I'm doing just that! Carlo doesn't want me. You're tired reliving the dead years through me! So I'm free. Good night, Father! I'll see you two in the car.'

Without a backward look, she hurried out. Landon shook the old man's limp hand and muttered a phrase or two, but he did not seem to hear. Only, when Ninette bent to kiss him, he stirred himself and patted her cheek and said softly: 'Bless you, child! Look after your man – and be gentle to each other!'

'You'll come to see us in Rome, *dottore*?'

'In Rome . . . ? Oh yes – yes, of course.'

They left him then, shrunken and defeated, in the big chair, and walked out into the cold moonlight where Valeria was waiting for them at the wheel of the car. Her face was wet with tears, but she said nothing and slammed the car fast and dangerously down the drive and out on to the moonlit ribbon of the Siena road. For the first mile or so, she was silent, wrestling the car savagely round the curves of the hill, while the tyres screamed and the offside wheels spun dangerously in the gravel of the verge. Then she began to talk – a low, passionate monologue that brooked neither comment nor interruption.

'Dear Carlo! Dear sweet Carlo! The noble boy with the great talent and the great future and the wife who didn't love him! You didn't believe me, did you? You thought I was just a cold bitch who was warm to everyone but her husband. The music was the trick, you know! Soft music for bleeding hearts. Nocturnes for unrequited lovers. God, if you only knew how much I hoped from that man! I was my father's girl. He gave me everything and I was grateful, but the one thing he couldn't give was myself. He couldn't surrender that, you see, and I didn't know how to take it from him. He made himself a partner, even in my foolishness. That's what I wanted from Carlo: what you two have and what I hated you for – partnership. I wanted him to stand with me, match me with love and anger, tame me and make me free at the same time! But he didn't want that. Not Carlo! He wanted possession, surrender – to grind me small and boil me down and swallow me up so that there was nothing left. He wasn't strong enough to do it one way so he tried another. The wilting smile, the melancholy mood, tantrums and tenderness. Take me back to the womb and let me eat your soul out like a grub in a walnut! . . .' The car lurched and skidded as she wrenched it round a hairpin bend, but she talked on, heedless of Ninette's cry and Landon's protest. . .
'I thought today his pride – or whatever it is that drives him – would be satisfied and I could go to him as a woman. But he doesn't want a woman! He wants a doll to play with, to croon over and spill the sawdust out of when he feels strong and cruel. That's why he's fallen for this Anna, a poor, empty pretty child, with nothing inside but what he's put there. Well, he's welcome to her. I'm free of him now – free of my father, too! I'm my own woman and I don't care what . . .'

She screamed and hit the brakes as a shadowy mass scrambled out of the ditch and ambled across the road in front. Ninette screamed, too, and threw herself against Landon. The wheels locked and they skidded in a sickening circle while the bumpers ripped open against the trunk of a roadside poplar. They ended, bruised and shaken, facing in the direction from which they had come. Ninette was breathless and trembling and Valeria sat slumped and sobbing over the steering-wheel. Landon was the first to recover. He said harshly: 'That's enough for tonight! We're going back to the villa!'

Valeria made no protest when he thrust her roughly out of the driver's seat and took over the wheel. They were all silent through the rattling, grinding drive up the hill, and when they reached the house Landon gave Ninette a curt order: 'Get her up to bed. Stay with her until I come. I'm going to talk to the old man!'

Ninette opened her mouth to protest, but, seeing his white, angry face and his tight trap mouth, she thought better of it and, taking Valeria's arm, she led her, submissive as a hospital patient, up the stairs to the bedroom.

Ascolini was still sitting in the library, slumped in his chair, staring in to the emptiness with a glass of brandy half-drunk at his elbow. Landon gave him no greeting but launched at once into a bitter tirade: 'This has got to stop, Doctor – all of it – now! If it doesn't there will be death in your house before the week is out. All three of us were damn near killed on the road ten minutes ago. Valeria's desperate. Carlo's a drunken mess. And you're sitting here feeling sorry for yourself because the bill collectors are in at last and you don't want to pay the score. If you want to destroy yourselves this is the way to do it!'

The old man lifted his white, lion mane and fixed Landon with a vague but hostile eye. 'And why should you care, Landon, what happens to us? Death, dishonour, damnation, what the hell does it matter to you?'

Landon's anger drove him on. He thrust an accusing finger in the old man's face and blazed at him: 'Because I've got debts to pay, that's why! To you, to Carlo, to Valeria. This is the only way I can pay them, and it's the last chance I've got. It's your last chance, too – and you know it! This is where it began – with you. If there's any hope at all it's in your hands. The bailiffs are in, my dear Doctor, and if you don't pay they'll tumble the house down about your ears!'

He broke off, splashed brandy into a glass and drank it at one swallow while the old man stared at him with cold, resentful eyes. Finally, with a hint of the old sardonic humour,

Ascolini asked: 'And what's the payment, eh, my friend? What's the penance from our confessor? I'm too old to scourge myself in the market place and crawl to mass on my knees!'

'You're old, Doctor,' said Landon with soft malice, 'and you'll soon be dead. You'll die hated and leave nothing behind but an unhappy memory. Your daughter will make herself a whore to spite you. And the man who could breed children for your house will die barren because there's no love to teach him better.' Swiftly as it had come, the anger died in him and he turned away with a gesture of despair. 'Damn it all! What more's to be said? Nothing is good enough for your gratitude, nothing can humble you enough to beg what the rest of us would give our eyes for!'

There was a long silence while the mantel clock ticked off the seconds like a death-watch beetle in the woodwork. Then, slowly, Ascolini heaved himself out of his chair and took a pace towards Landon. In a shaky, old man's voice that still had in it a note of dignity, he said: 'All right, Landon! You win. The old bull surrenders. Where does he go from here?'

Slowly, Landon turned to face him and saw in his aged face so much of ravaged pride, so much of pain long hidden, that he felt himself stifled by the sudden rush of pity. He gave the old man a pale, crooked smile. 'The first step is the hardest. After that it gets simpler all the time. A little loving, Doctor: a little tenderness, a little pity, and the grace to say one is sorry.'

'You think it's as easy as that?' A ghost of a grin twitched the lips of the old cynic. 'You overrate me, Landon. Now go to bed like a good fellow. A man has a right to be private before the last surrender!'

When he left the old man, Landon walked out on to the terrace and lit a cigarette. The moon was riding high and magical over the mountains and from the recesses of the garden he heard, for the first time, the sweet lament of the nightingales. He stood stock-still, one hand resting on the cold stone of the balustrade, while the plangent song rose and fell in the still air. It was a ghostly music, echoing the plaint of dead lovers and the ardour of passions long cold. It was a lament for lost hopes and vanished illusions and words unsaid but now never to be spoken. And yet there was a peace in it and the cool absolution of time. The moon would wane and the song would lapse into the sad silence of the cypresses, but in the morning the sun would rise and the scent of the garden would wake again, and so long as one was alive there was the hope of morning and maturity.

Not so long ago, he had come to this place, obsessed by the conviction of futility, convinced that the jargon of his trade was like a shaman's incantation – a passport to eminence in the tribe, but a fruitless remedy for the manifold ills of the soul. Now, for the first time, he began to see a virtue in their use, a virtue in the experience he had gathered, and perhaps a small promise of virtue in himself.

With Ascolini he had won the battle and paid one debt. But there were others still to be fought and he was grateful for the restoration of this hour of moonlight and nightingales. He finished the cigarette and then walked slowly upstairs to Valeria's room.

She was in bed, propped against the pillows, her face pale, her eyes absorbed in the painful self-contemplation of the sick. Ninette was sitting on the edge of the bed, brushing Valeria's hair. Landon stood at the foot of the bed, looking from one to the other, and groping for the words he needed. To Ninette he said affectionately: 'I want you to go to bed, sweetheart. Valeria and I have things to talk about. I'll come in to see you before I go to sleep.'

Ninette Lachaise nodded agreement, but he caught a swift flash of resentment in her eyes. She bent and kissed Valeria and then kissed Landon too. 'Don't be too late, chéri!' There was a note of caution which belied the lightness of her tone. 'I'll be waiting up for you.'

She left him then and Landon sat down on the side of the bed. Valeria Rienzi watched him, half curious, half afraid. Landon said, with professional casualness: 'It's been a rough day, hasn't it?'

Her eyes filled up with weak distressful tears, but she did not answer. Landon talked on, skirmishing round his theme, lest any injudicious word might destroy the relationship between them.

'I know how you're feeling, girl, because I feel with you. I know the danger you're in, because I've been dealing a long time with hurt minds. You had a look at death tonight, but at the last minute you drew back. If you get reckless and take another look, you may wait a second too long. After that – *kaput!* There's a cure for most things, but not for the kiss of the Dark Angel. You're asking yourself why I care what you do. I'll tell you. There was a night we had – and there was good in it, because there was some love. Not enough for a lifetime, perhaps, but enough for that little while. So I care! And there's more. I'm a physician. People come to me with soul-sickness and heart-sickness, but most of them come too late when the sickness has a hold and won't let go. You're not sick, yet. You're hurt and tired and lonely in a dark country. I'm offering you a hand to hold while you walk out of it.'

He could see the war in her: need and defiance struggling for the first utterance. She closed her eyes and lay back, dumb on the piled pillows. Landon laid a firm hand on her wrist.

'There are two ways you can have it. You can fill yourself with sleeping pills and wake in the morning with the ghosts still sitting on the bed. Or you can talk the troubles out and let someone else cut them down to size for you. Me, for instance. I know all the words – even the dirty ones.' He laughed softly. 'There's no fee. And if you want to cry, I can lend you a clean handkerchief.'

She opened her eyes and looked at him in doleful wonderment. 'You really mean that?'

'I mean it.'

'But what happens then? Do you gather me up and put me together again? Do you fill up all the empty places where there's no me at all?'

'No.'

'Do you pat me on the head and tell me I'm forgiven, provided I'm a good girl in future?'

'Not that either.'

'Do you teach my father to love me and Carlo to want me for a wife?'

'No.'

'Then what do you give, Peter? For God's sake, what do you give me?'

'Courage and a strong back! For the rest you need God Almighty. But without courage you won't find Him either. Well . . . it's the best offer I can make. Do you want to talk or do you want a sedative capsule?'

She broke then, and began to pour herself out, in tears first and then in a flood of talk, sometimes wild and incoherent, sometimes tragically lucid. Landon listened, prompted, probed and wondered, as he always did, at the miscellany of faces one human being could wear. Bitch, lover, liar, mother, mistress and lady in a mirror, small girl sitting on a father's knee and selling him the world for a kiss. In one night, or in a month of nights, there was no time to read even a single one of them. What he was attempting now was not a clinical analysis but the dispensation of a simple mercy: to conjure away grief for a few hours, to plant a hope that he knew might not survive the first dawn.

Finally the torrent of talk spent itself, and Valeria lay back, exhausted but calm and ready for sleep. Landon bent and kissed her lightly on the lips and she responded with a sleepy murmur. Then, bone-weary, he went to his own room.

Ninette Lachaise was sleeping fully dressed on his bed. He slipped off his coat and shoes and tie and lay down beside her. She stirred and muttered and threw her arm across his breast, then he too lapsed into sleep with her lips brushing his cheek. When he woke, she was no longer there and it was, once again, high noon in Tuscany.

When Landon came downstairs he found the villa bathed in a glow of triumph and familial unity. The maid-servant sang as she polished the furniture, the old gate-keeper whistled as he raked the gravelled drive, Ninette and Valeria were picking flowers in the garden, while Ascolini and Carlo Rienzi sat at coffee on the terrace working through a stack of newspapers and a pile of congratulatory telegrams.

They greeted him smiling. Ascolini rang for fresh coffee and then launched himself into an enthusiastic tally of Rienzi's successes. 'It is magnificent, Landon – like a great night at the opera. Read for yourself what they say. "A forensic victory..." ... "a vindication of the noblest principles of justice ...", "a new star in the legal firmament". I haven't seen anything like it for twenty years. And these.' He waved expansively at the pile of telegrams. 'Our colleagues in Rome are delighted. From this moment Carlo can have his choice of a dozen major cases. I'm proud of him. He has made me eat my words but I'm proud of him.'

Rienzi himself was flushed with pleasure. His face had lost its pinched and anxious look and he too launched into voluble compliments. 'It's your success, too, Peter. Without your counsel I should not have done half so well. I'm fortunate in my teachers, and, believe me, I know it.' Then, with boyish awkwardness, he made his apology. 'I'm sorry about last night. I hadn't eaten all day and I was very drunk.'

Ascolini laughed indulgently. 'A bagatelle, my boy! Forget it. I've seen better men than you carried to bed after smaller occasions. Besides, it's the future we have to think of. Before you came, Landon, we were discussing a partnership for Carlo. I'm not quite ready to pack up yet, but I will be soon. And then he can have the whole practice. But I still have a few lessons to give him, eh, my boy?'

There was so much patent goodwill between them that Landon wondered for a moment whether he had not read too much drama into the events of the night. Then Carlo said, casually enough: 'I had a call from Galuzzi this morning. They're transferring Anna today to the Sisters of the Good Shepherd. He says I can visit her this afternoon. I was wondering, Peter, if you'd like to come with me.' He gave a deprecating smile and added: 'I know how much I've asked of you, Peter, believe me. Valeria told me you and Ninette were getting married, and I know you want to be gone as soon as possible. But I would appreciate it if you'd take a last professional look at Anna.'

'If you like, of course, though I think there's nothing I can add to Galuzzi's knowledge. He's a good man. I would have great confidence in him.'

'I know. But he is, after all, a government official. I'd appreciate a little private guidance.'

'How would Galuzzi feel about my visit?'

'He's already approved it. Please come, Peter. We can leave about three o'clock and we'll be back here by five.'

'Valeria and I will look after Ninette,' said Ascolini. 'We shall all dine together tonight and then we shall send you away with our love.'

It was so simple and bland that Landon almost missed the point. Carlo needed a privacy with the girl. Ascolini needed Ninette as his ally with Valeria. Galuzzi was shrewd enough to want a monitor for this first crucial meeting between the advocate and the client whom he had started on the dubious road to freedom. They were still using him and there would be no freedom until Ninette and himself had left this home of troubled souls and made their own retreat in the green hills of Frascati.

The first touch of autumn was in the air as Landon and Rienzi drove out along the Arezzo road to the Hospice of the Good Shepherd. Carlo's good humour seemed to have deserted him and he was fretful and preoccupied. When they reached the first high ridges he swung the car off the road into a craggy indentation from which the land fell steeply away into a wild and sombre valley. When they stopped, he produced cigarettes, lit one for Landon and one for himself, and then began to talk in the nervous, staccato fashion of a man too long deprived of intimacy.

'We have time to talk, Peter. There are things I want to discuss with you.'

'Go ahead.'

'Valeria first. I'm sorry and ashamed for what happened last night, but in fact what I said was all true. I have no feeling for her any more. More than ever, at this time, I need a good marriage. I know what's going to happen. My career's going up like a balloon. You know what that means as well as I do. Pressure, demands, labour – from which there is no retreat. Without some kind of love in my life I shall be spending without renewal – a bankrupt's course. An understanding mistress would help, but I have not that either. I'm lonely, Peter. I feel old and empty beyond my years.'

His self-pity irritated Landon, but, remembering his debt, he tried still to be gentle. 'Look, Carlo. This kind of reaction is the most natural thing in the world. You've just fought a tremendous case. The pendulum is bound to swing back from triumph to depression. Don't be too hasty. Why don't you and Valeria give it another try?'

Rienzi's face hardened and he shook his head. 'We've forgotten the words, Peter. For me, too many nights in a cold bed. For her, too many other beds. Where do you start after that?'

Landon gave him Ninette's answer first. 'Someone has to make the first step and say "Sorry". I suggest it should be you.'

'And after that? How do you wipe out the waste and the hurt and all the memories?'

Landon gave him another answer to that, blunt and bawdy as anger could make it. 'You live with them, brother! You live with them and learn to be grateful for what you've salvaged. Damn it, Carlo! You're a big boy now! What do you want? A new book every night with the pages uncut and nothing written on them anyway? A new maidenhead every bedtime and people cheering when you hang out the sheets in the morning? Where's the comfort in that, for God's sake? It's a twelve-hour wonder – and a tedious business at best!'

To his surprise, Rienzi laughed. 'At least you haven't forgotten the words, Peter!'

'Neither have you. Neither has Valeria.'

'I'm afraid you'll never understand.' Rienzi smoked in silence for a few moments and then said, more calmly: 'You give me small credit, Peter. I'm not going to toss my cap over the windmill. I'm not going to go chasing the little models on the Via Veneto. I'm not built that way. I wish I were. Believe it or not, I've almost resigned myself to the situation. Convenient marriage is a very old institution in this country. Valeria can do what she wants so long as she's discreet about it. For myself, I can begin to see a kind of purpose in my life. Not wholly satisfactory, perhaps, but in part, yes.'

'You mean Anna Albertini?'

'Yes. In three years she'll be free. During that time she has to be prepared for an entry into the common world. When she does enter it she will need some kind of framework of interests and affection to step into.'

'And you think you can provide it?'

'I do.'

'At what price?'

'Less than I've paid for the little I have now.'

'Do you want to know what I think?' Landon's voice was chilly.

'That's why I'm talking to you, Peter. More than ever now I need your friendship.'

'Then for God's sake listen in friendship to what I'm going to tell you!' He broke off and gathered himself for a moment, then began to talk, warmly and persuasively, knowing that now or never the last debt must be paid. 'First let me explain to you, Carlo, that I don't agree with many of my colleagues who claim that every human aberration is a symptom of mental illness. I believe, as I think you do, that man is a responsible being, endowed with free-will. But this is no reason to confuse the issue. There is a moral infirmity as well as a mental one. There is evil in the world. There are calculated depravity and indulgence. And there is also a special sickness that follows from these things: a state of fugue, a flight from the knowledge of guilt, man pulling the blankets over his head to escape the beaks of the Furies.

'This is why modern psychiatry splits itself into two schools. The determinists say that man is not responsible for his actions. Therefore, when we've revealed to him the source of his disorder, he will cure himself by forgiving himself. You're a lawyer. You see where this ends – in the destructive absurdity that evil is its own absolution. The other school says, more reasonably, that when the source of the disorder is revealed, man must be given a hope of forgiveness, but he must also be led to the motions of self-reform. . . .' He broke off and laughed a little self-consciously. 'You wonder why I'm reading you this little lecture, Carlo? I'm no plaster saint, God knows. I know when I'm doing wrong and so do you. You're doing it now because you refuse any sort of forgiveness to Valeria and demand all of it for yourself. You know that you're preparing the way for a greater wrong. So you're creating a fiction that you can absolve yourself by the very act which will damn you – a cultivation of Anna Albertini.'

'You're lying to me, Peter,' said Rienzi coldly.

'Not this time, believe me.' He was pleading now and the knowledge of his own guilt lent him an urgent humility. 'Listen to me, Carlo, and think for a moment about Anna. You won your case on the plea you and I set up for her – that at the time of the murder she was mentally infirm, robbed of moral sense and legal responsibility by the shock of her mother's death. Now this could be true. On the other hand, it could be equally true that she was a responsible person, that she was conscious of guilt, and that after the act – after it, remember – she projected herself into the state of fugue in which she has remained virtually ever since. Think about that for a moment. And if there's half a chance of its being true, see where it leads. She clings to you because you are the only one who continues to absolve her as you did in the legal sense in court. This could be why she has no regret for her husband, because he rejected and did not forgive her!'

'That's a monstrous thought!'

'Monstrous indeed,' said Landon quietly, 'and the consequences are more monstrous still. You could be the one who robs her totally and completely of any hope of cure.'

'I don't understand that.'

'Then let me explain it to you, Carlo.' He laid a tentative, friendly hand on Rienzi's shoulder, but Rienzi withdrew resentfully from the contact. 'Believe me, man, I'm being as honest as I know how. I'm not raising bogies to frighten you. This is my profession, as the law is yours. All successful psychiatry depends upon the patient's willingness to seek a cure because of his knowledge that he is sick. He will resist treatment, of course, but if the distress is acute enough he will come to co-operate – except for instance in cases of paranoia where the mind closes itself utterly against reason. In Anna Albertini's case there is no distress, no sense of need. So long as she has you she is not sick, but cured, so her mind closes itself to further inquisition. You have forgiven her. Therefore she is totally forgiven. So the long fight continues and you, Carlo – you, my friend! – are her partner in the flight.'

'But only,' said Rienzi in the ironic fashion of the law, 'only if your guess is true, and in court you proved to the satisfaction of the judges that it was not. Where do you stand now, Peter?'

'On the same ground,' said Landon flatly, 'but for a different reason. You have made yourself a necessary prop to her infirmity. She will continue to cling to you. She will accept any condition, any relationship you impose on her, but you'll never be able to get rid of her. And if you fail her . . .'

He broke off and let the thought hang, a discordant note between them. Rienzi prompted him caustically: 'And if I fail her, Peter?'

'Death is familiar to her now,' said Landon sombrely. 'It holds no terrors and solves all problems. She will either kill herself or try to kill you.' It was out now, the untimely thought: death in the Tarot cards, death written on the palm of a man's hand, and he too blind to see it. Landon let him sweat over it for a few moments and then asked: 'Do you believe me, Carlo?'

'No,' said Carlo Rienzi, 'I'm afraid I don't.'

He started the engine, turned the car back on to the highway, and headed once more into the uplands towards the Hospice of the Good Shepherd.

In the late afternoon, Alberto Ascolini made his final capitulation to his daughter and to Ninette Lachaise. He sat with them on a low stone bench facing a small fountain where a dancing faun played his pipes and disported himself among the water jets. For once in his life, he gave no thought to stage management nor to the rhetoric of his trade. He did not attempt to persuade or to dominate the occasion, but sat, leaning on a stick, with a peasant hat perched on his white head, making the first and last apologia for his mountebank's career.

'This is the way it ends, my children. This is the way I think it is meant to end – an old fool sitting in the garden with the women. I used to be afraid of it, you know. Today, for the first time, I can see there might be a pleasure in it. When I was young, and that was a long time ago, the *signori* who owned this villa used to drive through San Stefano in their carriages on the way to Siena. They had coachmen and outriders, and the women – they looked like princesses to me – used to sit holding their handkerchiefs to their noses as they drove through the village. I remember myself, a snot-nosed urchin with his backside out of his breeches, shouting for coppers while the coachman flicked at me with his whip. A long time ago, but I remembered it every month, every year, as I was climbing up out of the dung-heap. One day I would have a coach and the woman with the lace handkerchief would be my woman, and I would sit in grand array at the opera and ride on to Corso in Rome and kiss hands in the *salons*. I did it all, as you know. I've dined with kings and presidents and walked into a reception with a princess of the blood on my arm . . . eh! What is it now? Not dust and ashes. I can't say that. A rich time? Yes. But every so often I would dream of the snot-nosed boy and reach out my hand to lift him into the coach – yet I could never touch him. Neither could I escape him. He would always come back and I could never be sure whether he mocked me or blamed me. So, for him, I think, I took my revenges on the world into which I had climbed, even on you, Valeria, my child. It has taken me a long time to understand that they were revenges on myself as well. When I married your mother I was poor and ambitious and I loved her. When I was famous and courted I regretted her. In you I tried to make her over again in the image of what I had desired. A strange thing, you know. She was wiser than I. She told me many times the price was too high and that when I had paid it I would regret it. You, child, I regret most of all. You were right, you know, when you said I made you pay for everything I gave. Nothing for nothing! It was the bitterest lesson my snot-nosed urchin had to learn. He could never believe in gratuity – the kiss that cost nothing or the hand to help a neighbour out of a ditch. He's learnt it now, from you, Ninette, even from that pig-headed Landon of yours. But you, my Valeria, have had to pay for the lesson. . . .' His voice

altered and he blew his nose violently. 'Forgive me, child, if
you can. If you can't, believe at least that I love you.'

'It's enough, *dottore*,' said Ninette Lachaise softly. 'The
loving is enough – and that Valeria should know that the
loving is there.'

She lifted the old straw hat and kissed him on the forehead and laid one cool hand for a moment on his cheek. Then
she left them, Valeria with tears and the old advocate with his
regrets, to the healing of the last summer sun.

'Now!' said the old man in his brisk, pragmatic style,
'now we dry our eyes and see if we have grown any wiser.
You will know now, child, that I am telling you the truth?'

'Yes.'

'Then let's see what we can do about this marriage of yours.
Tell me honestly now: what's the trouble between you?'

Valeria Rienzi lifted a ravaged face and stared at him
blankly. 'It's plain enough, isn't it, Father? I've been a fool
and Carlo needs something that I can't give him.'

'We'll admit the foolishness,' said Ascolini with his old
sardonic grin. 'We'll lock it away and bring it out occasionally
to remind us not to be fools again. But what about Carlo?
What does he want?'

She shrugged unhappily. 'I wish I knew. A mother, perhaps, or a child bride fresh from convent school!'

'He has the child bride,' said Ascolini cynically. 'But she's
no good to him because she'll be locked away for three years.
As for the mother, he can't do much about that unless he
finds a clucking widow with a forty-five inch bust.'

'Don't make jokes about it, Father. It's serious.'

'I know it's serious, child!' The old man was testy again.
'But we don't throw up our hands and go wailing through
the town. We do something about it.'

'What, for instance?'

'This girl, Anna Albertini. Ignore her. If Carlo wants to go
hanging around the convent garden with the girl on one arm
and a nun for a watchdog on the other, let him. He'll get sick
of it in time. Pity's a thin diet for a man of thirty-five. If he
wants to try the widow or a chicken from a pavement café,
ignore that, too. Swallow your pride and take him for what

he is, and while you've got him see if you can make him into something better. It's been done, you know. And you do have something to work on. You saw him in court. He was another man. You're a woman. You may be able to bring the same man out in bed. Look, child.' He turned to her and imprisoned her wrists in his old strong hands. 'There's always one who kisses and one who turns the cheek. Sometimes the one who turns the cheek learns to like the taste of kissing. It's worth a trial, isn't it? You've had your playtime. There's autumn after summer. If it doesn't work, what have you lost?'

'Nothing, I suppose. But don't you see, Father, I'm lonely now. I'm scared.'

'Wait till you get to my age,' said Alberto Ascolini with a grin '– the last winter, when you know for certain there'll never be another spring. Courage, girl! Go and put on a new face and let's see what carrots we can find for this noble ass you've married!'

The Hospice of the Good Shepherd Sisters reared its grey bulk over a spread of garden and farmland and dark cypresses. Its nearer aspect was forbidding: a big wall of tufa stone topped with spikes and broken glass, wrought-iron gates backed with a close mesh of chain wire, and, beyond them, the hospice itself, an old monastery building, four storeys high, solid as a fortress, with barren windows and a television antenna rising incongruously above its ancient tiles. An elderly porter opened the gates and raised his hand in a half-hearted salute as they passed. A pair of inmates shuffling across the lawn turned and stared at them with glazed, indifferent eyes. A young nun, with the sleeves of her habit rolled up, was clipping flowers, trailed by a group of women, aimless as hens in a barnyard. A vague oppression crept over Landon as he thought of all the misery penned in this place, last refuge of those who, by act of God and self-delusion, had failed to come to terms with life.

Yet not all the deluded were behind bars. There were all too many who, like Carlo Rienzi, created for themselves situations charged with explosive and destructive possibilities. Carlo had become, overnight, a public figure, thrust into limelit eminence, and yet the shrewd eye could see already how the pillars and buttresses of his personality were slowly withering away. The cracks were plainly visible, the dangerous cant towards indulgence and self-deception. How, or which way, he would fall was anyone's guess, but Landon was prepared to give long odds that he would decline inevitably in the direction of Anna Albertini.

Even for a middling sensual man, the association with an attractive young woman of twenty-four was fraught with danger. Add to that the character of the girl herself – her enforced dependence, her immaturity, her capacity for tragic decision – and there were all the elements of a classic melodrama.

How many times could the world blow up? The answer was plain to Landon now, plainer than it had ever been: as often as a man chose to reject the simple pragmatic rules of human experience and arbitrate his private destiny without respect to duty, obligation and his nature as a dependent animal.

The Greeks had a word for that, too: Nemesis – the ultimate and inevitable catastrophe, when a man pulled down the roof-trees of the world on his own hapless head. The trouble was that other heads were broken as well and he generally did not survive to mend them.

Landon was still chewing on that tasteless cud when the Sister Portress, a horse-faced woman with gentle eyes and an uncertain smile, opened the door to them. She showed them into the visitors' room, a large, bare chamber, furnished with high-backed chairs, twin statues of the Sacred Heart and Our Lady of Lourdes, and smelling vaguely of lamp-oil and floorwax; then she trotted off to find the Mother Superior.

Landon wilted at the thought of spending a couple of hours in this ascetic atmosphere, but Carlo reassured him with an unexpected smile: 'Don't worry, Peter. This is just to condition us to piety. They keep it for chaplains and doctors and visiting bishops. When Anna comes I imagine they'll give us the freedom of the garden.'

'Thank God for that!' said Landon dryly.

Rienzi gave him a rueful, boyish smile. 'Don't be too angry

with me, Peter. After all, this is my decision and I have to carry the consequences – good or bad.'

'Do you, Carlo?' Landon was still smouldering. 'If that's what you believe, then you'll do what you damned well please. I'm leaving tomorrow anyway, so why should I care?'

'I want us to be friends,' said Carlo Rienzi. 'I have a great affection for you, Peter. But that doesn't mean I have to agree with you all the time, does it?'

'A man who pleads his own cause has a fool for a lawyer, Carlo. A man who wants to be his own doctor is a bigger fool still. You've had my advice. I can't force you to act on it. Now please drop the discussion, like a good fellow.'

At that moment the Mother Superior came in: a small, grey woman with a fine-boned face, who reminded Landon of Ascolini's marchesa. She had the air of a great lady born to wield authority, and Landon thought she could be a very formidable superior indeed.

When Carlo presented himself she gave him a warm greeting: 'I followed your case with great interest, Mr Rienzi. The men of my family have been associated with the law for many years, so I had a special interest. You made a magnificent plea.' To Landon she extended a graver courtesy: 'We're very happy to see you here, Mr Landon. Professor Galuzzi speaks of you with great respect. If you would care to visit us at any time to see our methods or talk to our staff you will be most welcome.'

Landon bowed his acknowledgment and the Mother Superior went on with what was obviously a well-prepared exordium: 'We are all very interested in Anna's case, gentlemen. She was admitted early this afternoon, as you know, and we had none of the difficulty usual with new patients. Professor Galuzzi has given instructions that she is to be allowed as much freedom and responsibility as she can take. She will have all the privileges accorded to our advanced patients: a room of her own, time to read and sew, an hour of television each day, and a few cosmetics. These are special privileges, but so long as our people are orderly in their habits, obedient in their demeanour, there is no reason for them to be reduced. With regard to visits, there is a normal visiting day once a month. However, Professor Galuzzi suggests that for the present it would be best for Anna if we arranged a visiting day every six weeks. If she makes good progress, then we shall go back to the usual schedule.'

'Neatly done,' Landon thought. Galuzzi had a clear head and a shrewd eye, and in this little grey woman he would have a strong lieutenant.

She went on in her crisp, businesslike fashion: 'We have another rule, too, which we have found most useful. When visitors come they are generally accompanied – unobtrusively of course – by one of our Sisters. However, as Mr Landon is here with you today, I think we can dispense ourselves from the practice.'

For the first time, Rienzi was able to get a foothold in the conversation. Anxious as a Dutch uncle, he said: 'I have a great personal interest in Anna, as you know. If there is anything I can do to make her happy you have only to call me.'

The Mother Superior smiled indulgently. 'I assure you, Mr Rienzi, she will have the best of care. Our medical staff is well trained and devoted. Professor Galuzzi is a constant visitor. Our Sisters are especially trained to maintain a reasonable discipline while spending as much kindness as possible on our patients. Today you may find Anna a little restless. This is natural. It is her first day and she is new and strange; but she will settle down quickly. Also, she is a healthy young woman and it is natural that from time to time she will be irked by confinement and by the lack of the company of the opposite sex. But we are trained to watch for these things and to offset them.' She stood up and smoothed down the skirt of her habit. 'If you've brought any gifts for her I'd like to see them now.'

Awkward as a schoolboy, Rienzi displayed the packages: a box of chocolates, a hair ribbon, a religious medallion on a small gold chain, a sewing kit. The old nun passed them all with a smile, but insisted on taking the scissors out of the sewing box. 'Not because of Anna, Mr Rienzi, but because of the danger of their falling into other hands.'

Rienzi blushed and apologized. 'It was thoughtless of me. I'm sorry.'

'On the contrary, Mr Rienzi, you're a very thoughtful man. Anna is lucky to have your support.'

At the same moment, Anna Albertini walked hesitantly into the room and Rienzi held out an eager hand in greeting. 'Anna, my dear! How good to see you!'

'And you, Mr Rienzi.'

The formal address and the tentative handshake belied the pleasure in her eyes. Rienzi presented her to Landon. 'You remember Mr Landon, Anna? He was a great help to you before the trial and during it.'

'Of course.' She gave him a cautious smile. 'Mr Landon was very kind to me. I won't forget that.'

'You look well, Anna. I know you're going to be very happy here.'

The girl said nothing and the Mother Superior cut in briskly: 'I must be off. I have work to do. Take the gentlemen into the garden, Anna. Walk them down to the place where you saw the Sisters saying their prayers.' She explained herself with a smile to Landon: 'It's the Sisters' garden. You'll be more comfortable there. You won't be bothered by the inmates wandering around the grounds. Before you go, Anna will bring you back here for coffee.'

When she was gone, Carlo displayed his gifts, and while they were admiring them together Landon took a long look at Anna Albertini. She was dressed, like all the inmates, in a frock of grey cotton with long buttoned sleeves and a cloth belt sewn to the frock itself. She wore black stockings and black shoes. Her hair was shorter now, drawn back from her face and tied with a wisp of blue ribbon. Her hands were uneasy, but her face still wore the look of calm and classic repose which he had noticed on the day of their first meeting. There was more colour in it now, more animation in the eyes and in the voice. Her gestures were restrained, her movements studiously modest, so that she looked more like a fledgeling nun than a prisoner serving a sentence for murder.

For all his past judgements of Rienzi, Landon had to admit that he could see nothing but innocence in this first moment of meeting. There was no trace of sensuality, not so much as a hand's touch or a glance to hint at intimacy or collusion.

Anna was now calling Rienzi by his first name, but the most suspicious eavesdropper would have found nothing to blame in the tone or the inflection.

When her first excitement was over, Anna piled her gifts on one of the chairs and then took the two men out into the garden. She walked between them, reserved as a novice, rehearsing with simple pleasure the details of her first day after the trial.

'Everyone was so kind to me. At San Gimignano they made me a special supper and the nurses were allowed to come in and talk to me. One of them did my hair, another brought me a prayer-book. In the morning I was allowed to walk by myself in the garden and the warden's wife gave me coffee. Everyone said how lucky I was and what a wonderful thing you had done for me. I felt very proud. They've given me a nice room here. There are bars on the windows, but there are curtains, too, with flowers on them, and everything is white and clean. Sister Eulalia took me for a walk and showed me some new kittens in the gardener's shed. She told me funny stories about the people we saw, and tonight there is to be a concert with some very famous singers from Rome.'

Landon's first impression was of her extreme simplicity, her preoccupation with trivial things, her contentment with the narrow ambit of enclosed existence. But when Carlo began to question her about what she had read, about how she liked to spend her time, about the programmes she had watched on television, Landon caught a glimpse of a lively, if limited, intelligence and a very adequate judgement.

For the first time, she expressed an interest in what she might do after her release. She had once seen a fashion show and she wondered whether she might later qualify as a mannequin. If this failed, she thought she might like to train as a stenographer. She wanted to know whether there was any training available at the hospital. She asked questions about Carlo's work and Landon's, and her queries, if elementary, were still eminently sensible.

Carlo's method with her was sound. He probed for her interest, stimulated it with questions and then set about filling in the blank spaces in her information. His talk ranged widely, but he avoided any subject which might arouse her to discontent or revive old memories of childhood or married life. He made jokes for her and laughed at her mild comedies. And all the time he walked separate from her, hands clasped behind his back like a genial parent at finishing-school.

But for Landon there was something missing from the picture. It was too placid, too sober. Its pathos was too muted, its motif too mild. There was nothing in it to justify Carlo's desperate hope, or his own fears, or its importance to Anna herself. Landon could not believe that the performance was being staged for his benefit. Rienzi was too poor an actor to bring it off and Anna had had no warning to prepare for a deception.

Then understanding began to dawn on Landon. This was not the whole performance, but a prelude, a ritual entry into another stage of communion. He saw, or thought he saw, how they would both need something like this. They were poles apart in nature, education and experience. They would meet too rarely and for too short a time to leap at once into a high ground of understanding. The girl would be subdued by the daily disciplines of the institution. Carlo would have to discipline himself lest the exacerbations of his life drive him into indiscretion. So each of their meetings would begin like this : slow talk to skim the surface of the sleeping thoughts, a slow pavane along the garden paths – to what?

Their walk brought them finally to a low stone wall, broken by a wicket gate which led into the private domain of the Sisters : a croquet lawn screened on all sides by close-grown shrubs and, beyond it, more private still, a sunken garden with a fishpond and a shrine of Our Lady of Fatima.

This was where the nuns came for their recreation and to say the Rosary in the cool of the evening. This was their retreat from the thankless labours of the hospice and from the intrusion of the sick ones shambling about the grounds.

'Here –' said Anna suddenly, 'here I feel for the first time that I'm free. Not free as I used to be, but as I will be one day.'

She was not looking at her companions, but around the garden and over the tips of the cypresses to the pale sky where a solitary hawk wheeled and hovered in the slack air. Her eyes shone, her face was transfigured by a swift glow of vitality.

'You see that fellow up there? When I was a little girl in San Stefano, they used to call him the chicken-stealer. You know what I call him now? I call him Carlo. He hangs about up there for hours and hours and you think he's never going to come down. Then, all of a sudden, he drops – plop! – like a stone.' She turned to Landon, flushed and laughing. 'Just like Carlo! All the time I was in prison, all the time during the trial, he seemed to be so far away – miles and miles away among the great ones. Now – look! – he's here with me, in his garden.'

Landon stole a quick glance at Rienzi, but he was bending over a rose bloom, studious as any botanist. The girl laughed again in childish mockery.

'Carlo doesn't think he's a hawk. He likes to make out he's a wise old stork with long legs and a long advocate's nose with a pair of spectacles on it. You should have heard the lectures he read me when he came to see me! He sounded just like Mother Superior today. "Anna must be a good girl. Anna must do as she is told. She must learn her lessons and be tidy and patient and co-operative."'

'Anna's a lucky girl,' said Carlo coldly, 'but she laughs at the wrong things.'

'You told me once I needed to laugh!'

'I know, child, but . . .'

'I'm not a child! I'm a woman. That's what you want me to be, isn't it? That's what you were saying all the time, during the trial. Now you call me a child.'

She said it petulantly, as if it were an old complaint, and then stood, downcast, biting her thumbnail, waiting for Carlo to reprove her again. This time he was more gentle with her. He smiled benignly and said: 'Anna, the things I tell you are the things that will make you free. You're much better off than we ever expected you to be. Three years isn't such a long time and they'll go much quicker if you live each

day for itself. This is a good place to be. The Sisters are kind
people. If you're obedient and easy for them to handle we
may have a chance to get you out of this place sooner. That's
not a joking matter.'

'But I've been cooped up so long. Now I want to fly free
like the chickēn-stealer. I want to wear nice clothes again
and look in shop windows and . . .'

'I know, I know.' His voice took on a softer, crooning note.
'But I'll come to see you as often as I can. I'll bring you presents. You'll find the days will go faster and faster. Besides,
it takes a whole winter to make the spring flowers – but in the
end they come.'

She was penitent now, like a calculating child who ask
for cake only to win a caress. She said humbly: 'I'm
sorry, Carlo. I'll try to be better. I want so much to please
you.'

'I know you do, Anna. Now forget it like a good girl and
let's talk about something else.'

For Landon, it was an embarrassing experience, like
stumbling on a drunken courtship half-way down the stairs
Anna was seducing Carlo with pity while he struggled with
the clumsy fiction of paternal solicitude. How long they
could keep it up Landon did not know. By all the signs, they
had been practising for some time, and perhaps they had
developed a stronger tolerance than most for this courtship
by mutual deception. But sooner or later one would crack
The fairy-tale would come apart at the seams, and then – cap
over the windmill and hell to pay!

Landon had had more than enough for one afternoon, but
he endured it for another half hour, pacing with them up
and down the croquet lawn, listening to their talk, adding an
occasional banality of his own, and watching how easily and
unconsciously they lapsed into the conventions of their un-
conventional attachment. Finally, he gave up and suggested
to Carlo that it was time to leave.

Carlo looked at his watch and said, resentfully: 'Well, if
you feel you must . . . but it will be some time before I can see
Anna again.'

Anna was even more reluctant. She laid an urgent hand on

Rienzi's arm and demanded: 'Please, Carlo! Before you go, could we have a few words in private?'

'Would you mind, Peter?'

No, he would not mind. He would be glad to be rid of them for a while. He would smoke a cigarette and stroll for ten minutes more while they exchanged whatever secrets they had with the Madonna in the sunken garden. Carlo led Anna to the stone steps that separated the two enclosures and when she disappeared down the other side he came back for a hurried word with Landon.

'I'm sorry, Peter. All this must be very boring to you. But you see how it is. This is her first day here. She's restless. And I'd feel guilty if I left her unsettled. I shan't be very long.'

Guilty or innocent, Landon had to tell him. Once outside the gates of the hospice, chameleon love would change colour again and crawl back into the pigeon-hole marked 'grand illusions', a high, secret place beyond all reach of reason. He clamped a firm hand on Carlo's wrist and gave him the warning: 'Carlo, you're my friend and I've got to say it. You're walking on eggs in this affair. Whatever she says, however she says it, this girl is hot for you. And you're at least warm to her. Pull out now like a sensible man! Say good-bye to her and call it a day. Please, Carlo!'

Carlo tried to wrench away, but Landon held him as the other blazed in low, bitter invective: 'If today hasn't shown you the truth, Peter, nothing will. You've got a dirty mind! You've said all this before. Now it's once too much. Let me go, please!'

'One thing more, Carlo!' It was on the tip of Landon's tongue to tell him of his talk with Galuzzi and of the suspicion under which he lay already. Then he thought better of it. Why the hell play hangman to a man plaiting his own rope? Landon shrugged and let him go. Carlo stalked angrily out of sight into the sunken garden while Landon settled himself under an autumn tree and smoked a tasteless cigarette.

He smoked another, and a third. He paced the lawn for ten minutes, fifteen, twenty. Then, utterly exasperated, he went in search of Rienzi and Anna. He had hardly set foot on the first stone step when he heard their voices, and for the first time in his life he played the keyhole spy.

Rienzi and Anna were sitting on a stone bench in an alcove opposite the shrine. They were facing each other with half the length of the bench between them, but Anna was holding Carlo's hand and pleading with him: 'You've told me many times, Carlo, that no one can live without love – some kind of love. I know you're married, so I mustn't ask that kind. But I'm not a child, so you mustn't offer me that kind either. What have we got, Carlo? What can you give me to keep me alive in this place?'

Landon could not see Rienzi's face, but he could sense the uneasiness in him and his effort to hedge his answer in that bland dominie's voice: 'You're very precious to me, Anna, my dear – for many reasons. All those weeks I held your fate in my hands. You were and still are my prize. Of course I care for you deeply.'

'Is that all?'

It was the voice Landon had heard first on Professor Galuzzi's tape – dead, flat and colourless. Rienzi protested, feebly: 'No, Anna. You know it isn't all. But, for the rest, I'm not even sure myself. I doubt I could put it into words.'

'But I have words, Carlo . . . I love you!'

Rienzi was badly shaken, but he still tried to humour her like a child. 'Love is a big word, Anna. It means different things at different times. The way you love me today may be a lot different from the way you love me tomorrow.'

'Do you love me, Carlo?'

Landon saw him hesitate a moment and then heard him surrender: 'I – I love you, Anna.'

But she was not satisfied yet. She pressed him urgently, raising the reluctant hands and holding them to her breast. 'How do you love me, Carlo? How?'

It was Rienzi's last ditch and he knew it. Landon could feel him gathering himself, fumbling for the words that were his final defences against her. 'I – I don't know that yet, Anna. That's why you must be patient with me. I need time, we both need time to get to know each other, not in the crisis of a court-room, not here in this place, but outside, in a world of norma

214

people. This thing between us, Anna, needs to grow naturally, like a plant. If the flower looks different from what we expected, it will still be beautiful, still good for us both. Can you understand that?'

To Landon's surprise and Carlo's evident relief, she accepted it. She hesitated for a moment and then said, in her childish voice: 'Yes. I do understand. I can be happy now, I think. . . . Will you please kiss me good-bye?'

Rienzi looked at her for a long moment, then, with touching tenderness, but with no vestige of passion, he cupped his hands under her chin and kissed her lightly on the lips. Then he released her and stood up. Puzzled and disappointed, she faced him, picking a scrap of lint from his lapel with nervous fingers.

'You did that as if I were a little girl.'

Rienzi smiled gravely and shook his head. 'No, Anna! You're a woman. A very beautiful woman.'

'Then kiss me like one! Make me feel like a woman. Just once . . . just once!'

Landon wanted to shout at him: 'No, don't do it!' but shame held him back. The next moment the girl was in Rienzi's arms and they were kissing passionately like lovers, while the marble Madonna looked on dumbly and any wandering nun might shout their ruin over the roof-tops.

Then, without any warning, it happened. With a single, convulsive gesture, Anna thrust Carlo away from her. Her face was a contorted mask of terror and hate. As Carlo stared at her, unbelieving, she opened her mouth in a high, hysterical scream: 'They're killing her! They're killing her!' The next moment she was tearing at his eyes and face, tiger-wild and shouting in insane accusation: 'You're the one! You're the one who killed her! You . . . you!'

It took all their efforts to wrestle her back to the hospice, where four muscular nurses buckled her into a strait-jacket and carried her away. The Mother Superior looked at them with shrewd, dubious eyes and then called a Sister to dress Carlo's torn face.

Chapter Nine

TEN MINUTES later, in the bleak reception-room where Carlo's gifts to Anna still lay piled on the chair, the little grey nun faced them with the cold question: 'Well gentlemen, how did it happen?'

Carlo Rienzi was a very great advocate, but now he was in the dock and in need of another's counsel. Before he could open his mouth, Peter Landon hurried into an explanation: 'I think, Reverend Mother, I probably saw more of what happened than Mr Rienzi. All three of us were in the garden together. Mr Rienzi was just saying goodbye to Anna and I was standing about three paces away, watching them. Anna seemed perfectly normal, but when Mr Rienzi held out his hand she put her arms around his neck and tried to kiss him. He pushed her away gently and told her not to be silly. Then she started to scream that he was the one who had killed her mother. Immediately after that she attacked him.'

Landon hoped desperately that the narrative sounded as shocked and ingenuous as he tried to make it. This grey, competent lady held, at this moment, power of life and death over Advocate Rienzi, and Landon had no doubt she would damn him without mercy if she suspected the truth. So, for good measure, he added a professional opinion. 'This is a tragic business, Reverend Mother, but, speaking professionally, I am not too surprised. Both Professor Galuzzi and I were gravely concerned about certain unstable elements in this girl's case. I know Professor Galuzzi hoped to explore them more fully by deep analysis. If I could use your phone I think I should call Galuzzi from here.'

The Mother Superior gave him a cool, appraising look and then, apparently satisfied, turned to Rienzi. 'Mr Rienzi do you agree with Mr Landon's account of what happened?'

Shaken as he was, Rienzi was still a good lawyer. He knew that half a lie is worse than no lie at all. His answer came back pat and convincing: 'That's exactly how it happened.'

The Mother Superior nodded and then said in a crisp decisive fashion: 'I'm afraid it doesn't end here. You both know that people committed to our care from the courts are wards of the State. Everything that happens to them becomes the matter of an official report. I shall need affidavits from both of you – four copies, each copy notarized.'

She must have been convinced, Landon thought sourly, otherwise she would know that she was committing them to perjury, and the consciences of the worthy Sisters were too tender for such wilful irony.

Carlo Rienzi murmured some words of regret, but the Mother Superior waved them aside with an old, imperious hand. She had no time for lamentations. Her vocation was the care of sick minds and Anna Albertini was sick beyond recovery. She led Landon down a bare, echoing corridor into her office and then telephoned Professor Galuzzi.

Her own report was made first, in the clear decisive tones of a staff officer. Then she handed the receiver to Landon. It was a relief to him to hear Galuzzi's dry, academic voice from the other end of the line: 'So, my friend, it happened sooner than we expected, eh? Well, perhaps it's better this way – for everybody. Mother Superior tells me you were there and saw it all?'

'That's right.'

'I presume it's your version I've just heard?' There was an edge of irony in Galuzzi's question.

'Mother Superior reported exactly what I told her. I'll be attesting it in an official report.'

Surprisingly, Galuzzi chuckled. 'Our young advocate is fortunate in his friends. Your eye-witness report will, of course, close the matter, since it carries such a weight of professional reputation. If you have time, however, in the next few days, I'd like to drink a glass of wine with you – and perhaps consult you about our patient.'

'I'm very grateful,' said Landon, 'more grateful than I can tell you. But I'll be leaving Siena in a couple of days. I'm getting married.'

'My felicitations!' said Galuzzi warmly. Then he added dryly: 'I think you're wise. Miss Lachaise is a charming woman – and it's time you had some diversion. Good luck, my friend. Go with God.'

'Good luck to you,' said Landon softly. 'And thank you.'

The old nun looked at him with a canny, cultivated eye. 'So your case is closed, Mr Landon. Mine is just beginning. Thank you and good day.'

Landon drove Rienzi's car out of the iron gates and heard them close with a clang. As they climbed out of the valley towards the high road, Carlo sat huddled and silent beside him, fingering his scarred face and staring with blank eyes at the road ahead. After a while, he roused himself slightly and said, in a toneless voice: 'Thank you for what you did, Peter.'

'Forget it.'

'I can't say how sorry I am.'

'Forget that, too.'

Landon could hardly have said less, but he had no heart to say more. He knew that if Rienzi uttered one word of self-pity he would stop the car and punch him on the nose and make him walk every step of the way back to Siena. He understood what the man must be suffering, he was prepared to perjure himself to save Rienzi's neck, but the memory of Anna Albertini, lost to all hope, buckled in a canvas bag and carted off to oblivion, would haunt him for a long time.

Dusk was coming down when they reached the Villa Ascolini. Mercifully, everyone was dressing for dinner, so Landon settled Carlo in the library with a whisky decanter and a siphon of soda and then hurried upstairs to talk to Ninette. She heard him out in silence and then chided him firmly: 'I know you're angry, *chéri*, but you can't give way to it now. I know how badly you feel about having to perjure yourself. I agree that all your debts are paid. But we can't just work on debit and credit. This is a crisis for Carlo and we must help him to survive it.'

'Don't you think it's time he helped himself?'

'Do you think he can at this moment?' Her hands reached out to caress his angry face. 'Peter, Peter, can't you see What he's done today must seem like murder to him.'

'Wasn't it just that?'

'Who knows, *chéri*? Who knows how much or how little was needed to tip the balance for Anna? Who know whether without Carlo it might not have happened much sooner? Don't judge him, Peter. Not today. Not yet a while.'

He could not resist her then. He took her in his arms and kissed her and surrendered with a weary grin. 'All right, sweetheart, what do you want me to do?'

'Leave Carlo to me for a while. You go up and talk to Ascolini and Valeria.'

'Do you think it's wise to tell them?'

'I'm sure of it.'

Landon was far from sure, but at bottom he was too indifferent to care. A few moments later, Ninette went down to the library to see Carlo while Landon walked along the corridor to talk with Doctor Ascolini.

The old man took the news calmly enough. He made a quick canvass of the legal possibilities and then, satisfied that both Rienzi and Landon were beyond impeachment, he shrugged and said calmly: 'For the girl, of course, it's a terrible thing. For us – all of us – it may be the mercy we have been waiting for. Carlo is alone now. Perhaps he will turn back to Valeria.'

'Perhaps. It seems he has no other place to go.'

The old man cocked a quizzical eye at Landon. 'You've had enough, haven't you, my friend?'

'More than enough. We'll say goodbye tonight, Doctor.'

Ascolini nodded a grave agreement. 'You're right, of course. If I say I am grateful it will mean too little. Let me tell you simply that your debts are paid to Carlo and that we are now in debt to you. I have never perjured myself for any man, though often sworn false oaths to women. But that's a different matter. I thank you, Landon, and wish you well. I think you will be good for Ninette and I know she'll be good for you. Leave me, like a good fellow. I'll come down and see Carlo in a few minutes. What will you tell Valeria?'

'The truth,' said Landon flatly. 'What else? This is the end of the road.'

When he had told her the news, Valeria Rienzi echoed the tag of his own thought, 'It is the end of the road, as you say, Peter. If we can't come together after this there's no hope at all. We part and go separate ways. There are limits to all endurance.'

There was a question that had to be asked and he gave it to her baldly: 'How do you see this coming together?'

'Only with love, Peter.' She was very emphatic about it. 'No more of this cold salad of convention. I don't expect too much, I don't even count on an equal bargain, but there must be some love on both sides, a touch of passion sometimes. What else can we build on?'

'Nothing else. Do you love Carlo?'

'I can begin to, I think.'

'Does he love you?'

'I don't know, Peter. But he must tell me tonight.'

'Do you think he will know tonight?'

'If not tonight, then never!' She turned back to her mirror and began brushing her hair. 'I'll see you downstairs, Peter ... and when you go don't kiss me goodbye.'

He walked back to his own room, flung himself on the bed and closed his eyes. He was bone-weary, but there was no rest for him yet. By his own reckoning, all debts were paid and he was free to go. But there was still the last reaction and he had no heart to face it just yet. He lay, spent and empty, trying to set his own tangled thoughts in order.

It was not only Carlo Rienzi who had come to the end of the road. Peter Landon, too, had reached a moment of conclusion and a point of new departure. For a long time now he had been involved, knowing and unknowing, in the diverse and delicate anatomies of love and justice: in the loyalties of the one and the legalities of the other. He had found that while both were attainable, neither was perfect.

One arrived at each by conflict and contradiction. Love was affirmed by the contract of marriage, but the contract was not enough to preserve it. Justice was deemed to be preserved by the manifold provisions of the codex. But plead for both with a thousand voices, give a thousand advocates a thousand briefs and you would not attain to love or justice without the slow search, the meticulous balance of right and duty, the probe for truth, the ruthless weeding out of error and egotism.

A lifetime's efforts and you were not yet at the end of it

love was a flower of slow nurture, justice was a fruit of vigilant cultivation. The flower would wither and the fruit would drop under the hands of a shiftless gardener. And – God save their miserable souls! – men were all too careless of the charge committed to them: the love by which they might live happy and the justice by which they might live safe, two steps and a spit from chaos.

On which disturbing thought he heaved himself off the bed, splashed water in his face, ran a comb through his hair and went downstairs.

He found Ascolini and Valeria talking with Ninette outside the closed door of the library. Ninette looked strained and anxious and her eyes were swollen with weeping. When Landon asked her about Carlo she shook her head. 'I can't tell you, *chéri*, because I don't know myself. For a while it was quite terrifying. I've never seen a man so distraught. He told me everything – the most secret things of his life. Then he just sat on the floor with his head on my knees and didn't say a word. He's calm now, but what he's feeling or thinking I don't know. He wants to see us all now.'

'Did he say why?'

'No, just that he wanted to see us all together.'

For a few moments they stood, irresolute, searching one another's faces. Finally, Valeria shrugged and pushed open the door of the library.

The first sight of Carlo Rienzi stopped them all in their tracks. He seemed to have aged ten years in a couple of hours. His face was sallow and shrunken, his eyes burning like those of a man in high fever. His hair hung damp and lank over his forehead. He stood propped against the marble mantel as if the slightest move would topple him.

'Hello, Carlo,' said Valeria softly.

'Hello, Valeria.'

After that, there was a pause. Carlo looked at them vaguely and then blinked and shook his head as if to chase away the trailing mists of a nightmare. Then he said, in a dead level voice: 'I'm glad you're here, Valeria. I'm glad our friends are here. I want to tell you something.'

Landon could see Valeria struggling against a swift impulse

of pity, but she stood her ground and waited for Carlo to go on. Then he began to speak: 'I'm an empty man tonight. I am nothing and I have nothing. I've done a terrible thing today and I can't feel guilty about it any more. I can't even feel what I'm saying to you now. All I know is that I want to feel it and I want you to believe it because I will never be able to say it again. I'm not sorry for myself, but I'm sorry for what I've done and for what I've been – to you, Valeria, to your father, to Peter and Ninette here. This will sound strange from a man who cannot feel anything, but this too must be said. I love you all. I hope you'll forgive me and let me go in peace.'

'My God!' thought Landon, 'it can't be true!'

But it was true, and so patent that Landon wondered why they did not all burst out laughing. Advocate Rienzi was fighting his own case with the greatest piece of mountebankery he would ever pull in any court. He was pleading for the very thing he denied – the right to go on pitying himself, the right to have life always on his own terms and yet always have a breast to cry on. As a final stroke of genius, he was making himself the whipping-boy, knowing that, in the end, the stripes would fall on other backs than his own. He would never make a shrewder plea, never a less worthy one.

Landon thought he was winning it, too, when he saw Valeria move a pace towards him with hands outstretched. Then, abruptly, she checked herself and asked him, in a clear cool voice: 'Where will you go, Carlo?'

He turned vaguely towards her and said, almost apologetically: 'You mustn't ask me to talk about that. I've caused you enough grief already. But there'll be no more trouble, I promise.' He laughed, unsteadily. 'I told Peter today I didn't know the words. Funny! It turns out I knew them all the time. It's just that I'm saying them too late. That's always been my trouble. Too little a man growing up too late. I'm sorry.'

Landon almost expected to hear him say, 'The defence rests.' But he was too shrewd a craftsman for that – and besides he was exhausted, like every actor after a great performance. He heaved himself away from the mantel and began to walk with slow, dragging steps, towards the door. Then, clear as a trumpet, old Ascolini's rich voice challenged him: 'Nonsense, boy! Every damned word of it! So you've made a fool of yourself. That's every man's right. But you have no right in the world to inflict a maudlin confession on the rest of us! Pull yourself together, man! Cry in a tavern if you must, or in a bawdy-house, but in this place you stand up like a man and keep your mouth shut!'

For a moment, Rienzi stood blank-faced and rocking under the impact. Then, in a curious moment of transformation, his face seemed to harden and what might have been a smile twitched at his bloodless lips. He raised one hand in a mocking salute: 'You're a better advocate than I am, Doctor. You always will be!'

Then his knees buckled under him. Landon caught him as he lurched forward, and carried him over his shoulder to the guest-room. He tossed him on the bed and left him to Valeria. She said nothing, but gave him a small, bitter smile and began unlacing Rienzi's shoes.

Landon was grateful for her discretion. He had never liked curtain speeches and he had no patience with drunken actors. But Carlo Rienzi was a great actor – which in an advocate was a talent, and, for some women, a passable substitute for manhood. At least Valeria was accepting it without illusions. Or perhaps she was creating a new one, since love was a blind goddess, sister to her who sat with naked sword and scales in balance, peeping from under her handkerchief at the comedies enacted in her name.

'Time to go, Peter,' said Ninette Lachaise. 'Time to spend ourselves on ourselves. We've been too long in this town.'

They were standing together on the terrace of the villa, watching the rise of the moon and hearing the first solitary song of the nightingales. The valley stretched itself placid in the moon-glow and, above the crenellations of the mountains, they saw the pricking of the first faint stars. The land had surrendered itself to the night, and for Landon, too, it was the time of surrender. He drew Ninette to him and said, more gently that he had ever spoken before: 'I love you, girl. I never thought I could love anyone so much. But are you sure you want to risk me?'

'It's always a risk,' said Ascolini from behind them, 'but only the wise ones know it. Go home, both of you. Get your-selves churched if you must, but do it quickly. Time's the most precious thing you have, and who should know it better than I?'

He handed them the keys of the car and then fished out of his pocket two old and beautiful volumes, one of which he handed to Ninette with the sardonic dedication: 'For you, my dear. All the things your man feels for you but won't be able to say because he's a dull fellow who knows only the jargon of the clinic. They're Petrarch's Sonnets to his Laura and the book was made by Elzevir. It's a wedding present. My heart goes with it – and all my love.'

Ninette threw her arms round the old man and kissed him. He held her for a long moment and then pushed her gently away.

'Take her, Landon, before I change my mind and rush her to the altar. Here's something for you, my friend!' He handed Landon the companion volume, and said, whimsically: 'It's an Aretino – *The Luxurious Sonnets!* You're old enough to enjoy them and young enough not to need them!' He took their arms and urged them swiftly off the terrace towards the car. 'No more words! No long farewells. They remind me of death and I have enough reminders already!'

As they drove down the winding path to the gates, they could see him solitary and gallant on the terrace, the moon-light silver on his lion's mane, listening to the lament of the nightingales.